Asphalt Desert Blues
Second Edition

Primitive Road Publishing
Flagstaff, Arizona

Asphalt Desert Blues

by Avtar Khalsa

Primitive Road Second Edition
ISBN 978-0-9834902-2-7

Also available as an e-book at Smashwords.com
and other major e-book sellers

Disclaimer

Acknowledgements

The author is indebted to the following friends and colleagues who read various drafts of this book, and offered their feedback and encouragement: Bill Adair, Scott Baxter, Dennis Damore, Burt Gershater, Chris Gunn, Christina Norlin, Mary Sojourner and Wendy Weed.

Thanks also go to Randall J. Witte, who lent the magic of his graphic design talents to the cover of the second edition.

Special thanks must also go to Kathy Long Jura. She found flaws and helped us mend them.

Finally, a big thanks goes to Patti Lynn Wilson whose editing talents and fine attention to detail have been indispensable.

Primitive Road Publishing
Flagstaff, Arizona

-

For Simran and Kirin

Authors Note:

While *Asphalt Desert Blues* is a work of fiction, there are a few historically accurate details in this story. Arizona did experience a series of what were called Fifty and Hundred Year Storms between 1965 and 1981. During the drought years that followed, there were plans to build Orme Dam near the confluence of the Salt and Verde Rivers. And there were, in fact, people who advocated for cloud seeding to increase precipitation, and cutting down much of the Ponderosa Pine forest along the Mogollon Rim in order to increase runoff into the rivers.

One of the beauties of Arizona is the way it continues to provide abundant factual material around which a writer may weave an entertaining tale.

ASPHALT DESERT BLUES

PROLOGUE

The Mogollon (pronounced Muggy Own) Rim is a huge escarpment which pushes up out of the terrain of northern Arizona, cutting a wide swath from west to east across the state about a hundred miles north of Phoenix. It's beautiful country, with cool, clean air and tall Ponderosa pine trees.

The Rim forms the southwestern edge of the Colorado Plateau. North of the Rim elevations are some two thousand feet higher than the area below the Rim. Much of the Rim Country, the region immediately north of the Rim, has elevations between six and seven thousand feet.

At various times over the last few million years, there was a great deal of volcanic activity across much of the Rim Country. Some of those long-extinct volcanoes are now mountains. The biggest of these, the San Francisco Peaks, has a main summit over 12,000 feet in elevation.

The Rim is broken by a series of canyons, carved out over the eons by runoff from snowmelt on the Rim Country. Little streams, Oak Creek, Sycamore Creek and Clear Creek flow through these canyons to feed the Verde River, which winds its way east and south on its way to the desert.

In eastern Rim Country, another group of extinct volcanoes forms the White Mountains. Snowmelt from this range and the surrounding countryside finds its way into the tributaries of the White River and the Black River in eastern Arizona. These two small, scenic rivers come together to form the Salt River; their confluence about 100 miles east of Scottsdale on the San Carlos Indian Reservation. From there the Salt flows westward through the Salt River Canyon toward the desert.

About sixteen miles east of Scottsdale, the Verde River empties into the Salt. A couple miles further downstream the Granite Reef Diversion Dam routes the river into a series of irrigation canals. Some of these follow ancient canals that were dug by the Hohokam, native people who once farmed the Phoenix valley. The Hohokam vanished by the time the first Europeans arrived, though they likely were the ancestors of some present-day Arizona tribes.

The largest and northern-most of these canals is the Arizona Canal. It flows northwest and then west, cutting through the land of the Salt River Pima Indian Tribe before entering the residential neighborhoods west of Pima Road, then continues right through downtown Scottsdale. It was here, where the canal flows under the intersection of Scottsdale Road and Camelback Road, two young boys riding their bicycles along the canal bank early on a Monday morning saw something that looked like a body floating half submerged in the murky water of the Arizona Canal.

CHAPTER 1

Recovering alcoholics, those who have a few years in the program, will tell you nobody knows when they become alcoholic. But somewhere along the way, they crossed an invisible line. At that point, instead of them doing the drinking, the drinking was doing them. I didn't know it at the time, but I was dancing right on top of my own personal line.

It was comfortably dark inside Lucinda's. I sat in a corner eating green chile enchiladas, and washed them down with gulps of Margarita. I was already on my third, waiting for the tequila numb that was starting in my gums to spread to my brain. I don't especially like Margaritas, but Lucinda's doesn't serve straight shots of tequila.

It was June of 1992. I was sure of that much. And I guess if I had thought really hard about it and counted up the days that I'd been away, I would have eventually figured out that it was Tuesday. Beyond that, it was just a blistering hot summer gone ugly.

On the jukebox in another dark corner of the room—or maybe my mind—Hank Williams Jr. sang, *I OD'd in Denver and I Just Can't Remember Her Name.* Well Hank, that's what happens when you do too much booze and cocaine. I was killing the care cells because I could remember her name. And her face. And the way her hand felt on my skin. And the smell of her hair, like flowers in the rain.

I had been a soldier. Any soldier who has seen combat has more than enough reason to drink too much. A shrink at a VA hospital told me every soldier who makes it back from war, any war, has PTSD. The only question is how far into the darkness the demons will take them. But it wasn't the ghosts of war that were haunting me this time.

In Lucinda's I could hide in the darkness while I used the greasiest Mexican food in Phoenix as an excuse for midday alcohol consumption. I didn't really need an excuse—at least not another one. Not for having a cold drink or two in Phoenix in June when it's already 110° outside and the day is just starting to heat up.

Every so often the front door would open out toward the corner of Seventh Street and Indian School Road, and the blinding light of the noon sun would flood the doorway. I kept my face turned away from the light. You could lose your vision when the darkness returned and you'd barely be able to see the enchiladas on your plate. Consequently I didn't even see her as she walked up to my table.

It's unlike me to not notice a good looking woman. But it was dark in there, I had my back turned to the entrance, and my mind was elsewhere. It wasn't until she spoke that I became aware of her. "Excuse me," she said politely, "Are you Travis Jefferson?"

I glanced up, pulling my thoughts back from a few days before. At first I wondered if the magazine had sent her to find me, to hound me for the story. Or had she come to serve me a summons? I was undoubtedly guilty of something, ethical if not criminal.

I gazed at her before answering, weighing the possibilities. She was tall and not thin. Her long blond hair was braided and curled at the back of her head. She wore a light blue summer dress with thin straps. If she had perspired in the summer heat it was not evident.

I probably should have lied, denied who I was, denied my very existence. I didn't want to talk to anyone. But here was a young woman who had sought me out. What the hell, I said to myself. "What can I do for you?"

"Mr. Jefferson," she said, "My name is Heidi Charlayne. You know my older brother Charlie Gonnerman." The door opened again, and for a moment the sunlight shone through her summer dress. I was starting to feel the booze creeping up into my head. I stared at her. I couldn't help it. Then the door closed and it was dark. I pulled a chair back from the table.

"Please," I said, "sit down. How is Charlie?"

"That's why I'm here. He's disappeared." She took the seat I had offered. It was too dark to see her face. But there was tension in her voice. "He told me that if anything happened to him, I should find you. I've been trying to reach you for the past couple of days. Then when I called a little while ago, your voice mail said you were here. I'm sorry to bother you during your lunch, but I'm worried about Charlie."

I used to keep four out-going messages loaded on my voice mail. Any time I left the office I would select which one a caller would hear. One said I'll call you right back. It's what you got instead of a busy signal. One said I'm out of the office, but leave a message and I'll get back to you. One said I'm out of town but I'm checking my messages each day. And one said I'm down the street at Lucinda's getting my daily dose of bad cholesterol. Sometimes someone I needed to talk to actually tracked me down there. So I continued to use it.

The booze was beginning to cloud my brain. I had cut down on my drinking, and hadn't gone overboard in several months. But then I went to Denver to get an interview for a story that would never be written. And I had spent the last three days crawling in and out of one bottle or another, hoping to drown a pain that refused to die.

I tried to focus, tried to get a handle on what was going on with this girl, the younger sister of my old friend Charlie Gonnerman. "I'm sorry," I said. "I'm a little slow today." I wondered if I was slurring my words as I spoke. "Charlie said to contact me? I don't understand."

"I'm not sure I do either. He left a message on my machine Saturday night. He said he might have gotten into something dangerous. He left your number and said I should call you if anything happened. I tried to call him back as soon as I got his message. I kept trying." Her voice became softer then began to trail off into the darkness. "Now it's been three days."

Once again the light of the hot Phoenix afternoon rushed into Lucinda's. This time I focused on the silhouette of Heidi Charlayne's face, resisting the urge to let my gaze drop to the top of her blue summer dress. Her face was flawless, with high cheekbones, a small straight nose and teeth that had never needed braces.

Lucinda's returned to darkness. My eyes tried to find Heidi again. Her voice found me first. "Mr. Jefferson, can you help me?"

The waitress appeared. Did I want another Margarita? Of course I did. My brain wasn't completely numb, yet. But I told her "No thanks." I hadn't really had enough. But I had to be able to think.

"Look, Heidi," I said, "call me Travis. Why would Charlie tell you to get a hold of me? Why not the police?"

"He doesn't trust the police. You know Charlie. He gets pretty paranoid. But I know he trusted you. He told me you were the only journalist in town who had enough guts to do the story on Ace Martin."

Elmore "Ace" Martin had been publisher of the two daily newspapers that held a tight monopoly on the Phoenix print media market. Ace was a pretty good talker, and he had become the top guest speaker at Republican fund-raisers and VFW banquets. His claim to patriotic fame was his reputation as an ace fighter pilot during the Korean War. That's how he got his nickname. The story was he had been recalled to active duty during Vietnam.

But I'd heard him talk a few times, and began to notice some inconsistencies in his story. I was a veteran myself, and I'd heard my share of war stories full of overripe bullshit. So out of curiosity I began to do some checking. Everybody in town told me I was crazy to question Ace Martin's military record. He was a powerful man with powerful friends. But Ace had built a reputation on a lie. He was never in the Air Force, never in the war, never even in the military. He was nothing but a wannabe patriot, waving the flag for God and a country he had never served. After the local weekly tabloid ran my story, Elmore "Ace" Martin left Phoenix in disgrace. For a while after that you could see humorous bumper stickers around town that said, "I flew with Ace."

I guess to Charlie Gonnerman that story meant that I was not only a good investigative journalist, but that I was willing to lay it all on the line to go after the big boys when they were dirty. Charlie was sure all the big boys were dirty. And now, it seemed, Charlie might have been poking into that dirt a little too deeply. So he told his sister Heidi that I was the one to turn to if anything should happen to him, hoping that I could rake away whatever muck it was he had stumbled into.

In my current state of mind I had serious doubts about my ability to find Lucinda's front door in the darkness, much less find Charlie Gonnerman. "Heidi I wish I could help you, but this is really a matter for the police."

"Please," she said. She placed her hand on my forearm, leaning slightly forward across the table, bringing her face closer to mine. I caught the sweet, subtle aroma of gardenia. She was almost whispering, "I know you don't know me. I'm a stranger, and there's no reason you should want to get dragged into this. But Charlie thought you would help. He told me to find you so that's what I did. I don't know what else to do."

She was looking into my eyes. Her hand was still on my arm. My brain was numb, but my arm could feel the touch of every one of her fingers. They were soft but firm and strong. And the touch of a woman is something very, very hard to deny. "Okay," I heard myself say. I put my hand upon hers, "I'll see what I can do. Have you been to Charlie's place since he left you the message?"

She let go of my arm and sat up again. "No," she said. "He lives in a small apartment off of south 40th Street. I have a spare key but I haven't been there in a while. I could meet you there after work tonight." She looked at her watch, the hands glowing dimly in the darkness "I've got to get back to work. I came over on my lunch hour."

"Okay," I said, "How 'bout I meet you there at seven?"

She agreed, and wrote the address on a napkin for me. Then she stood up to leave. "Thank you, Mr. Jefferson," she said, "I mean Travis. I'll see you at seven." She hurried across Lucinda's dining room and out the door.

CHAPTER 2

I paid my check at the register, slipped on my sunglasses and stepped out the door. It's strange, but I always enjoy that first blast of heat when I step out of an air conditioned building in the summer in Phoenix. It's sort of like slipping into a warm Jacuzzi on a chilly night. But it only took a few seconds before that killer heat mixed with the tequila in my blood. There was a fuzzy feeling near the top of my brain, and I knew I couldn't stay out in the sun too long. Jogging across Seventh Street before the light changed, I felt the waves of heat radiating off the blacktop. There were no other pedestrians on the street. Even the homeless found some shade and stayed there.

I walked west along Indian School Road to my office. I had stopped in before I went to Lucinda's, but only long enough to drop off my camera, rolls of film, some notes, my tape recorder, and change the outgoing message on my voice mail.

My office was on the second floor of a building that had been a neighborhood drug store and five and dime years before. The family that owned those businesses had used the upstairs as their residence. The living space had long since been carved up into small offices. Mine was a single room with a window that looked out toward the Phoenix Indian School and the Veterans Hospital. A copper tinted film on the window reflected most of the sunlight. Even so, during the day I kept the curtains drawn. I sat down at my old wooden desk.

One wall was covered with pictures. They were photographs of people rock climbing, mountain biking, and white water rafting. Some were related to stories I'd written, others were pictures of friends, a few others friends had taken of me. They had been added one at a time, with no particular plan in mind.

I pushed a button on my telephone to switch it to the intercom mode. Then I pushed another, which automatically dialed my voice mail to retrieve messages. I had three new ones. The first was Heidi's call from two days before. She left both her home and work numbers. I listened to it a second time, writing down both numbers.

The second call was from the magazine: "Mr. Jefferson, this is Elaine Esser from Outdoor West. Mr. Rusnack asked me to call to say he is very sorry about what happened in Colorado. But he's sure that after you've had a few days to think it over you'll realize that you want to write the article after all. We're still saving space for it in the August issue. Please call and let us know when we should expect it."

I had called them from Denver and told them to forget it. I was drunk at the time. Perhaps they could tell. Maybe they figured that once I dried out and thought about the twelve hundred bucks they were willing to pay that I'd change my mind. Well fuck them, I thought. Fuck George Rusnack, and fuck his twelve hundred dollars. I hadn't dried out yet. And I wasn't going to write their fucking article if and when I ever did. It was genuine anger, but it was the stepchild of pain.

The third call was Heidi. She said she was going to try to find me at Lucinda's, but if we didn't connect would I please call her.

I sat in my quiet office. The only sound was the traffic on the street below and the hum of the air conditioning unit on the roof.

I looked at a small photo on my desk. In the picture are three young men in jungle fatigues. Jordan, Jefferson, and Johnson—me and my two best army buddies.

Leon Jordan was a dark brown, stocky brother from South Carolina who was facing the draft after he graduated from Moorhouse. So like me, he enlisted. Leon wanted to teach school and coach football, but his plans were put on hold. Allen Johnson was a big white kid from Ohio. Al wanted to be a police officer back in his hometown. But in 1970, if you wanted to work in law enforcement, you just about had to be a military veteran. Al enlisted.

And there I was between them, clean-shaven with short hair. A stranger in my office wouldn't have recognized me in that photo without reading the names on the uniforms. We were unlikely friends. But war does that to you. I kept the photo on my desk to remind me that I once had friends who would risk everything for me. And who expected the same in return.

I glanced down at the legal pad where I had written Heidi's phone numbers. What did Charlie expect me to do when he'd left Heidi that message to call me? I was a freelance writer, not a private detective. I thought about that for a moment. Then I pulled a phone number out of my Rolodex and dialed the number.

"Valley Views, Mr. Layton's office," chirped Ms. Janie Alterman.

"Janie, this is Travis Jefferson. Any chance of talking to his eminence?"

"Mr. Jefferson. You don't send flowers, you don't send candy, you don't even call just to say hello. Then out of the blue you expect me to just patch you through to the boss himself? Should we perhaps suspect drug abuse?"

Janie and I had become telephone pals when I was working on the Ace Martin story. Her boss, Michael Layton, ran the Valley's "alternative" newspaper. I'd contacted the Valley Views when I started thinking Martin's war record was bogus. Layton took a personal interest in the story, gave me a contract, and asked me to keep him informed as it developed. But there was no way to talk to Layton without first going through Janie Alterman. So for about six weeks the previous winter, Janie and I had talked on a regular basis.

"Janie, you're right, my behavior has been inexcusable. How can I make it up to you?"

"You know Travis, you have the two requisite qualities of a journalist."

"You mean I can read and write?"

"No. I presume you can read, and you do write beautifully. But that's not what I meant. During my few short years in the newspaper business I have observed that all freelance journalists have two notable qualities. You have the audacity to believe that someone will publish your work, and the optimism to think that anyone will actually want to read it. Now this same combination of audacity and optimism has got you thinking you can sweet talk your way around the fact that, after not hearing from you for four months, you call and don't even bother to say 'Hello Janie, how have you been?' before trying to get down to business with the boss."

It was another reason why I shouldn't drink. My social skills were never that good. I often forget to say things like "So, how's the wife and kids?" Get a little tequila under my belt and I'm hopeless.

She had me at a loss, so I opted for honesty. "Janie you are absolutely right. I'm very sorry. I hope you'll forgive me. I'm having a bad day that is only one in a series of bad days. But that's no excuse." I waited, wondering if I was going to get some sympathy or if I would have to grovel some more. "Will you give me another chance?"

"Well, okay," she said, "we can try again." She paused, then "Valley Views, Mr. Layton's office."

"Janie, this is Travis Jefferson. It's so nice to hear your voice again. How are you?"

"Why Mr. Jefferson, so nice of you to call. My, it's been such a long time since we've heard from you. You must stay very busy these days."

"Well, as a matter of fact, I have been working out of town." Last week, anyway.

"Really? Well, next time you must send postcards. I just love getting postcards. If I must be stuck in Phoenix in the summer, I would at least like some sort of vicarious vacation. Now, what can our humble weekly tabloid do for the traveling journalist today, Mr. Jefferson?"

Maybe I was forgiven. Maybe not. I made a note on the Rolodex card to send postcards. "Would it be possible to speak with Mr. Layton this afternoon?"

"Why Travis, your luck seems to be changing already. He just returned from lunch. I'll connect you now."

"Thanks, Janie," I said, but I don't know if she heard it. The next voice was Mike Layton's.

"Travis, good to hear from you. What's up?" Layton was friendly, but always had an eye on business.

"Mike, I need a favor. I'm starting to work on something that could turn into a story. And it's something I think you'd be interested in if it pans out."

"I'm all ears, Travis. Always looking for a good story. Where's the favor come in?"

"I'm going to be doing a little probing, asking questions, that sort of thing. I don't know yet where it's going to go. I'd like to say I'm working on a story for the paper while I'm doing it."

"No problem so far, Travis. But you haven't told me yet what it is you're working on."

"I'm reluctant to name names at this point, Mike. But there is a local environmental activist who disappeared a few days ago. His family has reason to believe foul play may be involved, but they're reluctant to go to the police with it. I'm not sure yet where all this will lead, but I'm going to pursue it. I'd like a contract to cover me."

There was no response for a couple of seconds. Mike Layton was thinking about it. I had built up some good credit with the Ace Martin story. Ace, through his two newspapers, used to bad mouth the Valley Views in general and Mike Layton in particular. There were probably few stories that Layton enjoyed publishing more than my Ace Martin story. Even so, I wasn't sure how far that would go toward Layton doing me a favor that involved his paper. I hoped my new idea would at least pique his curiosity.

"Let me see if I've got this right," Layton finally spoke. "You want a contract for a story you might pursue about an individual who may have disappeared but you're not going to tell me who that is. And family members who at this point remain anonymous don't want to report the disappearance to the police. Did I get that right?"

It sounded pretty flaky when I heard it repeated back to me. "Well, I think you've got the gist of it. Like I said, it would be a favor. But it could turn into a story you'd want." I was pressing my luck.

Silence again. Layton had taken some risks in his time. But he hadn't stayed in business for two decades by giving contracts to every two-bit writer who came up with some hair-brained concept. On the other hand, I had built up some credibility with him. "Okay Travis, here's what we'll do. We'll draw you up a contract for a story on a John Doe disappearance that says we'll pay a hundred bucks upon delivery. How long you think before you've got some hard facts on this?"

I didn't have a clue. "Give me thirty days?" I asked. It was a stretch. Essentially I was saying it might be a month before I'd know jack shit. Not real impressive.

"Thirty days. Okay, you'll be covered for thirty days, call it July 9th. At that point we have an option to offer a contract on the story at our usual rate. You come through with a good story, I'm a happy camper and we cut you a check. If not, you've used up the one favor you've earned."

"Michael, you're all right. I don't care what the mainstream media says about you."

"Don't even get me started on that one, Travis. Does Janie have your fax number?" I gave it to him. Some time in the next 24 hours I would get a fax that said I was working on a story for the Valley Views. It would make expenses related to the story tax deductible. It also gave me a reason to be asking questions about Charlie Gonnerman.

CHAPTER 3

Knowing I had a contract on the way began to change my perspective on my promise to Heidi Charlayne. I didn't know the first thing about finding old friends who had disappeared. But over the years I had developed a methodology for organizing and analyzing information. It had served me well.

I turned on my computer. By the early 1990s, software had become relatively versatile and user friendly. I'm no hacker, just a computer user. So I found a graduate student at Arizona State who created some customized software for my particular needs. It allowed me to track people and events, providing a visual representation of how they intersected over time. It was similar to tools I had used for intelligence work in the army.

I started a profile on Charlie Gonnerman. I entered the address Heidi had written for me on the napkin at Lucinda's.

Then my memory carried me back a couple of decades. Charlie and I had gone to high school together in the sixties. We weren't close friends. But we had been on the football team together. Charlie was never a star, just another body on the bench. For one thing he was sort of small, but he always worked hard and earned his spot on the roster. During the winter he was on the wrestling team, never more than an also-ran in that sport either. I didn't remember him having a girl friend, but I didn't think he was gay.

Charlie's father died of a heart attack when Charlie was seventeen. It must have had quite an impact on him. He told me once that life was short and you had to make every moment count. Consequently he lived his life differently than most of our classmates from the Scottsdale High School class of 1968.

He threw his heart and soul into the causes he believed in, whether it was the anti-war movement, social justice, or protecting the environment. While most of our peers were clawing their way up some corporate ladder or making a name in academia, Charlie lived a minimalist lifestyle while he saved the world.

I didn't see Charlie much during the seventies. I played a year of college ball as a wide receiver at San Francisco State. While my grades were good enough to stay eligible and keep my scholarship, I didn't carry enough hours to maintain my draft deferment. When the draft lottery was held during my freshman year of college, my date of birth matched up with number 26. That meant that without a student deferment it was a sure bet that my ass would be drafted. After considering my options I went to see an Army recruiter. I figured that if I could enlist for a job I might actually like, perhaps I could avoid playing 13 months in the Southeast Asian Conference. I wasn't very smart then, either.

When I finally left the Army twelve years later, I returned to Phoenix and enrolled at Arizona State to study journalism. That's where I ran into Charlie again. He had taken his time getting through college, dropping in and out as the years went by. By 1982 he was about to graduate with a degree in environmental studies.

I had an assignment in one of my classes to write an in-depth article on an issue of local concern. I had noticed a story in the local papers about wells in the Valley becoming contaminated after years of chemical dumping at several facilities operated by a large electronics firm. When I contacted one of the environmental groups to get some background information on water quality, they referred me to Charlie Gonnerman.

Charlie had become a local expert on the environmental politics of water in the desert. We got together. For several hours one afternoon and evening Charlie told me more than I ever wanted to know about water, water rights, irrigation, conservation, and a water table that continued to drop. He recited the entire history of western water projects, hydroelectric power, and an agricultural industry that was slowly committing environmental suicide.

Then he discussed the electronics firm that for years had been dumping solvents containing PCBs on their back lots. When the practice began, nobody knew that PCBs were carcinogenic. And no one apparently considered that the solvents would eventually seep into the aquifer that lay beneath the Valley of the Sun. Then traces of the PCBs began to show up in water from wells near the electronics plants. Those wells fed directly into the Phoenix water supply. While Phoenix's political leaders had historically been quite conservative, pro-business, and generally suspicious of environmental causes, even they tended to be sensitive to the possibility of carcinogens flowing into their homes (and the homes of their constituents) through the kitchen faucet.

The political questions tended to focus on money. How much would it cost to clean up the wells? What would it cost to clean up the dumping sites? What would it cost them to find an alternative means of disposing of the solvents? And who should pay? Always who should pay?

Charlie laid this all out for me in rapid-fire staccato fashion. If I hadn't brought a tape recorder I never would have been able to keep up with him. I got an A on the paper and actually sold a version of my article to the Rocky Mountain News.

I talked with Charlie from time to time after that. My Rocky Mountain News article opened up some doors for other stories on environmental issues, and I continued to use Charlie as a resource. If he didn't know the details on an issue he could refer me to someone who did.

He completed his degree, and started working as a substitute science teacher at local high schools. But he continued his work as a researcher and advocate with environmental groups. I knew substitute teaching didn't pay very much, but Charlie lived pretty simply.

I completed entering what I knew about Charlie in the personality data base file, then made a note check on what schools Charlie had taught at recently. I imagined him stepping into a classroom with his frizzy blond hair, frizzy blond beard, round, wire rim glasses, and what ever post-hippie attire he had scrambled together that morning.

That was about all I could do with the Gonnerman file. I flipped through my Rolodex for another number and dialed it. "East Phoenix Precinct," the dispatcher answered.

"Joe Diaz, please."

"Just a moment, I'll see if he's on duty." She didn't put me on hold, a good sign. "I'm sorry sir, Officer Diaz is not in the building at the moment. Can I take a message for him?"

"Yes, would you ask him to call Travis Jefferson. It's not urgent, but if he could call this afternoon I'd appreciate it."

"I'll give him the message, sir."

"Thank you very much," I said.

I went back to my computer to review projects that were either proposed, pending, or in progress. There weren't that many. Under "In Progress" there were only two. One was the new one on Charlie Gonnerman. The other was Juliette Skye Valdez.

I didn't want to think about her. This whole thing with Charlie Gonnerman was becoming just the sort of distraction I needed. But it wasn't enough. I stared at the computer screen, knowing that with the push of a button I could open her file. As simple as that: open the file; open the wound.

I needed a drink. I didn't know if I had a problem with booze, and I didn't care. I just felt like crawling into a bottle. I closed my eyes and placed my face into the palms of my hands, my elbows resting on the desk. And with my eyes closed I could see her, just like the first time I had seen her, in Denver at the climbing gym where she trained. I could see her black tights, the hot pink sports top, her long legs, tan lower back and shoulders, and that long, auburn hair that tumbled below her shoulders as she reached up for another hold.

The phone jolted me. I hit the intercom button, "Hello."

"Jefferson. That you, man?" It was Diaz.

I didn't want to come back. I wanted to close my eyes again, to hold on to that vision. "Yeah, Joe. It's me."

"They said you called. Wha's up, man? You sound like shit."

"Yeah, you got it. What time you get off?"

"Shift change is at four thirty. I should be out of the precinct house by five. You want me to meet you somewhere?"

"How about Brandi's on 44th? A little after five?"

"Choo got it, mon."

CHAPTER 4

I looked at the computer screen again. Need to think about something else, I thought to myself. Need to get back to work. Since I wasn't going to write about Juliette for Outdoor West, I was out twelve hundred bucks plus expenses. I needed to get some other projects moving.

I selected Proposed Projects. These included an article on climbing in the Eagletail Mountains, one on rafting on the Colorado through Westwater Canyon, one about the Grand Canyon Death March, an endurance run from the South Rim to the North Rim then back to the South Rim, all in under 24 hours. I also had a photograph from the Cabeza Prieta Wildlife Refuge that I thought perhaps I could peddle to either Outside Magazine or Arizona Highways.

Each of these had lain dormant while I focused on other projects. But with time on my hands and a hole in my future income, I knew I had better get on them. I spent the rest of the afternoon drafting query letters to editors, pitching my stuff.

By quitting time I had several query letters completed, each promising a fascinating article complete with professional quality photos. I printed them out and fed them, in succession, to my fax machine. Then I grabbed the rolls of film I shot in Colorado, and buttoned up the office.

My aging Honda Civic was in a covered parking space behind the building. The inside of the car was hot. I rolled down the windows as I backed out, and took the alley to Third Street. I drove south to McDowell Road, and dropped the film off at a photo lab. Then I forced a left turn back into the eastbound rush hour traffic. A flashing sign in front of a bank said the time was 4:54 and the temperature was 114. I stopped at the post office to pull a week's worth of mail out of my PO box, then continued east toward Brandi's Cantina, some cold beer, and Joe Diaz.

I got to Brandi's about ten after five. The air-conditioning inside was a welcome relief from the killer afternoon heat. Joe was already there. He was in plain clothes. He sat at a table in the far corner where he could observe the front door and the entire room. He already had a pitcher of beer and a pair of glasses for us.

"Man, you look like some kind of fucking hippie," Joe said, "long hair, scruffy beard. I think I should tell the Drug Division to keep an eye on you, see what kind of shit you're into."

"Yeah, well at least I still got some hair." I ran my hand over the hair on the top of my head. He grinned and poured me a glass. Joe's straight, black hair was combed back from a high forehead that had gone up an inch since I'd last seen him. He stood five seven and weighed close to two hundred pounds. His broad back and shoulders were the product of years of serious training with free weights.

"I see you're still working plain clothes," I said.

"Yeah, I've been on the organized crime task force for the past year. Doing a lot of surveillance work. Mostly it's the same old shit. But working with the other agencies is interesting sometimes."

"Weren't you telling me something about Internal Affairs the last time we talked? They were checking you out or something?"

"Shee-it," Joe replied, drawing the word out almost with affection. "Those fuckers couldn't find their asses with both hands and a road map. They pinched a couple of detectives who got caught taking payoffs. The I.A. guys were leaning on the detectives real hard, hoping they'd give up some other cops who were dirty. Well, one of them starts naming anybody he can think of who might be dirty, whether they are or not, including me." He picked up his glass and took a couple of swallows.

"Then what happened?"

"I.A. calls me in and they say they're investigating reports that I've done this and that. 'Course it's all bullshit. So I ask 'em 'You got pictures?' and they say 'No, only reports.' So I told 'em 'If you ain't got pictures, you ain't got shit.' They didn't like it, but fuck 'em. If the department was going to fire me, they would have done it years ago when I busted Senator Dowling."

As a young patrol officer on the night shift years before, Joe had caused a stir in Phoenix political circles when he made a DUI traffic stop, and the driver turned out to be Arizona's junior U.S. senator. While many a police officer back then would have escorted the senator safely to his home, Joe handled it by the book and cited Senator Dowling for driving while intoxicated. This did not endear Officer Diaz to Valley of the Sun's political elite.

"So," I said, remembering my earlier faux pas with Janie Alterman, "how are Shelly and the boys?"

"The boys are great. Mikey starts high school in August so he's all excited about football. Joey's playing little league, having a good time. But things are a little rough with Shelly right now."

"Yeah?"

"Yeah, she's been pissed at me for a couple of weeks, ever since she found out about one of my girl friends."

Joe was like a lonesome lady magnet. He'd been married to Shelly for nearly fifteen years, but was always looking to get a little more on the side.

He shook his head, "So, suppachoo mon?"

I took a long drink. The beer was cold and it felt good going down. "Well pal," I began, "I need to draw upon that vast wealth of investigative experience you've stored in that big *cabeza* of yours."

"Whoa," he said, glancing under the table. "The bullshit is getting deep already. You didn't tell me I needed to wear boots for this."

"No, seriously. I need your help with something. A guy I know has disappeared. His family doesn't want to call the police. They asked me to see if I could find out what happened to him."

Joe sipped on his beer. "So, how well do you know this guy?"

"We went to high school together, and I see him every now and then. He's helped me out with information on a few stories."

"What do you know about his family?"

"Not much. Middle class white folks. His dad died when we were in high school. I'd never even met his sister until she contacted me today."

Joe picked up the pitcher of beer and topped off both our glasses. He took a couple more sips while staring off at nothing. "There are generally three reasons why people don't want the police notified in a situation like this," he said. "The most obvious is that either the missing individual or someone else in the family is into something illegal and they don't want any cops snooping around. Second, there are cases where the family wants to avoid whatever embarrassment might result from the family name showing up in the news media. That's often the case with families who have serious money, usually real old, well established money." Joe looked at me with a sly grin. "If this guy was a friend of yours I'm guessing that's not the case in this situation."

"You been readin' my mail, pal. What's the third possibility?"

Joe looked at me for a moment, as if deciding how to phrase what he was about to say. "You said your friend is a middle class *gringo*, so this one probably doesn't apply either. But I'll mention it anyway since we're here, shootin' the shit over a cold beer just like the old days." He paused and took another drink. "Within some minority neighborhoods it's generally understood that no matter what kind of shit's going down, having the cops show up just makes it worse. So nobody calls the cops about anything. If something needs to be settled, they settle it. But they leave the cops out of it."

"That's an interesting analysis from a cop," I said.

"Hey, I grew up in South Phoenix. There used to be a lot of cops who were certain that part of their job description was making sure that smart-ass Mexicans like me knew their place. Same for the Blacks, only worse. And there's still guys like that in the department. They know they can't be as vocal about their sentiments anymore. City hall won't tolerate out and out expressions of bigotry. But when they get their chance it comes out. Just like those cops in L.A. who beat the shit out of that Rodney King guy. Now King doesn't strike me as being all that bright. But I know where he was coming from. 'Cause he probably thought they were going to kill him. Shit, I would have been trying to get away, too."

Joe drank more beer. He was not usually so candid, at least not about relations between the police and the minority communities. I smiled and said "I bet it put some of those ass holes through their changes when you joined the force."

"Yeah, maybe. But by then we'd had years of affirmative action. I'd spent time in Special Forces so I had some credibility coming in. And the department wasn't lily white anymore."

Joe looked across the room toward the door. Then he gave a half smile and waved at someone who had just walked in. "Speaking of lily white," he said in a low tone. "This guy who's coming over is a cop I work with. He'd be curious as to what I'm doing talking with a hippie-looking fucker like you. He might either think you're a source I haven't told him about, or else he'll think that maybe I'm into what ever dirty business he'll imagine you're into. So I waved him over. It's better than letting his imagination run wild."

The other cop walked to our table. He looked to be about forty-five. He had all the official cowboy accouterments: white hat, snap-button shirt, wide belt with buckle, tan pants which flared slightly over his cowboy boots. He even had him a Marlboro Man mustache. "Travis, this is Wayne Henderson. Wayne, this is Travis Jefferson, an old army buddy of mine." I thought I saw Cowboy Wayne's expression change ever so slightly upon hearing that my association with Joe Diaz was through the military. Maybe I gained some credibility. More likely, he was trying to decide if Joe was bullshitting him.

"So, you and ol' Joe here were in the Army together?" Wayne sat down and signaled the waitress for another glass.

"Actually we were in the Reserves together after we got off active duty," I said.

"Is that a fact?" Cowboy Wayne nodded. "And what do you do these days?"

"I'm a free-lance writer," I replied, looking the cowboy cop right in the eye. I was aware that a lot of cops don't care much for writers. Too fucking bad, I thought.

The waitress arrived with a third glass. "What do ya think?" Cowboy Wayne said. "Should we order another pitcher?"

Joe looked at me for an answer. I figured I didn't have to meet Heidi for another hour and a half, and more cold beer sounded real good. "Sure, why not." Wayne gave the waitress some cash for a second pitcher.

"What kind of stuff do you write?" Wayne asked. My interrogation wasn't over.

"Most of what I write about falls into the outdoor recreation genre. Mountaineering, rock climbing, white water rafting, that sort of thing."

"No kidding? I've always wanted to take one of those river trips through the Grand Canyon. But they're pretty darned expensive. Seems like either I don't have enough money or I don't have enough vacation saved up."

"They're definitely not cheap, Wayne. You're right about that. That's why I like what I do. If I'm lucky, I get paid to take the vacation I want to take, long as I write an article about it when I'm through."

"Damn," Wayne said, "you and me are in the wrong business, Joe."

The second pitcher of beer arrived. Joe announced he was heading for the restroom. "You know, Travis," Wayne said, "you're keeping dangerous company when you hang around somebody like Joe Diaz."

I didn't want to hear that kind of shit from Cowboy Wayne, especially when he waited until Joe wasn't around to say it. So I decided to fuck with him a little.

"Oh, I know exactly what you mean, Wayne. Trouble just seems to follow Joe wherever he goes. Even so, there's nobody I'd rather have cover my back during an ugly bar fight." I looked Cowboy Wayne right in the eye.

Wayne took another sip of beer. Then he asked, "You ever actually been in a situation like that with Joe?"

"Oh yeah," I replied, happy that Wayne had taken the bait. "A few years ago our unit was up in Alaska on an exercise. When it was over, Joe and I and a young lieutenant were in this little bar in Anchorage. You ever been to Alaska, Wayne?" Wayne shook his head no.

"Well, they party pretty seriously up there. Anyway we're with this lieutenant. It's a Saturday night and the place is packed. The lieutenant's a good guy, but after he's had a few he can get a little loud. I'm not sure how it started but the lieutenant said something to somebody who said something back and the next thing we know our young lieutenant is squared off and throwing punches with a guy about twice his size. But hell, the lieutenant's a Special Forces officer who has consumed a fair amount of alcohol. So despite that fact that he only weighs 140 pounds, he's confident that he can take on everybody in the bar.

"While he and this other guy are going at it somebody grabs him from behind. I don't know if he was just trying to break up the fight or what. All I know is that now the lieutenant's fighting two guys at once. So I went after the guy who grabbed the LT, and as soon as I pulled him off the lieutenant, two other guys jumped on me. Things got pretty crazy at that point. All I remember clearly is being on the floor with some guy's hands around my throat, and seeing Joe grab the guy who was trying to strangle me. Joe must have tossed him half way across the room. Then Joe hit another guy and knocked him out cold. He pulled me to my feet, kicked two guys off the lieutenant, smashed another in the face, and somehow got all three of us out a side door and down an alley. By the time we heard the sirens we were three blocks away from there."

Cowboy Wayne looked fascinated, trying to judge if it was all just bullshit. Some cops pride themselves on their ability to discern bullshit from reality. A lot of journalists, too, for that matter. If my story left old Cowboy Wayne scratching his head, all the better.

Joe returned from the can. Wayne couldn't resist the opportunity to check out the story I had told him. "Hey, Joe, ol' Travis here was just telling me about you saving his ass and some lieutenant when you were up in Alaska a while back." I noticed he was careful not to include too many details.

Joe looked a little embarrassed. He turned to me and said, "You told him about that? Shee-it!" he added, once again drawing the word out as though he enjoyed the experience of saying it. And didn't say another word about it.

"So how is my favorite lieutenant?" I asked Joe.

"He just made the captain's list. Won't be your favorite lieutenant for much longer. And between you and me, I think he's going to make a pretty good team leader."

"With NCOs like you and me to train him, I expected nothing less," I said. Joe grinned, but we both knew there was some truth to it.

Joe filled me in on what was happening with the guys who were in the Army Reserve unit I had left several months before. Wayne asked one more question. "So you guys never knew each other when you were on active duty?"

"Well, we were at Ft. Bragg at the same time for a while," I replied. "And we think we might have seen one another there. But Joe was in 7th Group and I was in 5th, so we never actually met."

By then it was past six thirty, and I said I needed to shove off. Joe and Wayne each said they'd had enough. I wanted to talk more with Joe about Charlie Gonnerman, but I knew I needed to wait for another time.

I said my good-byes and headed out the door. The sun was still shining high above the northwest horizon, the heat still brutal. I got into my Honda to drive to Charlie Gonnerman's apartment.

CHAPTER 5

I made my way south, past the construction of an interchange where a new east-west freeway crossed a new north-south parkway. It was all part of a never-ending effort to overcome gridlock in a city so bloated by urban sprawl that ownership of a car or truck was a necessity. My path wound around the east side of the airport where southeast Phoenix touched northwest Tempe, past the airport and south of Interstate 10, west to 40th Street and south past Broadway.

I found Charlie's place, a two-story apartment building a block east of 40th Street. The apartment building was one of three on the street, all a fading shade of yellow. They were three-sided, with the open end to the north. A stairway led up to a balcony for access to the apartments on the second floor.

The rest of the neighborhood was made up of low-cost single-family houses. A windowless wall on the west end of the apartment building was adorned with graffiti. Kids of various shades of white, black, and brown played baseball in the street, the outfield spilling over onto the worn grass in front of the apartment. I drove slowly through the game, giving the players a wave of thanks for allowing me to pass through.

The sun was now low enough to allow the apartment building to cast a long shadow. I found a space in the shade on the east side of the building, parked and got out. I saw no sign of Heidi, and wished I had had the presence of mind at Lucinda's to ask Heidi what kind of car she drove.

I walked to the front of the apartment building. Heidi said that Charlie lived in apartment G. Apartment G was at the far left of six 2nd floor apartments. An old black man sat near the bottom of the stairs, sipping iced tea and watching the children play. He wore a black baseball cap with the orange and purple logo of the Phoenix Suns basketball team. He wore a tan T-shirt, gray pants.

"Evenin'," he said.

"Good evening," I said. "I'm looking for Charlie Gonnerman. I'm supposed to meet his sister here."

"Charlie lives up in G. Haven't seen him in a few days, 'though. That his sister comin' now?"

I looked where he was gesturing. "Yes sir," I said. "That's her."

Heidi walked across the grass toward us. Her braided hair was still tied up behind her head. She wore a white sleeveless blouse, loose khaki shorts and brown sandals. Her legs were long. As she got closer I saw that she was taller than I had realized at Lucinda's.

"Hi Travis," she said. "Thanks. I really do appreciate you coming here." I caught a hint of fresh gardenia in the air. She turned, held out her hand to the old man sitting on the stairs and said, "I'm Heidi Charlayne, Charlie Gonnerman's sister."

"I'm pleased to meet you Ms. Charlayne. My name is Arthur Davis." Without getting up he reached out with a long arm and shook Heidi's hand. Then he offered his hand to me.

"I'm Travis Jefferson, Mr. Davis," I said as we shook hands. "Charlie and I went to high school together."

"Well I'm pleased to meet you, too, Mr. Jefferson," the old man said. I'm not sure why, but I got the feeling Arthur Davis knew Charlie Gonnerman fairly well. I was thinking about this when I noticed another black man walking toward us.

"Something I can help you folks with?" he said. He was smiling, but I suspected it was the smile he saved for white people, the smile that says, "'Scuse me, what are *you* doing here?"

"Rafer, this is Charlie's sister and her friend Mr. Jefferson," Arthur Davis said. Then to Heidi and me, "This is my grandson Rafer Malone."

I offered my hand to the man named Rafer and introduced myself. He stood about 6' 2" and had strong arms on a lean frame. His hair was closely cropped. He wore black trousers and a white T-shirt, the old fashioned kind with no sleeves. I guessed he was maybe five or ten years younger than me. Rafer shook my hand tentatively. Then Heidi offered her hand and said, "Rafer, I'm Heidi Charlayne. I think

Charlie has mentioned you. Haven't you two known each other for a long time?"

"A long time," Rafer agreed. "Since I was a young boy."

"Rafer, have you seen Charlie in the past few days?" Heidi asked.

"No, I can't say as I have. But that's not unusual. He and I often keep different hours. These days, a week or two could go by and we might not run into each other. Why?"

"Charlie left me a message on Saturday saying that he thought he might be in some kind of trouble. He said that if anything happened to him I should contact Travis. Since then, there's been no answer when I've tried to call him here. I've got a spare key to his apartment, and Travis came with me to see if we could find out what might have happened."

"*You* got any ideas?" Rafer asked, looking at me.

"Rafer, at this point you and your grandfather know as much as I do. We need to take a look inside Charlie's apartment. There might be something there that will at least give us a hint about what's going on."

"Well," said Rafer, now looking at Heidi, "you said you've got a key?" Heidi nodded her head. "Might as well go on up and check it out then. I gotta be going to the job soon. If there's anything I can do, you know where to find me."

"Thank you, Rafer," Heidi said. "It's nice to meet you after all these years."

"My pleasure," Rafer replied.

"Rafer," I said as he began to walk away, "is there some time in the next couple of days when we could talk some more?"

He looked at me warily. After a moment he smiled. It was the same smile he had greeted us with, his smile for the white folks. "Sure," he replied. "I'm usually around here late in the afternoon." With that he turned and walked back down the walk and through the door of apartment E. For the first time I noticed the sign in the window of that apartment which said "Manager."

"Mr. Jefferson," Arthur Davis said to me after his grandson had gone back inside, "Don't mind Rafer none. Sometimes it takes him a while to warm up to folks, that's all."

"Yeah," I replied, "Sometimes I'm a little that way myself, Mr. Davis." Then to Heidi I said, "Well, should we go take a look?"

She looked away, straightened her shoulders, and said, "We have to."

"You need help with anything, you just give a yell down here," Arthur Davis said.

"Thank you, Mr. Davis," Heidi said. We walked past him up the stairs to Charlie's apartment.

CHAPTER 6

Heidi knocked on the door of apartment G. There was no answer. She used her key, opened the door and called out, "Charlie, it's Heidi. Are you here, Charlie?" There was no sound but the hum of the air conditioning.

We walked in and I closed the door, shutting out the heat. The front room had an old couch against the wall to the left. In front of the couch was a low table covered with newspapers. Opposite the couch was what must have served as Charlie's office. There was a desk, with a computer that was beginning to show its age. An old, metal 4-drawer file cabinet stood to the right of the desk.

Beyond the living room/office, a Formica topped table marked the kitchen. Heidi called Charlie's name again and walked through a doorway to the right that led to the bathroom and small bedroom. I followed. Charlie wasn't there. After a quick look around Charlie's small bedroom and bathroom we returned to the front room.

Heidi stepped into the kitchen. She looked at the few dirty dishes in the sink, then turned to me and said, "Travis, I don't know what to do now. I was hoping maybe something here might tell us what's happened to him, but..." She looked at me, seeking an answer, and I thought she might start to cry. As I stepped closer she put her arms around me. I held her. She tried to sniff back tears, but then I felt their warm drops on my shoulder through my light cotton shirt.

While one part of my brain was trying to think of something to say, another was acutely aware of her breasts pressing against my chest. That, in turn, made me feel a little guilty. "It's okay," I whispered. "It's going to be okay." I wanted her to believe it, even if I didn't myself.

After a few seconds she released me. We both stepped back. I felt a little awkward from holding her when I barely knew her, and from thinking about the feel of her body instead of the strange absence of Charlie.

"Heidi, I want to spend time here looking around. Maybe he left some notes, something about what he was working on.

But I've had a rough day. Would you feel okay about loaning me the key so I can come back tomorrow? I could go through the stuff here, and I want to talk more with Rafer, too." I wondered if she knew that what I really needed to do was come back when I was sober, when I could think straight and keep track of the details.

"Oh, of course." She reached into the pocket of her shorts, pulled out the key, and handed it to me. "I guess there really is nothing else we can do here tonight, is there," she said softly, then took one last slow look around Charlie's front room before we walked outside. I locked the deadbolt with the key.

Outside it was still hot. To the west the sunset was turning the sky so red and orange you could imagine nuclear war had broken out somewhere along the Colorado River. We stopped at the bottom of the stairs to say good-bye to Arthur Davis and to tell him there was no sign of Charlie in the apartment. I mentioned that I'd be coming back the next day to look through some of Charlie's things, and talk to Rafer, if he was around.

I walked Heidi to her car, a white VW Jetta parked on the street to the west of the apartment. After she unlocked her door she turned back to me to give me a hug. A long hug. "Thanks, Travis," she said and released me with a kiss on the cheek. "Please call me as soon as you find out anything."

"I will," I promised. She got into her car. The engine started, the lights came on, and she drove away, windows up, AC on high. I drove home through the cooling furnace of Phoenix twilight, thinking about how Heidi's body felt against mine.

CHAPTER 7

I awoke reluctantly. Early morning sun was trying to crawl past the dark curtains of my bedroom window. I took a cool shower to help me wake up.

I wanted good coffee to get my mind kick-started. Three days of drinking had taken its toll. So I got dressed and drove over the Salt River Bridge to Mill Avenue in Tempe, near the Arizona State campus.

The riverbed is dry most of the time, especially in the summer. Up stream, above the confluence of the Salt and Verde Rivers, four dams on the Salt and two on the Verde store water and generate electricity. The water that is released downstream is channeled into a series of irrigation canals for the agricultural lands that surround the greater Phoenix metropolis. That water is also what allows two million people to live in that broad desert valley. It is the city's life blood. Without it we would die.

I entered Ragtime Cowboy Joe, my favorite Tempe coffee house, and walked up to the counter where a girl I knew as Shauna was taking orders. "Travis, right?" she said, remembering my name and my addiction. "Is it a double or triple mocha morning?"

"Let's make it a tall double," I replied. Any later in the day I'd have gotten the iced version, but it was still early enough in the morning to drink it hot.

"No whipped cream, right"? She had a good memory, straight brown hair that parted in the middle, a cute little body under her leotard top and cut off Levi's, and a ring in her nose.

"Right. No whip. Gotta watch my love handles." I paid Shauna and dropped a buck in the tip jar. Moments later she handed me my mocha.

Cowboy Joe is old town Tempe. It's in one of the few original buildings of the old downtown. The rest have been replaced through the renewal projects that have been ongoing in Tempe since the late-seventies. The building was once the town bakery. The walls are now decorated with old black and white photographs of Tempe at the turn of the century. That was back before the bridge was built. Before the dams were built on the rivers, too. Where the bridge is now was called Hayden Ferry back then, and when the river ran during the spring floods, cars making the eastward journey beyond Phoenix had to be ferried across the Salt River. Adjacent to the site of Hayden Ferry is the Hayden Flour Mill. It is from the flour mill that Mill Avenue got its name.

I found a small table by a front window, and took my seat among the summer school graduate students, ASU faculty, and local business people. I sipped the mocha, savoring the dark, rich mix of coffee, steamed milk and chocolate.

I thought about the previous day, how Heidi had found me and asked for my help. I needed to talk some more with Joe Diaz. I took a pen from my pocket wrote Call Joe on a napkin. I thought about my walk with Heidi through Charlie's apartment and made another note: Check Charlie's Files. Then I added Talk with Rafer.

I wondered about Rafer and that controlled hostility he had directed toward me. Was he just another angry young black man who carried hostility toward all whites? Hard to say. He didn't seem at all unfriendly toward Heidi. But Heidi was a fine looking woman. Maybe Rafer made exceptions for white girls with nice legs.

I was suddenly distracted. A girl with auburn hair passed by on the sidewalk. *A girl with auburn hair*, I thought to myself. *But it isn't her. It's not Juliette.* Then the girl who could not be Juliette was gone from view.

I stared out the window. The feelings began to well up inside me. No thoughts, not even questions. Just feelings. Just images of three days in Denver. Of Juliette climbing in the gym, dancing in a vertical world while I took pictures. Later, her smiles and laughter as we talked over dinner at a small Thai restaurant off Larimer Square.

It had all started with me asking questions, getting the interview, as they say, with the hottest young climber in the country. But before long she was asking as many questions as

I was. She admitted that she had actually hunted up some earlier climbing articles I had written, so as to know a little something about me before the interview. And she wanted to know more.

Her eyes were a strange shade of blue, maybe aquamarine. At first I thought they were contact lenses. But she wasn't wearing contacts. And somewhere in the evening I got lost in those eyes, and found something I needed very badly. It was later that night, in her little house, in her bedroom, on her bed, with her long red hair flowing down all around us, when she asked me if I would take her climbing, outdoors, on real rock.

I became aware how tightly I was squeezing the coffee mug I held in both hands. I relaxed my fingers and looked down into the cup. *Not much left*, I thought. I finished the last few luke-warm sips, thought about having another and decided against it. I was as awake as I wanted to be. I folded the napkin with the notes I had made and placed the napkin and the pen in my pocket. Then I stood up and walked out on to Mill Avenue.

In the late sixties and early seventies Mill Avenue had been the hub of the Valley's counterculture. The six blocks between the flour mill and University Avenue were sort of a mini-Haight-Ashbury. The low rent old buildings of a decaying downtown business district close to the ASU campus provided fertile ground for the head shops, bars, and clothing stores that sprang up there.

I missed most of that period. I'd left town in '68 to go to college. Left again the following year when I joined the army. But I remember noticing the changes each time I would return. Eventually the bars were all closed. The head shops disappeared, too. The buildings on the west side of Mill were all torn down, as were many of the old houses near by. They were replaced by bright, new, red brick buildings for boutiques, restaurants and offices.

Some of the old businesses survived urban renewal. A few even thrived on it. One of the survivors was the Co-op. It began in 1970 as a tiny store front on 5th Street, just a half block east of Mill. It carried the usual assortment of fresh juices, organic vegetables, whole grains, Deaf Smith peanut butter, and Dr. Bronner's peppermint soap.

In the late eighties when the Co-op was eventually displaced by a new resort hotel, Tempe's urban renewal funding allowed it to expand into a much larger location on University Avenue a few blocks west of Mill. I was certain that Charlie Gonnerman was an active member of the Co-op. So I decided to stop by to see if anybody could tell me anything about Charlie.

CHAPTER 8

In the Co-op I asked around until I found a manager who could help me. His name was Peter Sorensen. He looked to be about my age, maybe a few years older. What had once been a ponytail of straight blond hair that hung down all the way to his belt was now showing streaks of gray. He was checking the morning's produce delivery against what had been ordered. When I told him I was looking for Charlie and working on a story for the Valley Views he nodded. "Sure, I've known Charlie for years," he told me. "He was practically a charter member here. I think he works his hours every other Sunday. What sort of story are you working on?"

"Water in the desert," I replied, "and how long before it's gone." Not exactly true, but thanks to Charlie it was at least a topic I knew something about. And I figured a guy like Sorensen would be receptive to it. "Charlie has always been a good source for information on the environment. But now I can't seem to find the guy."

"He might be off doing some field research somewhere."

"That's true," I agreed. "You said he works here every other Sunday? Would that mean he worked last Sunday or he's on for this week?"

"Give me a minute to finish up here and I'll check." Peter Sorensen finished the produce order, and led me upstairs.

"Used to be we tracked everything on clipboards and a box of 5 by 7 cards. Now it's all on computer," he said, sitting down at a keyboard. He logged on, opened a couple of files, then stopped. "Well, he was scheduled for last Sunday but apparently never came in. That's unusual. Charlie's been a very dedicated Co-op member."

"If he had to go out of town, maybe do some research like you said, would he have rescheduled his hours?"

"Yeah, that's the procedure. You call and sign up for another day. Some people do just space it out. Then they'll come in a few days later and say 'Oh wow man I'm sorry but I just totally forgot'. But Charlie wasn't like that. If he couldn't make it, he'd let us know."

"Anybody else you can think of who might know where he is?" I asked. "Any other members he hangs out with?"

"You know, he and Connie Torelli are friends, I think. You might ask her."

"Connie Torelli? How do I find her?"

"She's our accountant. Comes in Wednesday and Friday around nine."

"And today is Tuesday. I'll stop in tomorrow morning. I appreciate all your help." I handed him my business card and started to leave the office.

"No problem. I hope it's a good article. I used to read the Valley Views all the time, but the last few years, I don't know, the paper seems to have lost its focus or something. Too many ads for car stereos and breast implants."

"Well, I don't publish the rag, Peter, I just try to sell them a story every now and then. Thanks again for your help." And with that I headed back down the stairs and out the door to my Honda, where the steering wheel was getting too hot to hold from sitting unprotected under the glaring morning sun.

CHAPTER 9

It was late in the morning by the time I got to my office. My contract from the Valley Views sat in the tray of my fax machine. I read through it quickly, then phoned the East Phoenix Precinct and left a message for Joe Diaz to call me. I had just turned on my computer to update the Charlie Gonnerman file when I got a call from the publisher of the Valley Views.

"Travis, Mike Layton. Does your contract look like what you need?"

"Yeah, Mike. Looks great. Thanks again for the favor."

"All part of doing business, Travis. I'm trusting your instincts on this one. Say, you've done some stories about water issues as I recall. I may have something you'll want to check out."

"What's that, Mike?"

"Some guy called the paper this morning saying he had worked on a water study for the state. He says the government is suppressing the results. I could put one of my own people on this, but you've already got the background to figure out right away if there's really a story here. You up for another assignment?"

"Sure, Mike. Who is this guy?"

"His name is Bill Seegmiller. Ever heard of him?"

"Don't think so. Got a number for him?"

Layton read off a phone number.

"Check out his story, Travis, and get back to me. If somebody at the state capital is trying to pull some kind of shit then the people have a right to know about it."

"Okay, Mike. I'll check it out and let you know. You got anything else on this?"

"That's it, amigo. Stay in touch."

Well, it was good news and bad news. On the up side I did need the work. On the down side, Charlie Gonnerman, my number one source on water issues hadn't been heard from in four days.

I was adding the names of Rafer Malone, Heidi Charlayne, and Connie Torelli into the computer when Joe Diaz called. "Jefferson, wha's up, man?"

"Hey, Joe, thanks for getting back to me. You remember the guy we were talking about last night?"

"Yeah. Your buddy nobody's seen for a few days. What about him?"

"His name is Charlie Gonnerman. I'd appreciate it if you let me know if you hear anything."

"Give me a spelling on the last name." I spelled it out. "Okay. What's he look like?"

"Caucasian male, about 42 years old. Five six. Hundred and forty pounds. Sort of frizzy shoulder-length blond hair. Frizzy blond beard."

"Another fucking hippie like you, huh? What's he drive?"

"Uh, let me think. Could be an old Toyota. Corolla, maybe. Dark blue. Probably late seventies or early eighties vintage."

"Okay, man. I'll keep an eye out and give you a call if anything comes up."

"Thanks, pal. Hey, you know that guy who was with us last night, what's his name, Henderson?"

"Yeah, Henderson. What about him?"

"While you were in the latrine he starts warning me that you were a very dangerous guy to be hanging around with."

"No shit? What'd you say?"

"I told him that you were very, very dangerous."

"All right! You always did have a way with words, Jefferson."

"You know me, pal. Always sticking up for a friend."

"Yeah, that's why I'll still hang out with you even though you look like a fucking dope dealer. You take care, man. I'll let you know if I hear anything about your buddy."

"Thanks, Joe. Talk to you later."

I hadn't had anything but a double mocha all morning. It was close enough to lunch time that I was thinking about heading down to Lucinda's. But I decided I had better try to follow up on the lead Mike Layton had given me. So I dialed Bill Seegmiller's number.

Seegmiller, it turned out, had been part of a team assembled by the state water commission to study the impact of the state's existing water supply on projected growth. Much of the study focused on the Valley of the Sun.

Green chile enchiladas were calling my name, and I didn't want to conduct a technical interview over the telephone. I asked Seegmiller if there was somewhere we could get together that evening to talk at length. He invited me to his house. He gave me the address and I agreed to come by around seven thirty.

I shut off the computer, changed my voice mail greeting, picked up my notebook, and headed for Lucinda's.

CHAPTER 10

By 1 p.m. I was done with lunch and driving south on Seventh Street on my way to Charlie's apartment. My route took me past the Phoenix Country Club, an inner-city anachronism less than a mile from Lucinda's. It was the first country club in the Valley, and was still the most exclusive. While the annual Phoenix Open pro golf tournament had moved out to the desert highlands of north Scottsdale a few years before, the Phoenix Country Club remained the prime spot for the Valley's rich and powerful to gather and plan for the future of the Valley of the Sun, and to cut deals that would make that future come to pass.

As a formal group these moguls were known as the Phoenix 40, a self-appointed assembly of the Valley's power elite. The organization was formed in the late 1940s when Phoenix started to change from a dusty desert backwater to a major Sun Belt metropolis. Over the years the number of members had fluctuated slightly, always remaining at or near forty. Membership was by invitation only. In Phoenix you could have money and you could be in politics. But to have any real influence on the big decisions that were made, you had to be a member of the Phoenix 40.

When I was just a kid there had been only three country clubs in the Valley. There was, of course, the Phoenix Country Club, there in the heart of the city at Seventh Street and Thomas Road. It was surrounded by stately old homes, which in turn were surrounded by not so stately working class neighborhoods. Six miles due east on Thomas Road, near where the old horse race track used to be, was the Arizona Country Club. It stood out among the citrus groves that eventually became upscale neighborhoods near the boundary between Phoenix and Scottsdale.

A couple miles north of there and a little further east, up near the base of Camelback Mountain, had been the site of the Valley Country Club. When I was in high school we used to go there at night. A bunch of us from the baseball team would sneak up on to the elevated 13th green with six packs of beer and whatever girls we could get to come along. From up there the lights of the entire city were spread out before us, and as we sipped cold beer on those warm spring nights it seemed like the best place in the world to be.

But the Valley County Club had fallen on hard times lately, fallen from financial grace somehow, and was now no longer a country club at all. The golf course and other facilities had been gobbled up by a real estate developer named Eldon Geetus. Geetus, through his Desert Diamond Development Corporation, was building what he promised would be the biggest, finest, most elegant resort hotel the Valley had ever seen. He called it simply The Jewel.

I thought about The Jewel as the light at Thomas Road turned green and I proceeded further south. Was that the sort of thing the Phoenix 40 talked about when they got together? Did somebody say to his golf or tennis or drinking buddy, "You know, what this town really needs is another high priced resort hotel"? Was that how it worked with the big boys? I didn't have a clue. And then I wondered if any of the Phoenix 40 might know what had become of Charlie Gonnerman, because I didn't have a clue about that either.

It didn't matter much where I parked when I got to Charlie's apartment. It was early afternoon and there was no shade anywhere. I pulled in where I had parked the previous evening, thinking that if I stayed long enough the apartments would eventually block the sun as it moved toward the west.

There were some young kids, brown, black and white, running shirtless back and forth through the water that sprayed from a sprinkler on the lawn in front of the apartments. They stopped to watch me as I walked across the grass from the parking lot, then returned to their play as I headed up the stairs.

I unlocked the door to Charlie's apartment and stepped inside. Shutting the door behind me, I took a quick look through the apartment to see if I had missed anything important the night before, but also to assure myself that I was alone. Then I sat down at Charlie's desk.

Charlie's desk seemed incredibly neat to me. Any time I had asked him for information, he always knew where to find it in a matter of seconds. Sitting at his desk I began to understand why.

On top of the desk, along with an old computer and a printer, was a stapler, a container of paper clips, a clear plastic floppy disk organizer, and a pad of lined paper with some names and phone numbers. One of the names was Bill Seegmiller, the guy I had talked with just a couple hours before. At first that seemed to be a rather strange coincidence. But then I thought about it and realized that, given Charlie's expertise in water issues, finding Seegmiller's name on Charlie's desk wasn't all that remarkable.

Below Seegmiller's number was a name and number that I didn't recognize, somebody named Don Applewhite. Under that was written A-1 Computers, a phone number, and the name Eddie. The last name on the paper was mine. Next to it was my office number, the number Charlie had given Heidi before he disappeared.

Partially covered by the legal pad was a pink copy of a service invoice from A-1 Computers. It was an estimate for file recovery, whatever that was. The estimated cost was $75.00. It was dated June 1st and said that the job should be completed by June 8th. I had seen a place called A-1 Computers before. It was a couple miles north, on McDowell Road near 48th Street. It looked like a low-rent operation, situated in a tiny strip mall next to a pawn shop. The address on the invoice matched that location. I decided I should pay them a call.

The desk had only two drawers, both on the left side. The smaller one on top held the usual assortment of office stuff: paper clips, staples, rubber bands, and yellow sticky post-it notes. There was also a stack of 3 or 4 computer disks which were not labeled and which looked as if they had not yet been used.

The lower drawer was a larger one with hanging files containing various file folders. I glanced through the labels on the folders. Charlie's files were arranged alphabetically.

Most seemed related to Charlie's environmental work. These had labels like Dioxin and Orme Dam. Other files had the names of environmental groups like Sierra Club and Earth First!. A few of the folders had labels any household might have. The first read Auto Maintenance. Behind that one was one that said Computer.

I pulled the Auto Maintenance file out of the front of the hanging files and looked at the stack of different colored receipts Charlie had saved. I found a recent one that identified Charlie's car as a '79 Corolla. It also showed his license plate number. I wrote that information down at the top of the sheet of paper that had the names and phone numbers.

Then I took out the Computer file. There were a couple receipts from a store where Charlie bought his computer. And there were three from A-1 Computers. The most recent was dated April 12. Charlie had them add 4 megabytes of RAM.

When I replaced the two file folders, I pushed the other hanging folders further back in the drawer to make room to put the two files in front where I had found them. As I did this I noticed that the hanging folders at the rear of the files wouldn't go all the way to the back of the drawer. Something was blocking their movement.

Pulling the drawer out as far as it would come, I pulled the back folders forward and looked behind them. There at the bottom of the drawer, behind the last hanging file folder, was a stack of six black 3.5-inch computer disks. A rubber band held them together. A yellow post-it note on top of the stack said *3D Originals.*

I had no idea what 3D Originals were. But if Charlie was hiding them they must have been important to him. They must have also been important to whom ever he was hiding them from. Between the disks and the phone numbers on the desk I figured maybe I finally had something to go on. Nothing else in the apartment seemed at all out of the ordinary. So I put both folders back in the file drawer and tore the sheet of paper off of the pad and folded it around the disks.

As I was getting up to leave something else caught my eye. To the right of the desk was a small plastic trash can. Sitting in the can were two empty boxes, each of which had once held 8 new 3.5-inch computer disks. I looked them over, then tossed them back in the can, shut off the lights and locked up the apartment as I left. I took the stuff down and locked it in the car. Then I went back to knock on the door of Apartment E.

CHAPTER 11

Rafer Malone answered the door. He raised his eyebrows. "So, you're back."

"Yeah," I said, "I'm back. Can we talk?"

"'Bout what?"

I was starting to get pissed off. It was hot outside, even in the shade. I could feel the air conditioning from inside the apartment slipping by me as it drifted past the door to be lost forever in the summer heat. I took a deep breath.

"You know," I said, "if I did or said something last night to start off on your bad side, I'm really sorry. I didn't mean to. If you wouldn't mind, I'd really appreciate it if you'd talk with me about Charlie." Rafer stared past my shoulder.

"Who's at the door, Rafer?" Arthur Davis called from inside.

"It's that friend of Charlie's who came by last night with Charlie's sister."

"Well, don't stand there talking with the door open, son. Invite him in."

"Yes, Grandpa."

"You know we can't be wasting cool air on the front yard, Rafer."

"Yeah I know, Grandpa," Rafer said. He looked back to me. "Come on in." He opened the door wider, inviting me inside.

Rafer's apartment seemed luxurious compared with Charlie's, furnished with thick off-white carpet, nice furniture, bookshelves and framed prints on the walls—good taste rather than big money.

"Well," Rafer said, "If we're gonna talk, you might as well have a seat." I took the tan love seat while Rafer eased into a matching chair. "But first let's get one thing straight. You did not do or say anything to get on my 'bad side' as you put it. I'm just a little baffled by you being an old friend of Charlie."

"How's that?" I asked.

"You see, I've known Charlie since I was eight years old. During much of the past twenty odd years I've spent more time talking with Charlie than with anybody else I know, including family. And in all those years the only guy named Jefferson he ever told me about was a white slave owner from Virginia who had the audacity to proclaim that all men are created equal. So I got to wonder just what sort of old friend of Charlie's you really are."

Rafer glared at me. "Yeah," I said, meeting Rafer's eyes, "I can see how that could make you wonder. Charlie and I did go to high school together, but we weren't best buddies or anything. Then I spent twelve years in the Army. When I got out I went to ASU to study journalism. I ran into Charlie again then. He's helped me out on a few stories. Helped me out a lot."

"Were you in 'Nam?" The question surprised me.

"Yeah, I was there. Why?"

"Just wondered. My dad died there."

"I'm sorry."

"Long time ago," he replied, shrugging it off. "If Charlie was helping you, he must have liked what you wrote."

"I think he did. Some of it I know he liked. Even so, I don't know why he told Heidi to call me."

"But you told her you'd help?"

"Charlie told her to call me. I couldn't tell her 'no'."

Rafer looked at me. He nodded his head ever so slightly for a moment. "Would you like a beer?"

"Yeah, I'd love one."

Rafer walked into the kitchen, brought back two open bottles. He handed me one and I thanked him.

Rafer sat down. I asked him to tell me about Charlie and how they knew each other.

"Back in the early seventies, " Rafer said, "when I was just a kid in grade school, there was this program to get ASU students to come down to my school in the evening to sort of mentor or tutor or whatever us inner-city kids. There was a bunch of them at first, but after the first couple of weeks all those bright, shining, middle class, suburban good intentions must have worn thin. Most of them stopped coming around. The few that still showed up were pretty irregular about it.

48

But not Charlie. Every Monday and Wednesday night he'd be there, helping kids with math or science or reading.

"By then I was living with my grandma and grandpa. They came a couple of times to check it out. Once they saw what it was they had me there all the time.

"Back then I was having trouble reading.   I wasn't keeping up with most of the other kids in my class, and it was affecting how I was doing in other subjects, as well. So my grandma, bless her heart, came one evening and talked with Charlie about it. From then on he became sort of my personal tutor for reading. He didn't neglect other kids for me, but he'd work with me once a week one on one in addition to the Monday and Wednesday nights.

"Even though he was like an adult to us, he told all us kids to just call him Charlie. We didn't even know his last name. Well my grandma would have none of that. She insisted that I call him *Mr.* Charlie."

"Just like *Blues for Mister Charlie*" I said.

Rafer's eyes opened wider at my reference to the play by James Baldwin. I had surprised him. "How do you know about that?"

"I've read it. Powerful stuff."

"How'd you come to read *Blues for Mister Charlie*?" Rafer asked.

"A long time ago an Army buddy of mine, a black guy from South Carolina, told me I needed to expand my universe a little by learning about people whose lives were different from mine. I asked him to tell me more, and he said there were some books that maybe I should read. I told him I was willing if he'd make the recommendations. So he wrote a list for me. *Blues for Mister Charlie* was on the list."

Rafer sort of smiled and nodded his head, then took another sip from his bottle of beer. Wanting to get back to Charlie I asked, "So how long was it before," I said, then hesitated, searching for the right words.

"Before I learned that Mr. Charlie had a meaning other than what I called Charlie Gonnerman?" Rafer said, grinning.

"Yeah."

"I was probably around 12 or 13 when I found a copy of *Blues for Mister Charlie* on my Uncle Phil's bookshelf. In the neighborhood I'd heard white guys referred to as Chuck all the time. But we never used the term Mister Charlie. So when I saw it there at my uncle's house, at first I thought somebody had written a book about Charlie Gonnerman.

"When I took it off the shelf and asked my uncle if I could read it, he felt obliged to tell me about the murder of Emmit Till down in Mississippi. He explained how James Baldwin had used that killing of a black teenager, a proud, young black man not much older than me, as the inspiration for his play. And that's how I learned about the other meaning of Mister Charlie.

I nodded my head. "So, you and your buddy," Rafer said, "the guy from South Carolina, were you in 'Nam together?"

"Yeah," I said as I gazed past Rafer, out the window – that old thousand meter stare.

"You ever see him these days?"

"No," I replied, my gaze drifting further than a thousand meters, out past a new resort development at the foothills of South Mountain, and then beyond to the mountain itself, "he didn't make it back."

"One of the names on the wall," Rafer said, "like my father." We sat in silence. I was aware of the sound of the television coming from another room where Rafer's grandfather was watching a ball game. "You read all the books on the list?" Rafer asked.

"Yeah. It took me a few years, but eventually I read every one."

I paused. "So how long did you have to call him Mr. Charlie?"

"Oh, probably less than a year. It's funny to look back on it now. But Charlie became sort of big brother to me," he chuckled, "a funny looking, white hippie of a big brother."

Rafer and I talked for another hour or so. I was hoping there was something he knew that would help me find Charlie, but by the time I had heard the whole story of Rafer and Charlie I still had no better idea of what had become of Charlie Gonnerman.

We drank some more beer and Rafer opened up some more about himself. When his father was killed in action in Vietnam, his mother was the beneficiary of the Serviceman's Group Life Insurance. Perhaps not trusting herself with a large sum of cash, his mother gave the bulk of it to her uncle Sedrick, her mother's brother, who was a partner in one of the two mortuaries in Phoenix that catered to the black community. She told Sedrick that the money was for Rafer to use for college.

Sedrick was a shrewd businessman who had seen Phoenix start to grow in the 1950s and knew that it would grow much larger. He invested the insurance money and much of his own into 5 and 10-acre parcels of uninhabited desert far out beyond the city limits. With no houses for miles around, there were no neighbors to object to the land being purchased by a black man. By the early 1980s the value of those properties had increased exponentially as the constant growth of the Valley's surging population pushed the suburbs further and further out from the city center. As Sedrick sold property he rolled the money into income producing properties.

In addition to the apartments where he lived, Rafer owned four other apartment complexes. He had not needed the money for college. Social Security had paid his tuition at Arizona State.

When Rafer was five, his mother, who worked as a nurse at County Hospital, was killed by a drunk driver as she was returning home from work on a rainy night in December. Her parents, Arthur and Matilda Davis, raised Rafer from the age of five. It was Grandma Tillie Davis who had approached Charlie Gonnerman about tutoring Rafer once a week. Tillie had arranged with her brother Sedrick to compensate Charlie for his time. Charlie wouldn't accept any money from Mrs. Davis, so she gave him the address of a service station in South Phoenix in which Sedrick was part owner. Any time Charlie's car was in need of repair, he brought it to the Gulf station on the corner of 24th Street and Broadway. Sedrick made sure that the blond, frizzy-haired white kid with the beat up old VW bug always got a good deal.

Rafer was in his mid-twenties when his Uncle Sedrick turned over management of the apartments Rafer owned. Rafer offered an apartment to Charlie at monthly rent well below what Charlie was paying in Tempe. Rafer said it was only fair. Tillie passed on in 1986 and Rafer convinced his grandfather, Arthur Davis, to move into Rafer's apartment. "I need you to help me manage it," Rafer had told his grandfather. "Got too many to work them all by myself."

Before I left, Rafer apologized to me for being less than hospitable at first. "I just couldn't understand why Charlie would have his sister call you instead of me," he said. "And that still bothers me some. But there's no use in blaming you."

I wondered about that as I drove back toward my office. All I could guess was that Charlie, still acting like the big brother, didn't want to involve Rafer in whatever shit he had gotten into.

I hadn't told Rafer the whole story about my conversation with Leon Jordan. It had been late in the afternoon. We were covered in sweat and dust, up by Nha Trang. Leon and I shared a beer, the last one we had until the next supply shipment arrived.

"Here's to racial harmony" I said, handing Leon the bottle.

Leon gave me a half smile. "Yeah, Trav, you like this. By sharin' a bottle with me you get to think that you don't have a prejudiced bone in your body."

Jordan and I had occasionally discussed racial issues a few times, but always at the national or societal level. It had never gotten personal before. "What do you mean, Leon? I'm not prejudiced. I think of you as a friend. What have I ever done to make you think I'm some sort of bigot?"

"I didn't say you were a bigot, Trav. I'm pretty sure you're not. But let's not confuse bigotry, and by that I mean racial hatred, with prejudice." He took another sip of warm beer and passed the bottle back to me.

I was brought up with fairly liberal attitudes about race, that everyone should be treated equally. It bothered me that Leon didn't seem to appreciate what an enlightened, fair-minded guy I really was.

"So, help me out here, buddy," I said and handed the bottle back, "just what is it you're trying to tell me."

He took another pull on the near-empty bottle. "Well," he said, "first of all, we are friends." He handed me the bottle. "Kill it," he said. "But that's pretty easy here. We're part of a good unit facing a common enemy. There are black and brown and white faces, but here, as long as were all in the middle of this shit, we are all green," he said, and gave a little tug on the bottom of his jungle fatigue shirt. "So as a result of our common situation, you and I, despite our differences, are very much alike. As the sociologists like to say, out-group hostility produces in-group solidarity."

I nodded my head. "Now," he said, "you told me yourself that you grew up in the suburbs and attended schools that were mostly white with a smattering of Chicanos and Indians thrown in. There were no Black people in your neighborhood. Your friends were white, you dated white girls, and I imagine that all your teachers were white, too. How'm I doing so far?"

"That's a fairly accurate description of where I grew up. But I don't see what that's got to do with it."

Leon cocked one eyebrow. "Trav, where you grew up, you were not only part of the dominant culture, it was literally the only culture. You had no reason to feel threatened by other races because they weren't even in the ball game with you."

"You mean I didn't feel threatened 'cause you weren't there lookin' to marry my sister?"

"More or less. Not that I'd want to marry your sister. 'Specially if she looks anything like you." Leon smiled. "But here's my point. Since there were no blacks around when you were growing up, your perceptions of black people, and that's what I'm talking about when I say prejudice, were shaped by white people, whether they were your friends, your family, or people who produced the movies and TV shows you watched.

"Let's take it one step further. There is a source through which you could have absorbed a good deal of authentic black culture and history."

"Why is it I suspect that it's not going to be listening to the Supremes?"

"Because the black music you hear on the radio, has, for the most part, been highly sanitized for mass marketing to white audiences." Leon smiled at me again, sort of reminding me that he had the benefit of a college degree from a very good school, while I had spent most of my single year in college playing football and getting high.

"No, my friend," Leon said, "what you really need, if you want to learn about people who are different from you, is to read books written by those people. They will tell you the stories of their lives, how they grew up, what they learned and how they survived. Then, whatever your perceptions and understandings might be, at least they will be based in reality."

Leon was my friend, and I valued what he had said to me. "I'd be grateful," I said, "if you'd give me some recommendations."

"It would be my pleasure," Leon grinned. He must have hijacked the clerk's typewriter during the night. The next morning, Leon presented me with a list. James Baldwin's *Blues for Mister Charlie* was at the top.

CHAPTER 12

A-1 Computers was more or less on the way back to my office. I was curious about why they were on the list Charlie had left, so I decided to stop in.

The storefront was low-key. Glass display cases lined the walls on three sides. These were stocked with software, modems, mice, small speakers, and some other items I couldn't identify. New computers sat atop the display cases. There were stacks of boxes of what I guessed were computer components on the floor. At the rear of the showroom an open door led to a workshop where a guy did surgery on a computer. Another guy moved in and out of view. I studied the fascinating array of computer goodies for a couple of minutes. The guy I'd seen walking around came out of the back room. He was tall and thin, with dark features and black, wavy hair that hung down to his collar. "What can we do for you today?"

"Would you be Eddie?" I asked.

"Yeah," he said, "Eddie Pelosi. What can I do for you?"

"Well, Eddie, I'm trying to track down an old friend of mine. Guy named Charlie Gonnerman." I thought I noticed Eddie's expression change ever so slightly. "I understand he's one of your customers."

"What'd you say his name was?" Eddie picked up a pen and suddenly looked like he had other things to do.

"Charlie Gonnerman," I repeated. "Kind of short. Blond beard, frizzy blond hair." I waited. Eddie tried to look preoccupied as he nervously scribbled what looked like meaningless figures on a piece of scratch paper.

"Hmm. No, can't say that I remember anybody like that," Pelosi said, without looking up at me. "Don't think I can help you." He picked up the paper, and turned to head back into the workshop. "Sorry."

"Anybody work here with you, Eddie?"

He turned back toward me. "Just Armando, my technician," his voice was clipped. "But he doesn't work up front here. His English isn't so good."

Armando, the technician, looked up. Pelosi turned again to return to the workshop. "Well, Eddie, that's kind of fascinating, don't you think?" I said. He stopped and looked at me. "I mean you're the only guy who waits on the customers, and here's this customer whose appearance is, well, let's say, a tad unconventional, the sort of guy you'd remember, right?" I was beginning to get a little loud. "This is the place he comes for computer service. In fact he's been here at least once during the last couple of weeks." Now I was getting real loud. "And you don't seem to have any fucking recollection of the guy. Now why the fuck is that, Eddie?"

Armando stared at me through the door. I wondered how much English he did understand. "You, you better get out of here," Pelosi stammered. "I told you. I don't know the guy. We're done talking. Done. Either you can leave or, or," he looked around for a second, "or I'm calling the cops."

"Fine, Eddie. It's been a pleasure." We had eye contact now. I figured that I'd pushed him as far as I could without getting my hands around his throat and choking the truth out of him. I knew he was lying, but I didn't know why. I wanted him to be able to reach me if he changed his mind. I put one of my business cards on the counter. "Your memory suddenly returns Eddie, you give me a call. Okay?" He didn't answer, but I still had eye contact. "Have a nice day," I said. And with that I left.

I battled my way through rush hour traffic toward my office. I needed to update my notes on the Charlie Gonnerman file while my conversation with Rafer Malone was still fresh in my mind. I also wanted to find out what was on the disks that Charlie had hidden in his file drawer.

There was another message from Outdoor West Magazine on my voice mail when I got to the office. Would I please call and inform them as to my intentions regarding the article? Maybe they were beginning to get a clue. I saved the message. I'd call them back when I felt more like talking about it. Like all journalists, my reputation was only as good as my last piece of work. No point in fueling rumors of becoming undependable, someone who accepts an assignment and then just blows it off. Still, it was a conversation I wasn't yet ready to have. Maybe tomorrow. Or some tomorrow after that.

I turned on my computer, opened the Charlie Gonnerman project, and began to enter notes from my conversation with Rafer.

In addition to tutoring Rafer in academic subjects, Charlie also felt an obligation to teach Rafer about music. Charlie was a serious blues fan. So once Charlie was certain that he had instilled the proper ethic in the care and handling of vinyl disks, Charlie allowed young Rafer to borrow albums by B.B. King, Ray Charles, Bessie Smith, Muddy Waters and Mississippi Fred McDowell. Later, as Rafer matured, Charlie introduced him to the avant-garde jazz of John Coltrane and Pharaoh Sanders. And for good measure, Charlie threw some Jimi Hendrix in the mix.

Charlie planted seeds that grew like weeds. Rafer bought an electric guitar when he was 15. But his grandparents insisted that his academic studies always come first. So at Arizona State Rafer majored in Business Administration, but he minored in music. By the time Charlie disappeared, Rafer was playing bass guitar four nights a week. His band, Them Changes, was the house band at an up-scale, uptown blues club called Suite 16. Them Changes played Sunday through Thursday nights, and the club booked headliner acts on the weekends.

Once I was done with the information about Rafer, I entered Eddie Pelosi into the Charlie Gonnerman database. I couldn't figure out why Pelosi would lie to me about Charlie being a customer. But I figured if I could get enough pieces of the puzzle, eventually some of them would start fitting together.

Next I tried to find out what was on the disks that Charlie had stashed at the back of his file drawer. The text editor on my computer couldn't make sense of them. They definitely weren't text files. Some of them had some words and numbers that seemed to be related somehow, but they were nothing I could de-code. Other files were pure gobbledygook, random clusters of letters, numbers, and symbols.

After sampling files from all the disks, I realized I was getting hungry as well as frustrated. So I thumbed through my rolodex until I found a number for Jay Fujiwara, the guy who had customized my computer software for me.

"Hey Fuj, it's Travis Jefferson," I said.

"Travis. How's it going? You're lucky you caught me, dude. I've been working so much, I'm hardly ever home at a decent hour any more."

"Don't tell me you got a real job."

"Finished my masters in May. Now I'm writing code full-time for a small software company called Dynamic Data. Long hours but I love it. I take half my pay in company stock, they keep the fridge at work stocked with Mountain Dew, and I can work any 80 hours a week I want. Pretty cool, eh?"

"Long as they order you a pizza every now and then, it sounds like you're set."

"Which brings up the question hackers are always asking: When are we going to get somebody in this town who delivers pizza 24 hours a day? I don't eat all that regularly, but when I'm hungry, I don't want to have to think about what the fuck time of day it is. Know what I mean, dude?"

"It's a valid question, pal. Phoenix will continue to be just another backward metropolitan cow town until basic human services like 24-hour pizza delivery are provided."

"You got that right. So what can I do for you?"

"Fuj, I was hoping you could help me out with something."

"Long as you're not in a hurry, anything is possible, my friend. Your computer starting to show its age?"

"Naw, it's running fine.   But you know me. I don't ask it to do megabyte back flips or anything. Here's my problem. I've got some disks that may have information relevant to a story I'm working on. But I can't figure out what's on 'em. Wondered if maybe you could check 'em out for me."

"Sure. No problem. You want to bring 'em by tonight?"

"Yeah, that would be great. I've got to interview a guy in about an hour, but that shouldn't take me too long. How late is too late to come by?"

"Think you can make it here by ten?"

"Yeah, I can make it by ten. If I get hung up I'll give you a call."

"Sounds good, Travis. See you then."

I shut down my computer and bundled the disks up with rubber bands. I grabbed my portable tape recorder, packed everything else away and locked up the office. I drove a few blocks to a little place on north Central called Thai One On for a plate of cashew stir-fry before heading to Bill Seegmiller's house.

CHAPTER 13

I'd spent enough time eating lunches and dinners at Thai One On that the staff knew most often I would come in alone and spend my time either reading or writing while I ate. The wall behind the cash register was adorned with a large plaque. Customers would indicate how hot and spicy they wanted their food by specifying a number of peppers, usually between one and five. Anyone who asked for their food spicier got their name placed on the plaque with little red peppers after their name. My name was up there, followed by eight little red peppers.

I first learned to love Thai cooking during my tour of duty in Southeast Asia. As I sat in Thai One On, savoring the subtle flavors of the spiced tofu, cashews and vegetables, I remembered sitting across from Juliette eating Thai food in Denver just a few nights before. That made me think about fate, or destiny, or karma, or what ever you want to call it.

We had talked about fate that night, how it seemed to dance through her life. Her parents had met at the Olympics in Mexico City in '68. Her dad, Steve Valdez, a world-class distance runner, ran the 10K for the United States. Her mother, Katie Skye, was an alternate in the 400-meter medley for the U.S. Swimming Team. When one of the American swimmers had to drop out due to a sudden case of appendicitis, Katie got to go to Mexico City. She met Steve Valdez at a party on the final night of the Summer Olympics. A year later they married. Two years after that, Juliette Skye Valdez was born.

Juliette freely acknowledged inheriting much of her athletic potential from her parents. She had trained and competed as a gymnast for several years as a young girl. But as she matured into a young woman her body began to betray her. She wasn't getting as much height on her release from the uneven parallel bars, or on her dismount from the balance beam. She had reached the point where she was no longer competitive against younger, smaller girls. By the age of 16 she was over the hill and knew it. So she walked away from gymnastics, and assumed that her days as a competitive athlete were over forever.

Then fate stepped in. A friend from school had a birthday party at the new climbing gym that had just opened in Denver. Juliette reluctantly put on a harness, laced up a pair of climbing shoes, tied into the rope, and took her turn on the artificial holds of the near-vertical climbing wall. In retrospect, no one should have been surprised at the unusual strength, balance, and agility she demonstrated on her first attempt to climb.

Within a year she was making a name for herself in local sport climbing competitions. After two more years of hard training and progressively tougher competition, she won her first big national-level contest. That was when fate drew me into the picture. Outdoor West wanted a story that would put Juliette on the cover of their magazine. Their first choice to do the interview was Jon Krakauer. Their second was David Roberts. Ironically, both of them were in Alaska, on separate assignments for Outside Magazine. So Outdoor West called me. I was in Phoenix instead of Alaska. And I was available.

Juliette wasn't kidding when she said she'd read things I'd written. Over dinner she was giving it back to me, word for word.

"When you did the first ascent of The Anvil, how did that feel, going up a line you knew no one had ever climbed before, reaching a summit where no one else had stood?"

"Well, I was mostly in a supporting role," I answered, fascinated she even knew about that climb. I'd written it up for Rock & Ice when she was still in high school.

"Don't give me that 'ah shucks' modesty," she said with a smile. "You led the final pitch. You were the first one to summit."

That was true. My partners had led the difficult pitches, leaving the final one for me.

Being a sport climber, Juliette really had no experience on mountains. She wanted to know what it was like being the first one ever to set foot on the top of some obscure desert peak.

"It felt great," I told her in all honesty. "It felt truly amazing."

"God, I would love to do that," she said. "I really would."

I could feel the passion in her voice, could see it dancing in her eyes. And I loved it.

I washed down the final bites of stir-fry with the last of my Thai ice tea. What I really wanted was a couple cold bottles of Singha, the national beer of Thailand. Thinking about Juliette made the prospect of something cold and numbing very attractive. But I drank the tea instead. I had an interview to do, a publisher who wanted the facts, and an old friend who was missing. I left some cash on the table and walked back out into the heat. As I moved through the parking lot to my car I tried to make sense of what had happened with Juliette. I could write it all off to fate, but I couldn't forget. One part of me didn't want to forget. The other part knew I had to.

CHAPTER 14

Bill Seegmiller lived in a little house on 18ᵗʰ Avenue just a few blocks north of Thomas. The neighborhood was typical of those built in the years just following World War II, before the mass-production of tract homes had created blocks of look-alike houses, one right after the other. Here each house had its own personality, and the mature ash and mulberry trees, some a half a century old, provided a little welcome shade and a calm dignity to the neighborhood. I parked in front of Seegmiller's house, grabbed my notebook and tape recorder, walked across the small front yard to the door, and rang the doorbell.

A young woman with a warm smile opened the door. "Hi," I said. "I'm Travis Jefferson, here to see Bill Seegmiller"

"Come on in," she said. "I'm Sally Hernandez." We shook hands. She had a firm, sort of reassuring grip. "Bill, Travis is here," she called.

Bill Seegmiller walked into the living room and held out his hand. "Travis, thanks for coming, man. Have a seat."

"Would you like something to drink?" Sally asked. "A beer? Iced tea? Water?"

"Some iced tea would be nice."

"How about you, Hon?" she said to Bill.

"Cold beer sounds good to me, Babe."

Seegmiller sat in a worn, upholstered chair across the small living room from where I was sitting. He was somewhere in his mid-thirties. His blond hair was parted in the middle and semi-long, thinning on top. He had a blond mustache and a reddish beard. His face looked as though he spent a lot of time in the out of doors. His big hands and arms looked like they had done some work in their time.

Sally came back in with a tall glass of iced tea in one hand and a pair of long necks in the other. She handed me the tea, and gave a beer to Bill. "Thanks Sally, this is great," I said. The tea was sweet with the taste of peaches. "Bill, let me tell you how this works. The Valley Views asked me to hear what you have to say. I take notes, check out any references you provide, then try to find other credible individuals who may also have knowledge on the subject. If I think there's a story, I write it up and the Valley Views will probably print it. No guarantees about anything, except about me listening to you, and then checking out whatever you tell me. How's that sound to you?"

"Sounds fair, man. Believe me, you're gonna want to write this story."

"Okay," I said, turning on the tape recorder, "it's June 10th, 1992, and I'm talking with Bill Seegmiller at his home in Phoenix, Arizona. Sally Hernandez is also present. Bill, if you wouldn't mind, first give me a brief summary of what you want to tell me. Then once I've got a handle on what we're talking about, I'll want you to start from the beginning and we'll fill in the details. Okay?"

"So you want sort of a big picture first. Got it. Okay," he said, "the state legislature authorized two million dollars for the state water commission to do a study assessing the impact of water on development in Arizona through the year 2020. I was hired as a researcher for a team that looked at current and potential sources of water. There were four other teams. They looked at current and projected water usage for commercial activities, residential, agriculture, and recreational uses. We all spent about eight months collecting and organizing the data. Finished in April. Then we turned the data over to the statistician, a guy name Don Applewhite. He crunched the numbers, and when you cut through all the statistical jargon, the bottom line was that the Phoenix metropolitan area won't be able to support any future growth beyond the year 2015." Seegmiller looked at me, a hard look. *2015! Did you get that?*

"Okay," I nodded, "No growth beyond 2015. That's a story. I'm surprised no one else has written this up already. The daily papers cover the capital pretty thoroughly most of the time. Did they somehow just miss this story?"

"No, man," Seegmiller said. "They didn't miss it. That's the story."

"I don't get it. What do you mean?"

"The story is that somebody doesn't want the story to get out."

"Are you saying that the state funded a study, and then doesn't want to release the results? Why?"

"I don't know, man. I don't know." I looked from Bill to Sally, then back to Bill again.

"It's hard to imagine," Sally said. "Bill spent eight months working on that project. A lot of people did. Everybody was dedicated, real energetic, worked real hard, thinking that they were doing something good for the state, for the environment, for their communities and families. Then it all just gets buried somewhere in the bureaucracy. Sometimes I just don't understand the government."

"You and me both, Sally." I paused. "Bill," I said, "this is getting interesting. And you may be right. There just may be a story here. How about you give it to me from the beginning, starting with when you first learned about the project."

"No problem," said Bill. "First let me give you a little background. The Arizona Water Commission is a semi-autonomous state agency. The legislature created it in 1987, following several years of trying to create a state-wide water policy with only the input from competing interest groups on which to base decisions. To their credit, key legislators saw the need for an impartial body that could advise them on water issues. So they created the State Water Commission, empowered to conduct research and provide information to the legislature, that the legislature might better serve the long-term needs of the state."

With a degree in Wildlife Biology and eight years of running the Colorado under his belt, Bill signed on to one of the research teams. While it meant missing a season on the river, the water study provided him with a good paying, temporary job in Phoenix. And he and Sally could be together.

"Bill," I asked, "do you know a guy named Charlie Gonnerman?"

"Charlie? Sure. Talked to him several times while we were doing the research. Funny little guy, but he sure knows his shit."

"When's the last time you talked to him?"

"He called me a month or so ago. Wanted to know what I'd heard about the results of the study."

"Yeah? What'd you tell him?"

"Same as I told you. Numbers got crunched and nothing happened. Told him he should call Applewhite."

Applewhite. The name had sounded familiar when Seegmiller first mentioned him. But I didn't think about it at the time because I was trying to follow what Seegmiller was telling me about the water study. But then I remembered. *Don Applewhite* was one of the names on the sheet of paper I had found on Charlie's desk. It was the name right under *Bill Seegmiller.*

"What do you know about Applewhite?" I asked.

"Not much. He does statistical work for government agencies on a contract basis. He briefed all the teams before we started to assemble the data. Gave us sort of a quickie refresher course on quantitative methodology. Kind of a dorky guy. Sort of an old-style computer geek. Big, thick glasses, pens in a pocket protector in his shirt pocket. And he walks with a limp, like he had polio as a kid or something."

"Any idea about his politics?"

"Not a clue. He didn't seem real political. Kind of like he was too geeky to be in politics. But hey, you never know these days. He could be running for State Treasurer for all I know. Using his big computer to count the coins in the coffers, you know?"

"Yeah," I replied, "You never know." I stood up. "Well Bill, I appreciate your time. I'll follow up on all this and see where it goes."

"Hey, no problem, man," he said, "I appreciate you coming over and listening."

I thanked Sally for the tea. "It was nice to meet you, Travis. I hope you can get to the bottom of all this." She led me to the door.

"I'm going to try, Sally."

I stepped outside. It was still hot. All that remained of the sunset was a faint glow on the northwest horizon.

CHAPTER 15

I drove across town and into Tempe to Jay Fujiwara's. Down near the Salt River the air was cooler, the heavier moist air settling into the slightly lower elevation of the dry river bed after sundown.

When I was a kid, the smell of the stock yards adjacent to the Cudahay meat packing plant at 48th Street and Washington used to drift up the river bed each evening, giving downtown Tempe a different ambiance than it enjoys today. I worked there at the meat packing plant during the summer between my junior and senior years of high school. By the time I quit the job and returned to school, I was a dedicated vegetarian.

Fuj lived in an area we used to call Sin City. It was a neighborhood of apartment complexes in Tempe, just east of the Arizona State campus, where students could live off-campus and entertain guests away from the watchful eyes of a dorm mother. I doubt anybody still called it Sin City in 1992. Our ideas of sin changed considerably over the past two decades. Maybe that's what happens when a generation loses its innocence.

It was pushing ten o'clock when I got there so I just handed Fuj the disks that I had found stashed behind Charlie's files. He said he'd check them out and give me a call the next day.

As I headed back toward Phoenix, I passed the Co-op where I had talked with Peter Sorensen earlier that day. Something he said got me thinking. Since I was so close, I headed back to Charlie's apartment to check it out.

As I pulled up in front of the apartment building I thought I could see light coming from the windows of Charlie's apartment. I parked on the street, wondering if I had forgotten to turn off the lights when I left earlier that day. That was just the sort of careless waste of energy that would drive Charlie crazy. I had another thought. Maybe Charlie was home, safe and sound. Heidi would be relieved. And I could focus on the water resources study of the State Water Commission.

When I got to the door of the apartment I knocked. "Hey Charlie, you there?" I waited a moment or two, and when there was no answer I reached for the doorknob and turned it. It wasn't locked.

I pushed the door open, and just as I was saying "Hey Charlie," again, a big fist hit me hard with a right cross to the jaw. The force of the blow threw me back against the balcony railing. As I was trying to grab hold to keep from tumbling over, whoever hit me ran past me, then down the stairs. I regained my balance and vision in time to see a large man with blond, curly hair. He reached the ground and dashed to the parking lot on the east side of the building. I stumbled through Charlie's apartment, and got to the window over the kitchen sink in time to see a red, late model Chevy pickup roar out of the parking lot.

I kept staring out the window after the pickup had disappeared. There was a salty taste in my mouth. I spit into the sink, bloody spit. Pain was talking to me from the left side of my face, telling me I was stupid for leaving myself wide open, for not expecting trouble, for letting a tall, good-looking blond with nice legs talk me into this in the first place. I felt for damage. It hurt just to touch my jaw. Whoever that guy was, he had nailed me pretty good.

I spat out more blood. Charlie's file drawer was open, and his files were scattered on the floor. Walking across the room I started to ask no one in particular, *What is this shit all about?* But it hurt to talk, so I stopped in mid-sentence.

A woman appeared at the open door. She wore cutoffs and a light blue tank top. "Who are you?" she asked in a voice that was flavored with Spanish.

"Friend of Charlie's," I said, wincing.

"Who was that other man?" she asked.

"Don't know. Probably not a friend. Who are you?"

"Elena Sanchez," she said. "I live next door. I heard some noise on the balcony. When I looked out I saw the other man running down the stairs."

"You ever seen him before?"

"No. But I have never seen you before either. Where is Charlie?"

"That's what everybody wants to know." I brought my hand to my jaw and winced again.

"You are hurt?" she asked.

"Yeah, but it's not serious."

"That other man, he hit you?" Her eyes were soft.

"Yeah," I said.

"Wait here," she said, and disappeared out the door.

I inspected the door. The lock looked normal. No sign of break-in at the window either. However that guy got in, it wasn't a forced entry. Either he was a pro at picking locks, or he had a key.

Elena returned with a damp washcloth folded around some ice cubes. "Here," she said, "hold this on your face. It will help." She set the ice pack gently against the side of my face. I brought my hands up to hers and took the ice pack. "You are very kind, Elena, *muy amable. Muchas gracias.*"

She smiled, perhaps at my limited Spanish, or maybe just to be nice. She was probably in her mid-twenties. Her dark hair hung well past her shoulders, in waves that looked like she had recently combed out braids. Her eyes showed kindness – and questions. She looked around the room, at the mess on the floor. "What happened here?"

"I think that he was looking for something. Don't know why. I must have surprised him, so he hit me and then he ran. Did you see him when he came in?"

"No, I was in my bedroom reading. I came out to the kitchen to get something to drink and that's when I heard the noise."

I walked over to the sink, and spit once more. Looked like the bleeding had slowed. The icepack was helping. Elena had started to pick up the papers and folders that covered the floor. I found myself noticing how her tank top and cutoffs did little to conceal a very nice body. She glanced up, catching me staring, then smiled demurely as she picked up the last of the papers and stood up, placing them on Charlie's desk.

"You did not tell me your name," she said, turning to face me.

"Travis," I replied. "Travis Jefferson. Charlie's been missing for a few days. His sister asked me to find him. I came by tonight to see if," and then, remembering why I actually had come, I walked out of the kitchen and around the corner, into the bathroom where I found Charlie's toothbrush. I picked it up and walked back to Elena. "I came to see if Charlie's toothbrush was still here," I said.

She stared at me. "And this toothbrush will tell you what happened to Charlie?"

"No. It tells me that wherever Charlie went, he thought he was coming home that night. And I'm guessing that ape who slugged me had something to do with him not coming home." And I suddenly felt silly, standing there with a bunch of ice cubes wrapped in a wash cloth in one hand and a red toothbrush in the other. I put the toothbrush down on the desk and handed the ice pack to Elena. "It's getting late, Elena. I need to go home. I'll talk to Rafer tomorrow and tell him what happened. Thank you again for your help."

"Are you sure you'll be okay? Maybe you should keep this tonight. Bring the wash cloth back when you can." She handed the icepack back to me.

"Okay, thanks. It's gonna hurt for a while, but I'll be okay." We walked out the door and I locked the deadbolt with the key.

As we got to her door she turned to me and brought her hand to my face. Touching me gently she said, "*Cuidado*, Travis Jefferson. Be careful."

CHAPTER 16

I awoke the next morning groggy, with a dull pain throbbing on the left side of my jaw. Before I went to bed I had tossed down a couple of Percocet tablets. They had eased the pain and let me sleep, but had worn off by the time I crawled out of bed.

I looked at myself in the bathroom mirror. There was swelling and discoloration on the side of my face. It was barely noticeable under my beard. I opened the medicine chest and reached for the Percocet. This time I only took one. I figured that would keep the pain at bay enough to allow me to function, while still letting me feel enough to remind me to be more careful. Even so, I took the pain killers with me.

An hour later I was sitting in Cowboy Joe, nursing a triple mocha while I made my notes for the day. I also ordered a pecan roll, but I was finding it painful to chew.

First I wanted to talk with Connie Torelli, Charlie's friend who was the accountant at the Co-op. So far, she was the only person I knew of who saw Charlie socially. I didn't know if they were lovers or just friends. In either case, I needed to find out what, if anything, Connie knew about Charlie's whereabouts.

I'd have to touch base with Rafer and let him know what had happened the previous night in Charlie's apartment. But I knew he had been playing with his band at Suite 16, so he probably wouldn't be up at the crack of dawn. The crack of noon was more like it.

I needed to talk to Don Applewhite. He appeared to be the next link in the Water Commission story, and he was on Charlie's list. I wondered if drinking another triple mocha would clear enough of the Oxycodone-induced fog to allow me to see a clear connection between the two. While it made sense that Charlie got Applewhite's number from Bill Seegmiller, and therefore Applewhite's name and number were under Seegmiller's on the list, it did not explain the connection to Eddie Pelosi, or, for that matter, me. But we were there on the list, too. I ordered another mocha.

I found Connie Torelli keying data into a spread sheet program in the upstairs office of the Desert Horizons Food Co-op. The sweet smell of cinnamon steamed up from a mug that sat next to the computer's mouse pad. The mug had the Co-op's cornucopia logo as well as its motto: *Food for People, not for Profits.*

She glanced up as I walked into the office. "You Jefferson?" she asked as I stepped inside, "Peter said you'd probable come by." Then, continuing her work, she added, "Give me just a sec to finish this part." Her voice had some east coast to it. Not New York or Jersey, I thought. More like Philly. I pulled up a nearby chair and sat.

Connie was in her mid-thirties. Her thick, reddish brown hair was beginning to show streaks of gray. She wore it pulled back and held with a barrette of silver and turquoise. She stared at the screen through frameless glasses. After a minute she put her pencil down, picked up her tea mug, and after taking a long, slow sip she turned to me and asked, "You're looking for Charlie?"

"Yeah. I was hoping you could help me."

"And I was hoping I'd have heard something from him by now," she replied, as her expression changed slightly, something making its way to the surface from deep inside. She made eye contact for the first time. "Tell me what you know," she said. It was more than a request, more than the terms of some agreement we might eventually come to. It was the price of admission to the lives of Charlie Gonnerman and Connie Torelli. I decided to make a down payment.

"Charlie left his sister a telephone message on Saturday. He said he might be in some trouble and if she didn't hear from him again she should call me. He had stashed some floppy disks in his apartment. Last night some gorilla was in there, tearing the place apart looking for something. I stopped by and surprised him and he ran off."

"Did he find the disks?"

"No. I found them earlier in the day and took them with me. Tell me about the disks."

Connie looked at me for a few seconds. She'd been holding the tea mug close with both hands, like a sort of ceramic security blanket. She took another sip. Then her expression changed again, her eyes suspicious. "Wait a minute. You're trying to find Charlie for his sister? Peter said you were looking for Charlie because of a story for the Valley Views. What's the deal?"

"Connie, I'm a journalist. That's what I do. I told Heidi that I'd try to find Charlie and I'm giving it my best shot. But if something has happened to Charlie, I'm going to find out what happened and why. And then I'm going to let everyone else in this town know, too. Charlie's helped me in the past, and I'm hoping you'll help me now."

Connie looked at me. "Why should I trust you?" she asked. "I mean, I don't know you. If Charlie was in some kind of," she paused for a second, "some kind of trouble or something, well..." She hesitated, unable to go where her answer was leading her. Her face showed both intelligence and the need to protect of somebody she loved. "Why the hell should I trust you?"

Why should she? She didn't even know me. Even so, I needed her to trust me—at least for a little while.

"Look, Connie, I've known Charlie since we were in high school together. He's helped me with several environmental pieces I've written. I need his help now and I want to find him. I'm not having any luck. If you'll help me, tell me what's going on, tell me what he was working on, maybe we can find him together."

She sat there in silence, looking down at her tea cup. Then she looked back up at me and out of the blue she said, "You're the guy who wrote the Ace Martin story, aren't you?" I nodded, hoping that maybe I could get just a little more mileage out of that one. "That was good work," she said, her face lighting up a little. "Charlie and I both loved reading it."

The somberness returned. She looked at me, "I'm worried about Charlie, afraid something bad has happened to him." She stopped for a moment, and looked away. I waited.

But she turned back to the computer. I thought I had blown my chance. She saved what she had been working on and took a floppy out of the disk drive and placed it in a disk holder on a shelf above the computer. Then she stood up, picked up her Co-op tea mug, and as she passed me on her way to the door said, "Come on. Let's go find some place to talk."

CHAPTER 17

Two hours later I was back in my office, checking my voice mail and wondering if it was time to take another pain pill or two.

Jay Fujiwara had called. "Travis, it's Fuj. Call me at work. There's some nasty shit on those disks you gave me." I called, got his voice mail, and left him the standard "phone tag – you're it."

I started putting what Connie had told me into my computer. She had taken me to her small accounting business. It was an older house just a few blocks south of the Co-op. The yard was neatly trimmed. Flower beds lined the walkway. A tasteful sign, Tempe Accounting Services, Constance Torelli, CPA, hung over the threshold to the front porch.

She had started working there a dozen years before while she was finishing her MBA at Arizona State. In her own forthright words, her work was good, and the old gentleman, Henry Foote, who, with his wife Evelyn, had owned the business for 30 years, took a liking to the shy graduate student from Philadelphia.

Despite her somewhat unconventional lifestyle, they appreciated the strong work ethic she brought to the business. She put in long hours when necessary and demonstrated remarkable attention to detail. Somewhat to their surprise, Connie developed an excellent rapport with the firm's clientele. And unlike most of her classmates, Connie wasn't interested in clawing her way up the corporate ladder at one of the big accounting firms. She said she was quite happy staying in Tempe and providing a valuable service to her friends and neighbors.

Henry Foote kept her on as an associate when she completed her CPA requirements. She convinced him it was time to computerize their work. Then she taught him how to use digital spreadsheets. In 1988 Connie bought the business from the Footes when they decided it was time to retire. She kept the business much the way it had always been: small enough to provide personalized service to the merchants in the downtown Tempe area. And each year she would take in an intern from the accounting department at the university.

Connie met Charlie through the co-op, but never really got to know him until he learned of her accounting expertise. Over the years Charlie had discovered that if you really wanted to know who was doing what in the realms of environmental politics, you had to follow the money. But Charlie couldn't make heads or tails out of a balance sheet. He had avoided business classes altogether during his many years of college, perhaps afraid some capitalism might rub off on him. So he approached Connie Torelli to aid him in his ongoing battles against corporate sloth and political greed.

They became friends and eventually lovers. She did not invite him to move in with her in the small second floor of the accounting office that served as her residence. And Charlie preferred to keep his apartment, which was also his office. They kept their separate spaces, and a close relationship.

Roughly three weeks before his disappearance, Charlie had presented Connie with a brown cardboard box. Inside was a stack of computer printouts a foot thick. They were financial records, both official and unofficial, of the Desert Diamond Development Corporation. When Connie asked Charlie where he had gotten the information, he said, "Don't ask, Connie. You don't want to know on this one." Nothing more about Charlie's source for the Desert Diamond files was ever discussed.

What Charlie wanted Connie to find was some financial connection between Desert Diamond and anybody in state government who was involved in the water study. Charlie had heard that somebody was being bought off in order to keep the study from being released. He wanted evidence. He and Connie began to follow the money. He gave her the names of people serving on the Water Resources Board and all the members of both houses of the state legislature, to see if any of them showed up in the Desert Diamond files.

"So," I asked Connie, "What did you find?"

"Desert Diamond, and the Geetus family, who are the majority stockholders, give money to a lot of politicians. They've donated hefty sums to the campaigns of the governor and all of Arizona's congressional delegation. In the last election they gave nearly equal amounts to *each* of the nominees in the governor's race. They also own a savings and loan in Houston, Texas, although I didn't find any money going from the S & L into any political causes. Eldon Geetus is personally bankrolling a group called the Citizens for Decency, some anti-pornography group. But I couldn't find anything linking Geetus or Desert Diamond to the Water Resources Board or the legislature."

"Any idea why Charlie was looking at Desert Diamond?"

"He had heard it from somebody, but I don't know who. I was so busy just going through Desert Diamond's finances that I didn't have the time to get into the rest of it. As I said, Charlie didn't want me to know too much. It was like he was protecting me. So if somebody should ask, I could honestly say I don't know where those statements came from."

Connie didn't even know that the disks actually existed. She recognized the printouts he gave her as coming from her old dot-matrix printer, one she had given him when she upgraded her office printers. But he did not mention the disks, and she did not ask. Even so, Connie knew enough about computers to know that much data must have come from several floppy disks.

They had been together the previous Friday, eating dinner at her house, then walking down to Mill Avenue to see a movie. When it was over, he walked her back to her house and stayed the night.

The last time Connie saw him was Saturday morning. She had to meet with some clients at 9 a.m., so Charlie was gone by then. She said that they usually met for coffee on Sunday mornings before he went to work at the co-op. But last Sunday morning he didn't show up at either place.

I was starting to think it was time to take another pain killer and then get some lunch when the phone rang. It was Joe Diaz. "Travis, it's Joe."

"Hey, how's it going, pal?"

"Same old shit, man. But I've got some info for you. I ran a check on the plate we were talking about yesterday, your friend Charlie's Toyota. City of Tempe had it towed on Monday morning. Parking violation."

"Where was it when they towed it?"

"Fifth Street, looks like about a half block east of Mill. You know the area?"

"Yeah, Joe, I know it real well. Anything else?"

"You ain't gonna like this one, but it's just a hunch. You know that body they fished out of the canal in Scottsdale the other day? The one those two kids found?"

"No. What body?"

"You know, it wouldn't hurt you to watch a little television every now and then. It was on all the local news shows. They pulled a John Doe out of the Arizona Canal, right by the intersection of Scottsdale Road and Camelback. Not exactly the kind of thing the good people of Scottsdale like to see floating through their lovely neighborhoods. Last I heard they still don't have an I.D. on the body. You might want to check it out."

"Thanks a bunch, pal. That ought to make for a real cheery afternoon. Where's the body now?"

"County M.E.'s got it until they identify."

"I've never been to see the medical examiner before. Where do I find him?"

"Her," Joe said. He gave me the address of the county morgue and dug up a phone number, too. I thanked him and hung up. I thought about lunch again and realized I had lost my appetite. What sounded good right then was a couple Percocet tablets and some very cold beer.

But I needed to get a hold of Don Applewhite, the statistician from the state water study who was on the list I found in Charlie's apartment. I dialed his number. Applewhite wasn't in, so I left him a message. I needed to talk with Rafer, but that could wait until later. I locked up the office and headed down to the county morgue.

CHAPTER 18

The county M.E., Dr. Devindra Suroop, was not cooperative—at least, not at first. Since I wasn't next of kin of any missing person, not even distant family, I was not really entitled to ask her to pull bodies out of the cooler for my personal viewing. Or so she said.

Dr. Suroop was an attractive woman in her forties. She wore her long hair pulled back and tied in a long, black braid that hung half way down the back of her white medical smock. She spoke with the impeccable English of someone from south Asia who has been educated in English schools, retaining just a hint of accent.

I took a moment to explain my unique situation. I was searching for a missing friend. I was also a member of the press, working on a missing person assignment. If she would care to call the Valley Views, my editor would be happy to confirm my status as a working journalist.

Dr. Suroop smiled. "Well that is entirely different," she said, her tone become quite pleasant. "I know most of the reporters who cover homicides."

I followed her into another room. There were four stainless steel tables in a neat row. There were no chairs around these tables. "Is that what we're calling this one," I asked, "a homicide?"

She walked to one of a row of handles on a long wall. She pulled out a body length stainless steel drawer.

"Prior to the autopsy," Dr. Suroop replied, "there was some doubt. The body was probably in the canal in excess of 24 hours. The Scottsdale police initially thought they had a drowning victim."

I moved closer to get a good look at the body. I stared for a moment, then felt the bile in my stomach retch. I swallowed hard, holding it down, then backed away quickly, trying to get some air.

Dr. Suroop glanced at me, then pushed the drawer back into the wall. "I will assume from your reaction that you've seen all you care to see, Mr. Jefferson, at least for the moment. Are you going to be alright?"

My head pounded. My throat burned from the vomit I was choking down. The grayish corpse in the steel drawer was marked by the coroner's mechanical cutting knife. The face was bruised, the nose broken, the lips split and disfigured. The skin lay wrinkled upon lifeless flesh. Much of the cranial and facial hair had been cut away to allow for a more detailed examination. The rest lay matted about the head and face. It was the most horrible sight I had seen in a very long time. And it was, without a doubt, the dead body of Charlie Gonnerman.

CHAPTER 19

By mid-afternoon I was back at my office. I knew I would have to call Heidi, but I didn't want to be the one to tell her about Charlie. Still, she was going to have to officially identify the body. I wondered how I would tell her about her brother—and how I would tell Connie and Rafer.

Doctor Suroop had given me the details, the same ones she provided Detective J. R. Ragsdale, the homicide investigator from the Scottsdale Police Department. In her opinion, Charlie was dead before his body ever hit the water. Probable cause of death was massive head trauma, which was likely the result of a powerful blow to the head with a blunt instrument. Conceivably such a blow could have resulted from a fall, from the skull landing on a hard, flat surface. But other damage to the facial features was consistent with prolonged beating. Additionally, marks on Charlie's wrists and ankles indicated that he had been bound, probably while he was being beaten.

In short, somebody tied Charlie up, beat the shit out of him, hit him so hard they killed him, and dumped his body in the canal. I tried not to think about it. I knew that if I gave in to the rage I was feeling I was likely to do some real damage to someone. And then the police would be looking for me instead of Charlie's killer.

I felt myself wanting to cry, grieving for Charlie, for Connie, for Heidi, too. And, I realized, for me. Charlie wasn't a close friend, but he was an old friend. And he had been a good friend.

One bad week had turned into another one. I considered that if I took enough pain killers and washed them down with enough tequila, maybe I could wipe the slate, erase the pain and grief of the last six days, and sleep without having to wake up sweating in the heat of an ongoing bad dream. I knew better, but even so, I had a pocket full of Oxycodone and Lucinda's was right down the street.

Applewhite called as I sat there wondering what to do. At the moment I didn't have much interest in pursuing a story about some apparent government cover up. But Applewhite agreed to talk with me, so we set up a time and place to meet the next day. That made me realize that I should bring Mike Layton up to date on both stories.

I called Valley Views.   After Janie Alterman and I exchanged pleasantries, she patched me through to Layton. "Travis, how's it going, big guy?"

"I've had better days, Mike. That missing person I was looking for is now in the county morgue. The Scottsdale police are calling it a homicide."

"I'm sorry to hear that. Did you know the guy?"

"Yeah. He's an old friend of mine. Guy named Charlie Gonnerman. We went to high school together and he's helped me out on some environmental articles."

"You still want to cover it?"

"I'll tell you the truth, Mike. Right now I don't know what I want to do. But I thought I ought to let you know what was happening."

"You get a chance to talk with that guy, what was his name, Siegfried?"

"Seegmiller. Yeah, I met with him last night. Looks like somebody at the capital doesn't want the results of the water study released to the public. I've got another guy I'm meeting with tomorrow, the statistician who actually crunched the numbers. I'll get back to you once I hear what he has to say."

"Okay, Travis. Sounds like you've got it covered. Let me know once you decide if you're going to pursue the story on your friend's homicide. If it turns out he was killed as a result of his environmental work, I'll be very interested in the story."

"I'll let you know what I find out, Mike."

"Do that, Travis. And business aside, I'm sorry about your friend."

"Thanks, Mike. I'll keep you posted." Then the line went dead.

I thought I had my courage up enough to call Heidi. I dialed her work number.   When she answered I was surprised by the way she answered the phone. I suppose I shouldn't have been. "Desert Diamond Development Accounting Department, this is Heidi."

"Heidi, it's Travis," I said. "I've got some bad news."

CHAPTER 20

I met Heidi at the morgue, warned her what to expect, then held her as she cried. Dr. Suroop was kind while she completed the official paper work required in the identification of a body.

Heidi asked me to follow her to her apartment. She poured us each a glass of wine. "God," she said, "I'm going to have to make funeral arrangements, tell my family." She began sobbing. I found a box of tissues and put them within her reach.

"Then there's the apartment," she said. "Charlie's things."

"I'll talk with Rafer, if you want," I offered. "I'm sure there's no hurry."

"Thank you, Travis. I appreciate that."

She sobbed, on and off, as we talked. I refilled our glasses. Maybe it was the wine, or maybe I'm just an insensitive jerk with no sense of boundaries. I was supportive and caring, but I needed to know the truth.

"Heidi," I said, "I'd like you to tell me about the disks, the ones with the Desert Diamond finances on them."

She caught her breath. "How did you know?"

"I didn't know for sure—until now. You asked me to find Charlie. I was too late. But I've found a few other things in the process. And before I'm done I'm going to find out who killed him—and why. So now it's time for you to tell me the whole story."

"You mean the Desert Diamond files? You don't think they had anything to do with whoever killed Charlie, do you?"

She worked in Desert Diamond's accounting department, but seemed to be struggling to put two and two together. My hunches might have been wrong, but I didn't think so.

"Heidi, at the moment I can't prove a thing. But I'm going to find out, and I need to know everything that you know. I know you'd lose your job if they ever found out about the disks. I'm not trying to get you fired. I just want to know how it happened, why you did it, anything Charlie might have said."

I looked in her eyes. She looked lost, like a scared school girl.

"Charlie came to me about a month ago," she said. "He said he needed a favor. Charlie never asked me for a favor in my whole life. Never. He said he would understand completely if I said no. It was literally the only thing he ever asked of me, and I couldn't say no."

"Even though you knew it might cost you your job?"

Heidi hesitated. I waited, hoping she would find the trust she needed in my eyes. But she kept looking down at her glass of wine.

"I've never told anyone else about this," she said.

It was an ugly story. Heidi and Charlie's mother remarried when Heidi was thirteen. Young Heidi was tall for her age and just starting to develop into a woman. After a few months the new dad started coming on to Heidi. It was subtle at first, like fatherly hugs that lasted a little too long, touching that initially seemed innocent grew bolder. She was afraid and confused, not wanting to anger her mother with accusations about Mommy's new husband.

As Heidi told me the story, I could see her as a teenager – big for her age, legs just beginning to lose their adolescent coltishness. She was just starting to get attention from the boys in her class, at least the few who weren't intimidated by her height. And at that vulnerable and confusing age, being pawed by the new man of the house who found her long legs and developing curves – what? Tempting? Enticing?

Heidi thought it was her fault, that she had done something to attract her stepfather's un-fatherly attentions. Certain that she was bound to cause her family great anguish, she even thought of killing herself, just to make it stop.

Unable to talk to her mother or any of her friends about what was going on, Heidi called Charlie. He picked her up from school the next day. Heidi confided in the one person she could trust. Charlie told her not to worry, that he'd take care of it. She had no idea what Charlie did or said. All she knew was that her stepfather's advances ceased.

I wondered what I would have done if I were her big brother instead of Charlie. I'm sure I'd have lost it. Probably would have shot the son of a bitch, somewhere low and painful. Maybe Charlie's way was better. Whatever he did, it must have scared the shit out of the old man. It worked.

"That's why I took the disks, Travis," her voice brought me back from my visions. "It was my chance to do something for Charlie, to try to repay him for what he did for me – for saving my life."

I wanted to reach out to her, to hold her again, to carry her safely through the pain and fear and darkness. But I felt afraid of touching her, afraid I might trespass, crossing some unseen boundary.

I was saved by the doorbell. We stood up. Heidi answered it. It was two Scottsdale police officers.

"Ms. Charlayne?" one of them said. Heidi nodded. "We're sorry to bother you during your time of loss, ma'am." Then looking at me he said, "Mr. Jefferson, we'd like you to come to the station with us to answer some questions."

CHAPTER 21

One of the cops stayed with Heidi to take her statement while the other followed me as I drove to the Scottsdale Police Station. The officer entered a code on a number pad next to a metal door. He then opened the door, stopped at a desk to say something I could not hear to another officer wearing sergeant's stripes. Then he led me to an interview room and offered me a chair.

"Have a seat," he said gesturing to one of the four chairs that were placed around a table. I slipped in to one of them. "Detective Ragsdale will be right with you." He left me alone.

I could feel my jaw starting to ache again. I wondered what Heidi would say to the other officer. Would she mention the files she pirated out of her Desert Diamond Development office? I wasn't sure she believed that Desert Diamond had anything to do with Charlie's death. I didn't know if I believed it either, but at the moment it was all I had to go on. I needed to talk with Heidi some more to try to find one or two more pieces of the puzzle.

Detective Ragsdale entered the room, closing the door behind him. He was a large man, tall and powerfully built. He was also very black. His hair showed no trace of gray, yet there was a maturity to him, something in the way he carried himself that made me guess he was in his mid or late forties. He was dressed impeccably in a sharply tailored dark gray suit, white shirt, red tie, and black shoes. The suit hung so well on Ragsdale's huge frame, I was certain he didn't pull it off the rack at Sears. And there was a confidence in how he wore his clothes. It made me think that, even if I were to dress as well, I could never look that good.

Standing rather than sitting in the chair opposite me, Ragsdale opened a folder he'd brought with him and scanned its contents.

After a moment or two he said, "Thank you for coming here to speak with us, Mr. Jefferson." I waited for Ragsdale to continue. The ache in my jaw had begun a slow, rhythmic pace, keeping time with the pulse at my left temple.

"I take it you were an acquaintance of Mr. Gonnerman?" Ragsdale asked.

"I've known Charlie since the sixties. We went to high school together. And I've talked with him occasionally during the past few years."

"And how would you describe your relationship with Mr. Gonnerman?"

"We were friends. Not close friends. I'm a writer. Charlie knew a lot about environmental issues, especially water. I've used him as a technical resource on a number of occasions."

"When did you last see Mr. Gonnerman alive, Mr. Jefferson?"

"I'd guess maybe seven or eight months ago."

"Do you know of anyone who might have wanted to harm Mr. Gonnerman, anyone he might have offended, either personally or professionally?"

"I don't know anyone who didn't like Charlie. He may have offended people as the result of his environmental work. But I never heard of anything directed at him in particular. So, no, I can't think of anyone who might have wanted to harm him."

"I understand you brought Mr. Gonnerman's sister, Ms. Heidi Charlayne, to the morgue to identify the body this afternoon?"

"That's right."

"And then you and Ms. Charlayne were later at her apartment?" I didn't know where Ragsdale was going with this, but I didn't like it. My pulse seemed to drive the pain in my jaw. As soon as this is over, I thought to myself, I'm going to need several of those pills.

"That's right, Detective," I said curtly.

"And how would you describe your relationship with Ms. Charlayne?" Ragsdale continued. If he had noticed a change in my attitude, he didn't let it show.

"I'd never met her until a few days ago. She told me Charlie was missing and asked me to help find him."

"And how was it that she came to you, Mr. Jefferson, if, as you said, you did not know each other until then?"

"She said that Charlie had left a message on her answering machine, that if anything was to happen to him, she should contact me."

Ragsdale glanced up from his folder for the first time. Three deep wrinkles furrowed Ragsdale's forehead. He continued to look at me instead of his folder, then let his glance drift slightly upward and to the side, though he was looking nowhere in particular. He seemed to be pondering something distasteful.

"Tell me Mr. Jefferson," Ragsdale said, "how is it that you came to look for Mr. Gonnerman in the morgue?"

"It was a long shot. But I'd heard about the body some kids found in the canal. I thought I should check it out." Ragsdale nodded, as though my answer sounded plausible. There was another pause while he scanned his folder.

"Do you know anyone else we should talk to Mr. Jefferson, anyone who might be able to shed some light on Mr. Gonnerman's whereabouts or activities prior to his death?"

I certainly had some ideas, but I wasn't ready to talk about them yet. So I told him the obvious. "Charlie had a girl friend. Her name is Connie Torelli. She's a CPA with a practice in Tempe called Tempe Accounting Services. It's in the phone book."

"Anybody else?" Ragsdale asked as he jotted down notes in the folder.

"Not that I can think of. Tell me Detective, did you have anything to go on, any clue at all about Charlie, before you talked to me?"

"This is a criminal investigation, Mr. Jefferson. We don't discuss details of an on-going investigation."

"Does that mean that we're finished? I can go?" I could hear the Percocet calling my name as the pain in my jaw throbbed harder.

"Not yet, Mr. Jefferson. There is something else I'd like to ask you about. Are you familiar with an individual named Edward Pelosi?"

90

"Pelosi?" I knew that name from somewhere. But at the moment I couldn't connect it to anything. "The name rings a bell, but I can't recall why. Who is he?"

"Were you, by chance in a computer shop on East McDowell yesterday afternoon?"

Right. It was Eddie Pelosi who ran the computer shop, and who told me he'd never heard of Charlie Gonnerman. I was surprised that Ragsdale had connected him to Charlie's murder. Maybe he knew more than I was giving him credit for.

"Okay, I remember him now. What about him?"

"You spoke with him at his computer shop yesterday, is that correct?"

"That's right."

"You were heard to speak to him in what could be described as a threatening manner, Mr. Jefferson."

Where the fuck was he going with this? "You want to tell me what you're driving at?"

Ragsdale looked perturbed. "I'm the detective, Mr. Jefferson. It's customary for me to ask the questions and for you to answer them."

"And I'm a reporter, Detective..."

"So you said."

"...working on the story of a homicide victim who also happened to be an old friend," I felt the pain in my jaw surge with my anger, "so it's customary for me to ask whatever fucking questions I want, of you or anybody else."

Ragsdale stared at me for just a second, and then continued as though my little outburst had never happened. "I'd like to know about the conversation you had with Mr. Pelosi yesterday at his computer shop."

At this point I began to wonder how much to actually tell Ragsdale. Was it possible to tell him everything I knew and still protect Heidi? I was fairly certain that it was a felony to withhold information pertaining to a criminal investigation. I decided to answer Ragsdale's questions truthfully. But I'd wait before volunteering anything additional until I could check out a few more things myself.

"I asked Pelosi if he had seen Charlie recently. He said he'd never heard of him. He was lying. He had done some computer work for Charlie a few weeks before, and on a couple of other occasions, as well. I'd seen the receipts. I couldn't figure out why Pelosi would lie about something like that. It pissed me off. I guess I yelled at him. You want to tell me why you think that's important?"

Ragsdale scribbled some notes in the folder. He looked up, hesitated a moment. "Mr. Pelosi's body was found early this morning lying near the center of a poorly lit section of Pima Road. Given the harsh words you and Mr. Pelosi exchanged yesterday, Mr. Jefferson, at the moment we have to consider you a suspect in his murder."

CHAPTER 22

I had to sympathize with J.R. Ragsdale. He had two cold bodies. Both turned up in his jurisdiction, although their murders may have very well occurred elsewhere. He'd found a suspect he could connect to both victims.

And I had witnesses who could swear that I was doing something other than committing homicides at the time. The previous night was easy. Dr. Suroop had fixed the time of Eddie Pelosi's death at right about when Bill Seegmiller was telling me the details of the state water study. Both he and Sally Hernandez could cover for me then. And I had the recording of our conversation.

Pelosi's body was found on Pima Road just about the time Elena Sanchez was handing me an iced wash cloth to put on my face. And in between, I had stopped at Jay Fujiwara's apartment.

For tax purposes, I save receipts from all my work-related travel. They're an absolute necessity when it comes time to file. Consequently I had a significant paper trail including airline tickets, motel receipt, and restaurant tabs from the long weekend in Denver. Ragsdale could check them out if he wanted. He stepped out of the room for a few minutes.

I didn't tell him about Juliette. That would have been a little too much to go into. I'd been trying not to think about her. But telling Ragsdale that I was working in Denver when Charlie was killed brought it all back.

...We'd gotten off to a late start on Saturday morning. Juliette woke me up at sunrise, already half dressed, eager to go climbing. I told her I couldn't imagine anyone choosing to thrash away on some crag when the alternative was making love with the most fascinating girl in Colorado.

We compromised. She peeled off her sports bra and stepped out of her shorts and panties. "One time," she said as she slipped into her bed, "then you're taking me climbing." I pulled her over on top of me and compromised my journalistic ethics once again.

I was falling in love, hard and fast. It was the kind of love I hadn't known for a very long time, the kind you just throw yourself into without caring where it goes, as long as it keeps going...

Detective J.R. Ragsdale looked perplexed. Those forehead wrinkles were back. "You know, Mr. Jefferson, given the nature of your vocation, and your involvement with two recent murder victims," he paused a moment, "I can't tell if you are unusually sharp or incredibly stupid."

"That's funny, Detective," I laughed, "there was a colonel over in Vietnam who said nearly the same thing to me once."

Ragsdale raised an eyebrow. "Is that so?"

"Yes indeed. Except I think the term he used was 'incredibly *fucking* stupid,' but I believe the meaning was about the same."

He almost smiled. "Who were you with over there?"

"Originally the 173d Airborne. When the brigade was due to return to the states, some personnel REMF* decided that, since I hadn't completed my full 13 months in country yet, I should be reassigned to another unit to finish up my tour. So I spent my last 8 months with a Special Forces battalion. And what about you, Detective?"

Ragsdale hesitated. It was clear that he was not in the habit of revealing aspects of his personal life. Even so, there is often something between veterans, especially those who saw combat in the same war, which can break down long-held reservations about self-disclosure. Ragsdale looked me in the eye, "I had the honor of serving my country in the 2nd Battalion, 5th Marines, '68 and '69."

I waited, but he said nothing more. He probably said more about himself than he intended. From then on, he was

---

* Rear Echelon Mother Fucker

back to business. But I was no longer a suspect – at least once he verified my alibis.

We came to an understanding. He understood that I was investigating the murder of Charlie Gonnerman for the Valley Views, "that bastion of phony liberalism and car stereo ads," as Ragsdale put it. And he understood there was a chance I might stumble upon some information he would find useful. I understood that if I managed to interfere with his criminal investigation, he would find some way to lock me up, good alibis or not.

We talked some more. I answered his questions as honestly as I could, without divulging more than I should. And he told me a little more about the Pelosi case. Before we concluded our little talk, I mentioned the water study and that I thought it was what Charlie was looking into when he disappeared. I did not tell him about the big ape who slugged me when I surprised him in Charlie's apartment the previous night. For the moment, at least, I was still trying to keep the focus of his investigation away from Heidi.

I asked Ragsdale if he already knew Charlie's car had been towed from a downtown Tempe street for a parking violation. "The '79 Corolla?" he replied. "Yes. Tempe P.D. had it towed on Monday morning."

We regarded one another once again, each of us reassessing our earlier estimate of the other. I was impressed that he had done his homework in the short time he had between when the county medical examiner notified him that his John Doe had been identified, and when I showed up at the station. I suspected he was surprised that I had contacts within the law enforcement community who would run a license plate for me. We both knew it was a good bet that each of us had some cards we hadn't put on the table.

CHAPTER 23

Out on the street the night air felt like a fever over the Phoenix valley. I headed back toward my office. My pills were there. I was hungry, too, having missed dinner. But my first priority was stopping the pain that was throbbing on the side of my face.

Driving west on Indian School Road, I thought about the murder of Eddie Pelosi, and wondered how it was connected to Charlie's death, if at all. Pelosi certainly seemed like an asshole. But let's face it, there are a lot of assholes out there on the streets, and most of them don't get shot in the head and dumped in the middle of Pima Road.

I had asked Ragsdale about the location where Pelosi's body was found. He remarked that it was interesting from a jurisdictional standpoint. Pima Road marks the border between Scottsdale and the Pima Indian Reservation. The center line down the road marked the official boundary. While the reservation police are responsible for law enforcement and public safety on the reservation, capital crimes are the jurisdiction of the FBI.

A citizen who was driving north on Pima spotted the body in the southbound lane about a quarter mile north of the intersection of Pima and McDowell. The citizen stopped, called 911 on his car phone, and remained on the scene until a patrol car from the Scottsdale PD and paramedics from Rural-Metro arrived. Ragsdale said if the body had been lying just a few feet to the east, his colleagues at the Bureau would have had the pleasure of solving the Pelosi case.

I wondered if it was just a coincidence, or if someone who knew about the jurisdictional issue made sure that it was local cops and not the feds who would be trying to find Pelosi's killer.

Out of curiosity, I had asked Ragsdale if my business card was found, either on Pelosi's body, or in his shop. Ragsdale told me no. He added that Armando had given him a very accurate description of me.

Back in my office I popped three Percocets and wished I had a cold Corona to wash them down. My voice mail had messages from Heidi and Jay Fujiwara. Heidi thanked me for all I had done, said she was taking a few days off work, and she'd like to talk some more when I had some time. Fuj's message said we needed to talk in person, how about tomorrow morning before nine? He said to call and leave word about to the location, he would be there. I called his apartment and left a message that I'd be at Cowboy Joe at 8 a.m.

The Percocet hitting my empty stomach made me want to puke. I gulped several swallows of water from the water cooler. I was back in my chair, staring at the picture of the three young soldiers that was a permanent fixture on my desk, wondering if I should turn the computer on and begin a major update of the Charlie Gonnerman files, when the Percocet kicked in. My brain began to drift from pain to mild discomfort to euphoria. I felt great. People were dying all around me, state government was rife with payoffs and corruption, we would soon run out of water, but I felt just fine, thank you. No pain. No worries.

The picture on my desk caught my eye. Young Jordan, Jefferson, and Johnson stared back at me. I could hear Leon Jordan's voice in my head, just as clearly as 22 years before, "So Trav, is that the way it is now? You made it home safe and sound, back to the land of the Big PX, and as soon as the going gets a little rough you just pop a couple of pills and say 'Fuck it. Don't mean nothin'. Ain't my problem.' Well I shore am glad I got wasted savin' your sorry ass."

With that, Big Al chimed in with "Shit, Leon, I told ya you should have just left him out there. Hell, there wasn't hardly a scratch on him. He probably would have woke up in the morning and wouldn't have noticed a thing until he had to take a shit."

I started to chuckle. Al had always made me laugh. But the laugh got stuck halfway between my belly and my throat. The faces in the picture blurred. Before I knew what was happening, I was sobbing.

Leon and I had been working the night shift together in the battalion TOC*. I was out in the crapper when the attack began. The first mortar round landed near the latrine, blowing it to pieces and leaving me unconscious on the ground, my fatigue pants still down around my knees. Leon was moving to his fighting position when he saw me lying in the open, covered with shit and splintered wood, illuminated by flares our guys fired into the air to make it easier to see the approaching enemy. Mortar rounds continued to fall in the compound, machine gun rounds poured in from the tree line. Leon ran out through the VC fire, pulled my body out of the debris, and was dragging me back toward the TOC when a burst of AK fire tore through him.

Big Al, who had been asleep, rolled out of his cot as the first round exploded. He was staggering from his hootch when he saw Leon running out to get me. Al tried to cover Leon with M-16 fire, but it wasn't enough. There were rounds coming in from every direction. When Leon went down, Al ran out and grabbed both of us. We were within a few yards of the CP when shrapnel from a nearby mortar round ripped into Al's spine. His legs crumbled beneath him. He crawled the last few yards, dragging each of our bodies with him to shelter.

The rest of the guys managed to hold off the attackers. None of the VC made it through the wire. I came to just as the medivac choppers were coming in. Al and I and the other wounded were loaded aboard. The bodies of our dead went out with us. Leon Jordan was one of them.

The medic said I had a bad concussion. It was nothing serious. I couldn't hear very well for a few days, and I felt like someone had run me over with a truck. But I got over it. They flew me back in the following day. I spent my last 5 weeks in-country training the new kids who arrived to replace Jordan and Johnson.

---

* Tactical Operations Center

I'd been back in the states about three weeks when I learned that Big Al Johnson put a .45 to his head and blew his brains out shortly after he was rolled out of the VA hospital in a wheel chair.

The phone rang. I still had tears in my eyes. "Yeah," was all I could manage to say.

"If you're smart you'll forget about Charlie Gonnerman and stop asking questions." It was a voice I did not recognize, a middle-aged male, Southern, though I couldn't place it.

"Who is this?" I didn't get an answer. He had already hung up.

CHAPTER 24

I got to Cowboy Joe shortly before 8 the next morning. My jaw felt a little better. As I walked up to the counter, Shauna smiled. "Hey Travis, how's it going?"

"Too early to tell, Shauna. How's it going with you?"

"I've been working too many double shifts," she replied, "trying to cover my fall tuition. Consequently I've had no social life for the last few weeks. Other than that, I guess it's going okay. You should come in here after dark sometime. You'd be amazed how many people drink coffee at night. Must be the heat or something." Then she raised an eyebrow and said, "Double mocha this morning? Or is this a triple mocha day?"

"Let's make it a triple. Seems like I'm living dangerously these days. Might as well be awake for it."

"Triple it is. No whip," she said with a smile and a wink. I paid her and dropped a buck in the tip jar.

Fuj came in just as Shauna called my name. He wore dark sunglasses, faded blue jeans, penny loafers with no socks, and a white tee shirt with red lettering that said *BYTE ME* with the logo of some obscure software company. He carried a newspaper folded under one arm.

Fuj didn't speak as we passed, so I nodded at him as I went back to my table. He joined me after placing his order with Shauna. "Nice shirt," I said as he sat down.

"Picked it up at a trade show this spring." He set the newspaper down on the table, still folded, then removed his sunglasses and placed them on the table, too. Making sure he had eye contact with me, Fuj looked down at the newspaper. My eyes followed his. He lifted the corner of some pages just enough to show me that the computer disks were taped to a page inside. He closed it as quickly as he had opened it.

"I'll leave it here when I go," he said, "in case you want to read it." He hesitated a moment. I had never seen him look so serious before. "Or maybe you should just leave it here and walk away, too."

I waited, sipping my mocha. It was clear he had something more to say. Then he asked, "Where did you get those disks, Travis?"

"From a friend who was murdered a few days ago." Fuj raised his eyebrows, then glanced around the room. "He had a source inside who copied them for him," I continued. "He was looking for evidence of bribes, political pay offs, that sort of thing. How about telling me what you found on them?"

"You know what a GIF file is Travis?" He pronounced it *jiff.*

"Never heard of it."

"Or some people say GIF." This time it sounded like *giff.* "It's a type of computer file. Stands for Graphic Interchange Format. It's a way of digitizing a picture so it displays the picture on the computer screen."

"So," I said, nodding at the newspaper, "what we've got here, in addition to financial records, are some pictures?" Fuj nodded.

Shauna called out, "Jay, your order's ready." Fuj walked over to get his cappuccino and maple walnut scone.

He sat down again. "Pictures of what, Fuj?" I asked.

"Kids," he said. "Kids with their clothes off. Kids having sex, sometimes with other kids, sometimes with adults." He shivered and glanced down at the folded newspaper. "I'm pretty sure that possession of those disks is a crime. I made the mistake of loading them on my hard drive in order to speed up the time it took me to look at every file. I had a hell of a time making sure there was no identifiable trace of those files on my computer once I deleted them."

"What do you mean? Once you delete them, don't they just disappear?"

"No, Travis. That's a common misconception. When you delete a file, the computer just erases the first letter of the file name. That serves as a sort of a marker that says the space is available to write on. But if nothing gets written there, the file remains virtually intact."

"Wow. I never knew that."

"Most people don't. It's something to keep in mind, though, if you have something on your computer you don't want anyone to ever see again."

"How would somebody get files like that?"

"People buy them, trade them. All done with the computer, through a modem, over the phone line. There's a couple different ways." He dipped his scone in his cappuccino and took a bite. With his mouth full of soggy scone he asked me, "You ever hear of the internet?"

"Yeah. Computer network linking the government to universities, research centers, that sort of thing."

"Right. That's how it began. Basically it provides a communication link to send digital files from one place to another. At first it worked sort of one on one. Like, I would send a message to you in the form of electronic mail or e-mail, asking about something. You then transfer a copy of a file to me so I can check it out. It would go back and forth like that.

"That worked okay for two people. But sometimes you might want to collaborate with a whole bunch of folks. So the internet community added a feature called newsgroups. These are like electronic bulletin boards where everybody can comment about a given topic and everybody else can see what they said."

"What kind of topics? Nuclear physics? Thermal dynamics?"

"That's how it started. But the concept of newsgroups took off like no one had ever imagined. Pretty soon there were newsgroups about everything from golden retrievers to the Grateful Dead."

"And you think those pictures came off of one of those, what did you call them, newsgroups?"

"Maybe. The internet has grown so fast in the last couple of years that nobody can keep track of all the stuff that's out there."

"Well, I'm still a little perplexed about something. How does somebody get access to the internet outside of the government and academia?"

"They don't, at least not yet. But all that is about to change."

"Change how?"

"There's legislation in Congress right now that would open up the internet to anybody who wants to log on. And there are a number of people, including the guys I work with, who think that is really going to be a big deal. Bigger than anyone realizes today."

"Okay. Cool. But back to how somebody gets files like these. You said there were two ways. The internet's one. What's the other?"

"They could have been downloaded off of a BBS."

"What's a BBS?"

"Bulletin Board System. Like the internet, but on a smaller scale. They've been springing up all over. Most big cities have dozens of them. Basically some computer geek sets up a file server on a computer in his home. The average BBS has a couple of main features. One is a chat room where anybody who is logged on can type in a sentence or two that everyone else in the chat room at that time can see. Somebody else responds. The conversation appears on the screen. A BBS also usually has a bunch of files that can be downloaded."

"What kind of files?"

"All kinds of stuff. Games, utilities, shareware stuff."

"Shareware?"

"Yeah. Let's say I develop a program that I think is pretty neat. Maybe it's a computer game like black jack or solitaire, or a compression utility that shrinks your files so they don't take up so much disk space, or maybe it's a program that lets you view pictures you've downloaded."

Fuj paused to dip his scone and take a bite. "Maybe I can't get a big company to buy my program. I have another option. I post it to a bunch of BBSs. You download my little file, and when you open it the first thing that comes up is a caveat that says *This program is shareware. Try it for 30 days free. If you like it and decide you want to use it, please send me $20.*"

"And people actually send money?"

"Some do. Some don't. Most computer geeks are pretty ethical. They know they might be on the other end of the deal someday."

"So these pics could have come from a BBS instead of the internet?"

"Possible. But it would be a huge risk for whoever is running the BBS. This is definitely go to jail shit. Maybe there's some offshore BBS where the laws are looser. Or more likely, somebody is running a BBS and just doesn't have the time to check out every file that's uploaded to his system. I don't know."

"So how hard is it to connect to a BBS?"

"Piece of cake. All you need is a computer, a modem, a little communications software to make the computer dial a number and interface with a computer at the other end, and a phone line. If a computer at the company is set up that way, that's all it takes.

"Okay. And assuming that they do, any way of knowing who actually acquired—is there a better term?"

"Downloaded."

"Okay. Anyway to know who downloaded those files or where they actually came from?"

"Depending on how big the company is, what kind of computer system they have, they probably have a system administrator, a guy who keeps everything running, makes changes and upgrades, stuff like that. He's the guy you'd want to talk to."

"I appreciate your help with this, Fuj," I said, "I owe you big time."

"Forget about it, Travis. After all, you were the first guy who ever paid me to write code." He smiled as he said it. "But there is something I'd like you to do."

"You name it, Fuj."

"You said the guy who got you those files was killed?"

"Yeah. I'm trying to find out who did it and why."

"Well man, in that case," Fuj said, looking me right in the eye, "what I'd like you to do is be very, very careful."

"I intend to, pal," I replied as I touched the tender spot on the side of my face.

CHAPTER 25

My head was spinning by the time Fuj walked out the door. I wasn't at all sure how to integrate all the information he'd given me. But I knew I needed to talk with Heidi to find out who was keeping the computers running at Desert Diamond.

Thinking back on the events of the past couple of days, I went through them one by one. I was making a list on my note pad – something I should have already done on the computer, but I was a little behind – when I mumbled to myself, "Travis, for a smart fellow, sometimes you're not real bright."

"You say something, Travis?" Shauna was bussing the table next to mine.

"Nothing important, Shauna." But then I asked, "Hey, any chance you were working last Saturday night?"

"Yeah. It was actually slower than usual. Kind of a disappointment in terms of tips. Why do you ask?"

"You know a guy named Charlie Gonnerman?"

"I know a few guys named Charlie. Don't catch many last names, though. What's he look like?"

"Kind of short. Early forties. Frizzy blond hair and beard."

"Yeah. Charlie. I know who you mean. He comes in here a lot. Usually orders the French Press."

"Any chance he was here Saturday?"

"Let me think. Yeah. Yeah he was here on Saturday. In fact he sat with this other guy who was pretty weird."

"Really? Weird how?"

"Well, he was a really big guy. And he looked kind of nervous and, I don't know, just sort of out of place in here. Kind of like he'd rather be drinking coffee at Denny's or something."

"Let me guess, Shauna. Curly blond hair?"

She picked up a tray of dirty dishes. "Yeah, that's him. Let me take these back to the kitchen. I'll be back in a sec."

When Shauna returned she told me how the big guy had come in first, looked around for a minute or two, then come up to the window. He ended up just ordering a house coffee. Shauna remembered because the guy seemed so perplexed by the array of gourmet choices on the big overhead menu.

"That's real interesting, Shauna. Any chance you remember his name?"

"Let me think a sec. Jerry? No. Something like that." I gave her a moment. "No. Larry. That was it. He said his name was Larry."

"So he waited a while and then Charlie came in?"

"Yeah. Charlie came in. I don't think he ordered anything. They talked for a couple minutes. Then they left together."

"You seen either of them since then?"

"No. Sure haven't. You looking for these guys or something?"

"I was looking for Charlie, but somebody killed him a few days ago. Other than that Larry guy, you might have been the last one to see him alive."

"Holy shit! You mean it? Somebody killed Charlie?"

"'Fraid so, Shauna." I let that sink in for a second. "There's a detective in Scottsdale—that's where they found Charlie's body—who's probably going to want to talk to you. Guy named Ragsdale. My guess is you'll be hearing from him real soon."

"Holy shit!" Shauna said again.

I stood up, placed my notepad on the folded newspaper Fuj had left me and picked them both up off the table. I put my arm around Shauna and said, "Thanks, Shauna. You've been a big help. Just tell Ragsdale what you told me. Shouldn't be any more to it than that." And then I added, "Sorry you got dragged into this."

"Yeah, Travis," Shauna muttered, "thanks a lot," as I was headed out the door.

CHAPTER 26

I stopped by Connie Torelli's office to give her the bad news about Charlie. She said Ragsdale had already phoned her. I offered my condolences as well as I could. Connie tried to maintain a tough exterior, but she broke down and cried when I told her I was sorry that I hadn't found Charlie in time.

"Don't be sorry," she said. "It's not your fault. Charlie always went off and did whatever it was he thought he had to do. There was no stopping him once he made up his mind."

I reached out to hold her but she stopped me. "No. I'll be alright." She pulled a tissue from the box on her desk, wiping her eyes and then blowing her nose. "Thank you for coming, Travis. It was kind of you to come in person to tell me." She walked me to the door.

"Connie, if you get a chance to give those financial records a thorough review, I'd like to know if you find anything interesting." I took a card from my wallet and handed it to her.

"That is what Charlie would want, isn't it. I'll see if I can find anything more." And then as I stepped out the door she said, "Take care of yourself, Travis."

My next stop was Rafer's apartment. He looked like he had just got up, but he invited me in and poured me a cup of coffee.

"I got a message on my machine to call J. R. Ragsdale. Any idea what he wants?" Rafer said.

"Yeah." I hesitated. "Charlie's body is in the morgue, Rafer. I'm sorry."

"Shit!" Rafer looked down at his feet and shook his head. He'd lost both of his parents as a child, then the grandmother who raised him. Now Charlie. It hardly seemed fair.

"What happened?" he asked.

"Police are calling it a homicide. He was beat up pretty bad. Then they threw his body in the canal. Some kids spotted it in Scottsdale. That's why Ragsdale's got the case. You know him?"

"Jackie Robinson Ragsdale? I've never met him. But everybody I know knows who he is. First Black on the Scottsdale Police. First Black detective in the east valley. When I was a young buck in high school I used to hear the other dudes talk about him. They'd say 'don't get caught doin' wrong in Scottsdale, 'cause besides bein' Black in a rich White town, J. R. Ragsdale would come down on you extra hard for makin' the race look bad, makin' it harder for people like him who were tryin' to succeed in the White world.'"

"So you steered clear of him?"

"You kiddin'? My grandma made it real clear that I shouldn't be goin' anywhere I didn't have any business goin'. And I didn't hardly ever have any business in Scottsdale."

"Well, my guess is Ragsdale will want to have a look in Charlie's apartment, and maybe talk to you and some of the neighbors. That reminds me, did Elena talk to you yesterday?"

"Yeah. She said some big white guy was in Charlie's apartment the other night. Said you came by and he popped you a good one and then took off."

"That's about it. Big blond guy with curly hair. Drove off in a pretty, new, red Chevy pickup. Ring any bells?"

"No. I'd remember somebody like that. I went up there yesterday. No sign of a break in. You sure you locked it up when you were there that day?"

"Yeah. I'm pretty sure I did."

"Well, I had my grandpa change the lock yesterday, so let me know if you want in again. Elena said something about Charlie's toothbrush."

"Yeah. I had some brain storm the other night that if Charlie planned on being gone he would have taken his toothbrush with him. But it was still there. Guess that doesn't matter much now."

"No, guess not."

"What can you tell me about Elena?"

"She's studying education at ASU. Wants to teach school. Works as a waitress at a bar in Tempe called El Zarapé or something like that. Been here not quite two years. Pays her rent on time. Keeps her place clean. Why?"

"No special reason. She seemed to know Charlie fairly well."

"Yeah, I think Charlie might have helped her out learning her way around the university, how to do registration, student services, stuff like that."

"Figures."

"Yeah," Rafer said, nodding his head slowly. "That guy who slugged you, what do you think he was after?"

"I'm only guessing, Rafer, but Charlie had some computer disks hidden in the back of a file drawer. The goon who slugged me pulled all the files out and threw them on the floor, like that was what he was looking for."

"So he found 'em?"

"No. I've got 'em. I took them with me the other day. I've got a friend in the computer business and I had him check them out for me to see what was on them."

"What did he find?"

"Rafer, you've been in the real estate business for a while. What do you know about Desert Diamond Development?"

"Eldon Geetus and Company? He's a shit bird trying to buy respectability by being a big-time developer. I know somebody who can tell you lots about Geetus and his whole operation. What's he got to do with Charlie?"

"Charlie thought Desert Diamond might have been making payoffs to cover up a study done for the State Water Commission. He had somebody inside Desert Diamond who copied their internal financial files."

"So that's what was on the disks?"

"Yeah, that and some other stuff I'm still checking out. You say you know someone I should talk to about Geetus?"

"Yeah, a lady I used to see on and off. She works for the Gazette. Writes for the business section. Her name is Allison Rowe."

"Should I mention your name, or is that a bad idea?"

Rafer smiled just a little. "Yeah, you can tell her I told you to call her. We haven't gone out together for a while, but she'll help you out if she knows I sent you."

"Thanks, Rafer. I appreciate that."

"Anything else I can do for you, Travis?"

I thought for a second. "Couple of things. Forget I said anything about those computer disks."

"You don't want Ragsdale to know about 'em?"

"Not yet. The person who got them for Charlie could be in a lot of trouble if that got out."

"Okay. I don't know nothin' 'bout no disks, boss. What's the other thing?"

"Next time you're playing at Suite 16, play something for Charlie."

CHAPTER 27

I had about an hour before the meeting I'd set up with Applewhite. I stopped at my office and unlocked the bottom drawer of my desk, the only one of the three that locked. I kept two things in there. One was my camera bag containing my camera and additional lenses. The other was a box that held my Model 1911A1 Colt .45 (loaded) and two additional magazines (also loaded). I took the newspaper Jay Fujiwara had left for me and placed it in the drawer, closed it and locked it. The six diskettes were still taped to an inside page.

I called Ragsdale. To my surprise, I caught him on my first try. "This is Detective Ragsdale," he said politely.

"Travis Jefferson, Detective. Think I've got something you might want."

"You don't say, Mr. Jefferson. Could it be about the large Caucasian gentleman who tried to punch your lights out at Mr. Gonnerman's apartment the other night? That one that you forgot to mention when we talked at length yesterday evening?"

He had already talked to Rafer. "I'm sorry about that, Detective. I owe you one."

"It's a felony to withhold information regarding a criminal investigation, Mr. Jefferson. I'm disappointed in you. I thought we had an agreement." I couldn't tell from his voice if he was toying with me, or if he was genuinely disappointed, or both. I decided to push my luck.

"Funny you should mention it, Detective. That's exactly why I'm calling you."

"Is that so?"

"That large Caucasian gentleman, who uses the name Larry and drives a red, late model Chevy pickup truck, may have been the last person who saw Charlie Gonnerman alive."

Ragsdale was silent. Maybe he was considering what I told him, maybe he was writing it down. "Go on, Mr. Jefferson. Tell me why I should be looking for Larry the mystery man instead of locking your ass up for withholding evidence."

"Three reasons, Detective. One, Charlie and Larry were seen together at a coffee house in Tempe called Ragtime Cowboy Joe. A waitress there named Shauna can put them together on Saturday night. Two, there was no sign of a break-in at Charlie's apartment. Larry must have had a key, and he must have got it from Charlie. Three, you don't have cause to lock me up. I answered all your questions truthfully. I will continue to do so to the best of my ability with one caveat. I've got some sources I'm going to protect." I paused a second to let him digest that. "What are your questions, Detective?"

"Only one, Mr. Jefferson. What will you do when the county attorney gets you before the grand jury and forces you to testify?"

"You disappoint me, Detective. By the time you got me before a grand jury, the leads in this case will be so cold you'll need an ice pick to sort them out. And trust me on this, Detective. If I decide that this afternoon is the time to go on that wilderness hike I've been promising myself, there isn't a summons server anywhere in the country who can find me if I don't want to be found. On the other hand, you give me 48 hours, and I might be able to hand you all the evidence you and the county attorney will need to solve this and get convictions. I want to work with you, Detective. I think we need each other's help. Just give me two more days."

There was silence again on the other end. "Very well, Mr. Jefferson," Ragsdale said, "You've got 48 hours. I assume Officer Joe Diaz will know how to reach you in case I need to contact you and you're not at your home or office numbers." He hung up.

Ragsdale threw me a curve by mentioning Diaz. It only took me a few seconds to reason that he must have had someone at the Scottsdale P.D. run a query to see who had checked the license plate on Charlie's car. Officer Joe Diaz, Phoenix P.D. would be the response.

I tried to reach Heidi at her apartment. There was no answer, so I left her a message saying I needed to talk with her. I called the Valley Views. I wanted to pay Mike Layton a visit once I had talked with Applewhite. Janie Alterman was at lunch, so Layton himself picked up the phone. He suggested I come by around two.

When I phoned the Gazette, the operator patched me through. "This is Allison Rowe," a warm, cultured voice answered.

"Ms. Rowe, my name is Travis Jefferson. Rafer Malone said you could tell me all I want to know about Eldon Geetus."

"Rafer Malone, huh? Wait. What'd you say your name was?" I repeated my name. "You're not the same guy who wrote the article about...?" She couldn't finish the sentence with "Ace Martin." He had been the publisher of her paper. I suspected that my name was one that shouldn't be spoken in her newsroom.

"Ace Martin," I finished the question for her. "And yeah, I'm the guy." Allison agreed to meet me at 5, somewhere other than downtown. I took her meaning. She wanted to meet away from the newspaper office, minimizing the chance a co-worker might see us together. I suggested Lucinda's, but it was too close to the downtown commute route to suit her.

"How well do you know south Phoenix?" she asked. When I told her I knew it well enough to find my way around she said, "There's a Mexican place on South Central, about a block south of Broadway. It's called Tia Maria's." I knew the place. The food was very good. It was the only Mexican restaurant in town that served calabacitas, a traditional New Mexican dish made of squash and green chiles. And it was dark enough to provide some anonymity. I told her I'd be there.

I connected with Applewhite 15 minutes later. We met at a little Chinese place called the Shanghai Buffet, just about a mile north of the state capital. I recognized him from the description Seegmiller had given me. Applewhite was tall, lanky, and walked with a pronounced limp as he shuffled through the buffet line. He wore blue jeans, a red pinstriped short sleeve shirt, and a green and blue striped tie.

The place was just starting to get busy. Moving through the buffet line, I found some fried rice and a broccoli tofu dish that didn't look too bad, got some iced tea, and made my way to the table where Applewhite was sitting.

We made our introductions. I took a seat across from him. "How's the food here?"

"You're about to find out. I like to spice it up a little, myself." He spooned some hot mustard sauce onto what looked like Kung Pao chicken. "Best thing about it is I've never seen anyone I know from work in here," he said smiling.

I had placed my small tape recorder on my tray. Gesturing toward it, I asked Applewhite if he minded me recording our conversation.

"I'm in a bit of a dilemma here," he replied. "I believe the government should be open and honest with its citizenry, and in keeping with that philosophy, I'd like to tell the press things the people have a right to know." He paused, taking his first bite. "My problem is that most of my work comes from one government agency or another. And I want to keep working. There just aren't a lot of protections in place for an independent contractor like me."

I needed information. He needed options. I was willing to trade. "Okay," I said, "no recordings." I pushed the slim recorder across the yellow Formica tabletop. He picked it up, pushed the button that ejected the micro-cassette, and set the recorder back down on the table.

I opened my note pad and began to offer more options. "I still want to hear what you have to say. I could call you a knowledgeable source close to the state capital."

I glanced up and our eyes met. He shook his head. "Still too risky for me."

Option two. "Okay. How about if I just use you as background. I'm guessing that at this point you know more about the water study than anyone else. So you tell me what I need to know. I won't quote you or mention your name in any way."

"Even to your editor?" he asked.

"If that's the way it has to be, not even to my editor. But you have to tell me who else I need to talk to, and you help me sort through whatever political doubletalk I encounter. That way the truth and the public are served, and you stay out of the line of fire."

He stared at me for a couple of seconds, the thick lenses of his black framed glasses magnifying his eyes, making them look larger that they were. He grinned. "You going to refer to me as Deep Throat?"

I pondered that. I needed to give him a code name, if only for my notes. "No, Don," I said. "Officially you don't exist. Why don't I call you U.F.O?"

His smile broadened. "That'll work."

CHAPTER 28

An hour later I was back on the streets of Phoenix. The sun was cooking the city like raw meat under a broiler. I had some more answers and just as many new questions.

We call it a dry heat, but that's misleading. There's not much humidity, but plenty of sweat. I had my windows down and was heading east along Roosevelt. But the Friday afternoon stop and go traffic made it hard to generate much air flow in my little car. Seemed like everybody was leaving work early, hoping to beat the rush of cars, trucks and motor homes heading for the cooler weather of the mountains for the weekend. They clogged the streets and movement slowed to a crawl.

It took me thirty minutes before I got to the parking lot of The Valley Views, soaking in my own perspiration. The air conditioning, 40 degrees below the outside temperature, gave me a chill when it hit my sweat-soaked clothes as I walked through the front door into the foyer.

The receptionist, a small, middle-aged, Hispanic woman named Anna, recognized me. She smiled, asked if I was there to see Mr. Layton, and said he was in. She picked up the phone. "I'll let Janie know you're on your way." That let me know it was okay to head down the long hallway and up the stairs to Layton's office.

I wondered if I was still in Janie Alterman's dog house for my earlier lapse of social skills. She smiled as I walked in. Her eyes were gentle. "Travis, I was really sorry to hear about your friend."

"Thanks, Janie." We were talking about a brutal death and there just wasn't much more to say.

She led me into Mike's office. He stepped out from behind his massive oak desk. "Travis, I'm glad you stopped by."

"Janie," he said, "why don't you sit in on this. Since Travis may have two different stories in the works for us, I want you to know the details so we can stay straight on what's what." He looked at me, "But maybe we're getting ahead of ourselves. What do you think, Travis? Do we have two stories, only one, or should we just call this a social visit?" He gestured for me to sit on a couch.

"At least one, Mike. Maybe two."

Mike got down to business. "Okay, Travis, let's take them one at a time. First, the murder of Charlie Gonnerman." I was surprised and impressed that he could recall Charlie's name so easily. But he'd been a newspaperman for more than twenty years. He knew how to recall important details. "First question: is it a story our readers will want to read, and by that I mean was he killed for some reason other than robbery, drugs, or a jealous lover? Especially, was Charlie's death connected to his work as an environmentalist? Second: Travis, if it is a story we'll want to run, do you still want to work it? I don't have a good read on how Charlie's death has affected you, whether you're too close to it to do the job right. No offense, but despite what the local dailies say about our paper, we do insist on objective, verifiable reporting."

Both had their eyes on me now. "Here's what I know," I said. "Charlie was tipped off that the water study was being suppressed. He suspected that Eldon Geetus and his Desert Diamond Corporation were paying off one or more people in order to keep the report from the public. The essence of the report is that the Valley has only enough water from available sources to sustain the current level of growth until 2015." I gave them both a couple of seconds to let that sink in. Layton made a note on the legal pad on his desk then nodded his head in my direction.

"Charlie had a source inside Desert Diamond," I said, "who copied Desert Diamond's financial records on to floppy disks. The disks were hidden at the back of a file cabinet in Charlie's apartment. A couple of nights ago a guy was in Charlie's place going through the file cabinet. He got in the apartment without breaking anything so there's a reasonable chance he had the key. I surprised him when I stopped by to check something I had overlooked earlier. And he didn't find the disks because I had removed them that afternoon.

118

"Charlie's car was found in downtown Tempe, just around the corner from a coffee house called Ragtime Cowboy Joe. A waitress there says that on Saturday night Charlie was in there, and he left with a guy who matches the description of the same guy who was in the apartment the other night.

"The results of the water study were given to a guy named Sandy Dominguez who runs the State Water Board and is responsible to report to the legislature on water issues."

"And who is running for Congress in the new district created by the 1990 census," Layton added.

"No shit?" I hadn't known that. In truth, I hadn't been following local elections much. And Applewhite hadn't mentioned it either.

Remembering my manners I said, "Sorry Janie."

"I've heard the term before," she smiled.

"Know anything about his platform?" I asked.

"A lot of the usual stuff," said Layton, "continued growth for more jobs, more efficient government. But he's also making an issue of adult businesses like topless bars and video stores, saying he would introduce legislation to let the states regulate them out of existence."

"So, he's going for the Latino pro-family vote?"

"Something like that. It's a brand new district, so maybe he's trying to play both sides of the street by running as a conservative Democrat."

"Interesting. So anyway, Dominguez gets the results of the water study, looks them over, and decides that they are inconclusive and that further research is required."

"Were they?"

"Not according to somebody who knows."

"And who's that?"

"Somebody who won't go on the record. Somebody who does a lot of work for the state and wants to keep it that way. I've agreed to keep him out of it. I won't quote him, even as an anonymous source. But he's giving me good background information, and he'll keep me pointed in the right direction."

"And you're not going to tell me who he is?"

"Sorry, Mike. I gave him my word. In my notes I call him UFO."

"UFO?" Layton said, giving me a quizzical look. "This puts me and the paper in a position I don't much care for, Travis. We have to be able to check sources to verify our stories. You know that."

"I hear you, Mike. That's why he's not a source."

Layton stared at me for a moment, then at Janie. He turned back to me. "You said Charlie had a source inside Desert Diamond?" I nodded. "And does that source have a name?"

"Not yet, Mike. It's somebody who owed Charlie a big favor, big enough to risk a good job, maybe even criminal charges for stealing the files. At any rate, it's someone who won't be quoted."

Layton glanced at Janie who then looked at me. "You used the masculine gender in referring to your government source, Travis," she said, "but not with your Desert Diamond source. Should we suspect that your other source is a woman?"

"No, Janie, not necessarily," I replied. No wonder Layton had her sit in on our meeting.

"Let's cut him some slack, Janie. Travis has to protect his sources. We'll help him as much as we can."

"Travis, I want to bring our editor in on this. Janie, would you ask Susan to join us?"

As Janie got up and walked out of the office I wondered why Layton hadn't just picked up the phone and asked his editor to come to his office. Layton said, "Travis, I got a call from a Detective Ragsdale this morning asking if you were, in fact, working on the Charlie Gonnerman homicide. Do I need to ask if you are maintaining cordial yet professional relations with the local law enforcement agencies?"

"Detective Ragsdale and I are working on the same case, Mike. He wants me to tell him everything I know, and he doesn't want to tell me squat. So our relations at the moment, while still more or less professional, are somewhere south of cordial. I patched things up with him as well as I could a couple of hours ago. He's giving me two days to get to the bottom of Charlie's murder or he's going to haul me before the grand jury."

"Well, that would be the end of your confidential sources, I guess."

"Either that or I stand up in front of the grand jury and tell the county attorney to go fuck himself. Of course in that case I'd be trying to finish the story from a jail cell while I wait to see if the ACLU wants to take up another First Amendment case."

"You do that and you may want to think about working on a novel instead of just an article," Layton chuckled. Janie walked back in with the managing editor.

"Susan," Layton said, "you remember Travis Jefferson."

"Of course," she replied as we shook hands. "Nice to see you again, Travis." Susan Alexander was a big woman in her late thirties. She wore her light brown hair pulled back in a bun. Wire frame glasses gave her a look of intelligence and her light brown pants suit suggested good business sense. Her Chicago accent added a taste of street smarts. Her smile conveyed both warmth and honesty. We had met five months before when I brought in my completed story on Ace Martin. "I hear you're up to more journalistic mischief."

"Just trying to do my part for truth, justice, and the American way, Susan. Nice to see you, too."

She took a seat next to me on the couch, and Mike quickly brought her up to date, including my two unidentified non-sources. When he had finished, Susan looked at me and smiled. "So Travis, who ya got that'll go on the record?"

"Guess my next step will be to talk to Sandy Dominguez. Political candidates always want to talk to the press. Let's see what he has to say."

"Want me to call and set it up?" Susan offered. "Let him think it's about his campaign. Then you can slip in a question or two about his work on the water board."

"Susan!" Layton said in mock surprise, "I can't believe that you'd contribute to such a devious scheme, much less encourage a nice guy like Travis to participate in such underhanded reporting tactics."

"Just good investigative journalism, boss," she answered. "I'm sure Travis can make the transition so smooth that Dominguez won't even know he's being hustled." Then, turning to me she said, "Whadaya say, Travis? Think you can be that smooth?"

"Who knows, Susan. If I'm really good, maybe he'll even say he flew a few missions with Ace Martin."

Susan said she'd call me as soon as she set up the interview with Sandy Dominguez.

"You mentioned some computer disks," Layton said. "Find anything useful on them?"

"Lots of financial files, Mike. Charlie printed out a bunch of it and gave the printouts to a friend of his, a CPA, to scrub. Nothing juicy so far, but she's still working on it." I didn't say anything about the kiddie porn that Jay had uncovered. Figured it was better to have more information before opening that can of worms.

"Okay," said Layton. "What's next, besides talking to Sandy Dominguez?"

"I'm meeting with a woman in a few hours who, I'm told, knows everything there is to know about Eldon Geetus."

"Another unnamed source," Janie nodded, "or is she the same one who copied the files for Charlie?"

"No, and no, Janie. Her name is Allison Rowe. She's a business reporter for the Gazette."

"The Gazette?" exclaimed Layton. "And she agreed to talk with you?"

"Yes, Mike. Apparently I'm revered with a certain degree of covert awe by some of the rank and file of the Phoenix dailies."

"Interesting," said Layton. "Let me know how that goes." "Susan, Jamie, anything else?"

"Just give me a heads up when you've got some copy for us, Travis," Susan said. "I'll try to find some space for it." Susan, Janie and I stood up.

"Than99ks for checking in," Layton said. "Sounds like this might be going somewhere. I really hope it is."

Outside of Layton's office Janie asked me, "Just wondering, Travis. Are you talking to anyone at Central Arizona Water and Power?"

"Not yet, Janie, but that's not a bad idea."

"I know a guy who works in CAWAP's community relations department. Our kids go to the same Montessori school. I'm sure he'd talk with you if I ask him."

"That would be real nice, Janie. Give him a call, and let me know what he says. Now I've got to get out of here. That air conditioning is so cold in here I think I'm starting to catch a chill." I headed for the front door.

CHAPTER 29

There were three voice mail messages waiting for me at my office. Susan Alexander had spoken with Sandy Dominguez's campaign manager. They were interested in doing an interview. She left a number. Janie Alterman had called Alan Davies, her friend at Central Arizona Water and Power. He'd be happy to talk to me. She left his number. Heidi had returned my call. She said that she'd been making funeral arrangements and she would be back by five, and that I could either call or just drop by.

I was starting to feel the effects of the chill I had gotten in Mike Layton's office. My spine ached. As it spread to my head I could feel the pain in my jaw begin pounding. I couldn't afford to have a nagging summer cold slow me down. So I took a couple more pain killers and within a few minutes was feeling better than I had all day.

I called Heidi back first. She wasn't there so I left a message, saying I'd stop by around seven.

I called the Dominguez campaign office. Cecilia Montoya, his campaign manager, said Sandy could give me 45 minutes at his campaign headquarters the next morning at eleven. He was speaking at the West Side Christian Women's Club monthly luncheon at 12:30. I gave her my fax number and ask her to send me copies of Dominguez' position papers so I could get up to speed on where he stood.

I reached Alan Davies at his office in the Community Relations department of Central Arizona Water and Power. CAWAP was a product of some early 20th century reclamation projects that built the hydro-electric dams on the rivers east of the Valley. It sold water and electricity.

Davies asked me how tight my schedule was. It was Friday afternoon, but I needed some answers before Monday. Davies said his daughter was playing soccer on Saturday morning. If I didn't mind talking with him in the bleachers of an east Valley soccer field, he'd be happy to meet with me there. I agreed and he gave me the location. I told him I'd be the guy with the beard and legal pad.

I spent the next 30 minutes updating my computer files, inserting what I'd learned from Applewhite and adding Sandy Dominguez into the database. I looked at my event matrix. Couldn't see an obvious trend. Charlie had phoned Heidi, obviously apprehensive about something, maybe his meeting with Larry. Larry and Charlie were seen together at Ragtime Cowboy Joe. Charlie was killed. Heidi contacted me. I went to see Eddie Pelosi. That night somebody put a bullet in his head. Larry showed up in Charlie's apartment, probably looking for the computer disks.

Pelosi was still a mystery to me. I looked back through my notes, then added one more entry. On June 1, a few days before Charlie was killed, he dropped off something at A-1 Computers. There was a claim check on his desk. The service was described as "file recovery." I wished I knew what that was all about, but with Charlie and Eddie both dead, it seemed unlikely I ever would.

I decided I had time for one more call. It was one I should have made after I'd talked with Joe Diaz a few nights before. I found the number and dialed it. A woman's voice answered after one ring, "First Valley National Bank, how may I direct your call?"

"Merritt Donovan, please."

"May I tell him who is calling?"

"Yes, of course. My name is Travis Jefferson."

"One moment, Mr. Jefferson." Elevator music came on.

A few seconds later David Merritt Donovan, First Lieutenant (promotable), U.S. Army Reserve, who also happened to be a branch manager for First Valley National Bank, came on the line. "Travis, what's happening?"

"Hey, *Trung Ûy*, I hear we're going to have to start calling you *Dai Ûy* pretty soon.[*] Congratulations."

---

[*] In the Vietnamese language, Trung Ûy and Dai Ûy mean First Lieutenant and Captain, respectively. Ûy sounds a bit like the French word oui.

"Thanks, Travis. Looks like for once, those pencil necks up at headquarters managed to not screw up the paperwork. What are you up to these days?"

"Same old stuff. Just trying to make a living without having a real job. I was wondering if you had some time this weekend when we could talk?"

"You thinking about rejoining the unit?"

"No, LT, nice try. I was wondering if I could pick your brain for a while about the banking industry. I need background for a story I'm working on."

"You want to meet after work? Split a pitcher of beer? I could eat some wings and you could eat whatever rabbit food they put out at happy hour."

"No, that won't work for me. I've got to meet somebody in a little while. Got any time tomorrow?"

"It's possible, Travis. You interested in doing a run tomorrow morning?"

"I'll tell you the truth, LT. I'm 42 years old, my legs are shot, and I haven't been able to keep up with you since you were a butter bar*. But sure, why not? A little sweat might do me some good."

"Okay. How about we meet at 40th Street and the canal? Run the canal bank? Say about six thirty?"

"Yeah, I guess if we're going to beat the heat we'll have to start early. I'll see you then."

It was almost 4:00 when I got off the phone with Donovan. I had an hour until I was supposed to meet Allison Rowe in south Phoenix, so I shut my computer down, locked up my office, and headed home for a shower and change of clothes. The pain killers had me feeling pretty perky, and I wanted to look my best for my dinner with a fellow journalist.

• Second Lieutenant

CHAPTER 30

I got to Tia Maria's just a little after five. The hostess asked if I was joining someone, and when I said I was meeting Ms. Rowe she directed me to the booth where Allison was waiting.

She smiled as we shook hands. She was dark, her black hair cut fashionably short. She was attractive but not flashy, wearing a maroon top and black crepe pants, small gold earrings, and minimal makeup. Her appearance suggested more class than one usually finds among reporters, at least in Phoenix. "So you're the legendary Travis Jefferson. I feel honored to be in the company of such greatness."

"Must be confusing me with somebody else, Ms. Rowe. I'm just a humble, hard working freelancer, trying to make a buck and keep my facts straight."

"Yeah, right," she chuckled. "The humble, hardworking freelancer who sent Ace Martin packing to journalism Siberia. And please, call me Allison."

We ate chips and salsa and placed our orders. Allison got the chicken taco salad with a light beer. I ordered the calabacitas burro. I was tempted to have a beer, too, but pain killers were still in full force and I was working, so I just asked for water.

"I'm curious about two things," Allison said. "How do you know Rafer, and why do you want to know about Eldon Geetus?"

"Rafer and I had a mutual friend, an environmentalist named Charlie Gonnerman."

"Had?"

"They found his body floating down the Arizona Canal about a week ago."

"Oh. I heard about that. And he was a friend of yours? I'm sorry." There was an awkward moment of silence. "Do the police have any idea who or why?"

"Not much, at least not yet. I'm trying to follow up on a few things myself, which brings us to your second question."

"You mean Eldon Geetus?"

"Before Charlie disappeared he was looking into the Desert Diamond finances trying to find a connection between them and a water study?"

"You mean the Water Commission study? What sort of connection?"

"Charlie thought maybe Geetus was paying off somebody to keep the report from being released."

"The way I heard it," she said, "the study team left out an important variable that would have a significant impact on the results. So Sandy Dominguez decided to wait until the research was complete before releasing any results."

"And that important variable was the construction of Orme Dam?"

"That's the way I heard it at the paper."

"You know," I said, "the team that did the research on present and future sources of water did not consider Orme Dam a viable alternative."

"Yes, I've heard that, too. Dominguez apparently felt that the researchers demonstrated an obvious bias in excluding Orme Dam as an alternative."

"Is that what you think, Allison?"

"I'm not sure," she replied carefully. "Given the dire predictions for the business community without additional sources of water, I think any viable alternative has to be considered."

"There's that word *viable* again," I said. "How do regular folks like you and me decide what's really viable and what's just another political boondoggle?"

"And," she continued, "you're also wondering how a young man with political aspirations like Sandy Dominguez decides."

"Allison, I'm beginning to think the answer to that question is not so difficult. Based on my extensive experience in these matters, if you want to know how a young man with political aspirations, as you so eloquently put it, decides what's viable and what's not, you must follow the money."

"Which, I imagine, brings us back to Eldon Geetus."

CHAPTER 31

It was well after seven when I called Heidi from the pay phone at Tia Maria's, telling her I wouldn't be at her place for about another 30 minutes. Once Allison and I had finished our dinners we'd continued to talk. She went through several bottles of Corona. "Hey, why not?" she said, "since you're buying and I don't have a date tonight." In just a little over two hours, Allison told me more than I ever wanted to know about Eldon Geetus, and almost as much as I needed to know. I walked her to her car. Before getting in she smiled and said, "You know that I want to hear about it if you do find out anything more on Geetus. And you tell Rafer that my phone number is still the same."

The long drive from south Phoenix to Scottsdale gave me time to digest everything Allison had told me. She was the youngest of 5 children. During her junior year at Florida State her father, Ernie Rowe, a Senior Master Sergeant in the Air Force, told her that he and Allison's mother were buying some land in the Florida panhandle for their retirement home. It wasn't far from Hurlburt Field where Ernie had spent much of his career, just a few miles outside of Fort Walton Beach.

The land sales office was a slick operation. The salesman drove Ernie and his wife around on a golf cart that was equipped with a two-way radio. They saw another couple riding back toward the sales office as they were riding out, and heard another salesman say over the radio that those folks were going to buy one of the last remaining lots. The salesman with Ernie and Florence told them they were lucky they came out the day they did because there were only 3 lots left, and it didn't look like they'd still be available by the end of the week.

Ernie and Florence liked the lots they saw. They had trees and seemed to be some of the best land in the area. The salesman said that a number of military folks, from Eglin, and Hurlburt, and as far away as Fort Rucker and even Fort Benning had been buying lots for their retirement homes.

And while they were free to choose any builder and design they liked, the company had some wonderful floor plans. In fact, their model homes would be going up soon.

Once back at the sales office, convinced by the sales staff that they'd better make a commitment if they wanted one of the remaining lots, Ernie wrote a check for the land they wanted and they signed papers to buy the lot.

Unknown to Allison's parents, they purchased a different piece of property from the one they were shown. The land sales office would change the signs in front of the five desirable lots each morning. Properties that were identified as lots 21 through 25 on one day, became lots 26 through 30 the following day. Then they would attach "Sold" signs to two of those lot number signs.

A lot matching the legal description on Ernie and Flo's deed turned out to be – once Ernie paid to have a survey done – a tiny, bare ridge which dropped off quickly into a mosquito-infested bog. Because it was difficult to prove wrong-doing, no criminal charges were brought against the land company. There was, however, a great deal of consistency in the numerous complaints that eventually made their way to the state attorney general's office. He referred the matter to the state licensing board, which held a hearing on the matter. After listening to many people, including Allison's parents, tell how they were cheated by Gulf Coast Land and Development LLC, the board revoked the license of GCL&D.

It was a hollow victory. GCL&D had ceased to exist by the time its license was revoked. Its president and CEO, Eldon Geetus, had moved on to take advantage of another business opportunity, leveraging the small fortune he had made in Florida real estate to open a savings and loan in Houston, Texas.

It was really hard, Allison told me, to wring the details out of her parents. They were both proud, hard working people who hated to admit that they had been swindled. By then Allison was in her final semester of college and interning at the Tallahassee Tribune. She wanted to write an expose on

GCL&D's shady land deals. But despite doing the ground work and digging up the relevant files at the state capital, her editor wasn't interested. "It's old news," he told her. "Nobody cares about another Florida land deal gone bad."

Maybe so, she thought. And maybe nobody in north Florida wants to see the by-line of a young, Black woman on the business pages. The experience convinced her it was time to leave north Florida. She had good memories of a time her father had been stationed in Arizona. The winters were mild and the summers were no worse than they were in Florida, only without the humidity. So with graduation approaching, she sent her résumé off to some Arizona newspapers. To her surprise, the Gazette gave her an interview and hired her. "My timing was good," she told me. "They were under pressure to diversify. By being Black and a woman, they got to check off two boxes when they hired me."

It wasn't quite three years later when the name Eldon Geetus crossed her desk at the Phoenix Gazette, this time as the head of the newest big home builder in town, Desert Diamond Development. He was getting underway with large developments of tract houses in three different parts of the Valley, plus a gated community in the desert northeast of Scottsdale. There was even talk of a big resort hotel in the Scottsdale area.

Allison approached her boss, the editor of the paper's business section, an old school newspaperman from Chicago, telling him what she knew about Geetus from her Florida days. "Was he ever indicted?" her boss asked.

"No," she replied, "but his company lost its license."

"Well, that's too bad. Without an indictment and conviction, he's just another developer who had some administrative problems along the way. They're a dime a dozen, and you got no story." Then, with a more sympathetic tone, her editor continued, "But hang on to your notes Allison, and keep an eye on this guy. I mean, as much as you've got time to, anyway. Arizona's had its share of crooked real estate deals, just like Florida. Who knows? This guy Geetus could screw up somehow. And when he does, you'll be ready.

In the mean time, get back to work on the America West story. I want to know how long they're gonna keep flying to Hawaii and Japan with a plane full of empty seats."

Allison did keep an eye on Geetus. She maintained a permanent query with the wire services for Geetus and Desert Diamond Development. And she maintained a hard copy file of clippings. She slowly developed contacts within the industry who would slip her a little inside gossip.

In a way, Geetus became her personal, if not professional obsession. Once she learned about Geetus' foray into the banking industry, she added the Diamond Savings and Loan in Houston to her wire service query. And over time she filled four cardboard file boxes with clippings on Geetus and his business ventures. And twice she used vacation time to go back to Mobile, Alabama, where Geetus and his family had lived before coming to Florida.

"People tell me he's real frustrated that he hasn't been invited to join the Phoenix 40," Allison had told me. "He wants to position his son to run for Congress in a couple of years. Apparently he thinks that rubbing elbows with the rich and powerful is the way to make that happen."

"Tell me about his son," I said. It was the first I'd heard about him.

"Delbert Geetus, 38 years old, Vice President and Chief Financial Officer of Desert Diamond Development. Doesn't seem to have the old man's drive to make money, but certainly likes to spend it. Been married for twelve years, has four kids, but has a bit of a wandering eye when it comes to the ladies." Allison was giving me sort of a funny grin at this point. The beer was beginning to take its toll. "I've heard," she continued, "that all of the young women who work for him, who, I'm told, he hires personally, are quite attractive. Just rumor, of course. Never actually seen them myself."

I pictured an office of young women who looked like Heidi Charlayne. "What's his daddy think of that?"

"The old man is kind of funny about it. Seems that as long as Delbert maintains the appearance of the good husband and father, everything is okay. And so far, that's been the case.

But I guess the old man was pretty strict with him when he was growing up. There must have been a time when the family was real religious or something. Somebody in Mobile told me a story about the old man going crazy one time when he caught Delbert reading a Playboy in his bedroom. Delbert must have been in high school at the time. Anyway, they say the old man lost it, and started yellin', slappin' Delbert up side the head, and carryin' on about what would Delbert's mother think if she knew he was bringing such filth into their home. Stuff like that. The guy said it was a 'genteel southern womanhood' kind of thing. Sort of like good old boys will be good old boys, just don't bring it in the home or let your mother see it. But nobody really knows."

"Interesting. That brings us to his Citizens for Decency thing. What's that all about?"

"There's a couple of ways you can look at it. On the one hand it's strictly business. The old man's in the business of selling homes. The more people who move to the Valley, the more homes he's likely to sell. So he wants Phoenix and the surrounding communities to be nice, wholesome places for families to live, free of smut and sleaze."

"Makes sense, I guess. What's the other way I can look at it?"

"It gives him an inroad into local politics. Through CFD he can promote certain candidates, collecting favors he hopes to cash when he runs Delbert for Congress."

"Okay. So, who's he promoting this time around."

"Sandy Dominguez. I've got a friend who covers politics for the Gazette. He says there's a lot of soft money involved."

"Please help me out here, Allison. I'm real ignorant when it comes to elections. What's soft money?"

"Well, in this case, instead of just funneling cash into the Dominguez campaign, CFD is preparing radio and TV ads. They won't come right out and say Vote for Sandy. Instead they'll say something like CFD has examined the positions of all the candidates on important family value issues, and Sandy Dominguez is, far and away, the candidate who will stand up for families and fight against the degradation of the moral fabric of America, or some shit like that. Or more likely, they'll say that Sandy's opponent is soft on pornographers and won't protect your children. But, either way, they never say 'Vote for Sandy.' Geetus can use company money and it doesn't get counted in the official records of how much candidates receive and how much they spend. And, of course, since it comes from CFD instead of Geetus himself, it looks as though it came about through some wellspring of community support, rather than just one real estate developer with his own agenda."

"That's real interesting, Allison. While we're still talking about money, how about telling me about his bank in Houston."

"Savings and loan," Allison corrected me. "And not your typical one, either."

"How's that?"

"Your normal S & L lets people deposit money in a savings account that pays them something like three or four percent interest, then loans the money back to them at eight or nine percent for the mortgage on a house, or maybe for a car loan. The profit is the difference between the two minus expenses. Geetus has been offering up to a half a point of interest above the other institutions to get people to deposit their money there. And while they do make the occasional home loan, most of their money goes into the booming real estate market in Arizona."

"Are you telling me Geetus loans the money to himself."

"Not at all, Travis," Allison replied with a smile. "Geetus doesn't loan money to himself. Diamond Savings and Loan of Houston buys land in Arizona, which, through an agreement with the Desert Diamond Development Corporation of Arizona, is then subdivided into residential properties. The value of these properties is enhanced significantly by Desert Diamond adding amenities like streets, water, sewers, gas and electrical hook ups and nearby parks and playgrounds. That pumps up the value of the assets Diamond S&L has on its books so it looks good to the regulators. When the lots are sold as part of a new housing development, Diamond S & L makes a handsome profit on its land investment and is able to maintain the required cash reserves. Desert Diamond makes money on the construction of several hundred new homes without the need to buy big chunks of land. The fact that Eldon Geetus happens to be the president of both entities is merely a business coincidence."

"Right. And if I believed that, I bet you've got some land in Florida to sell me."

She smiled, really only about a half of a smile. "That would be funny if, well, you know."

"Sorry," I said. "Bad choice of words. So anyway, the S & L makes money, Desert Diamond makes money, everybody's happy. What a great deal! Is there a down side?"

"As long as people keep moving to the Valley, the demand for housing remains high. Geetus has gone from tract homes for the masses to a gated community for the rich and paranoid. Now he's one of the ten largest employers in the Valley." She paused, draining the last of her final Corona. "If I didn't hate the man so much, I'd be writing articles about what a wonderful asset he is to this sprawling wasteland of a city." She took a pen and a business card out of her purse, wrote something on the business card and handed it to me. "That's my home number and my pager number in case you need to contact me. And now, Travis, I should go home while I can still drive."

CHAPTER 32

It was almost sunset when I pulled into the parking lot of Heidi's Scottsdale apartment. Sprinklers, triggered by a timer hidden somewhere among the shrubbery, turned on automatically as I made my way along a sidewalk bordered by green lawn, over-planted palms and green plants that typified the landscaping concepts of most of the apartment complexes in Heidi's upscale neighborhood. It provided the illusion of a lush, green environment where an orchard of citrus trees had once grown, fed through an irrigation ditch from the nearby Arizona canal. Before the canal was built and the orchards planted, it was just hard scrabble desert with little growing except mesquite, creosote, and cactus—hardy plants that can go months without a drink, and take full advantage of the occasional gully washer when it does rain.

I knew that somewhere toward the center of the maze of apartments there was bound to be a swimming pool and probably a jacuzzi and sauna, too. That led me to think about how good Heidi must look in a swim suit. Thoughts like that would only distract me from questions that needed answers. Reminding myself that I was involved in a serious business that had already cost Heidi's brother his life, I knocked on her apartment door.

Heidi invited me in, giving me a hug as though we were old friends sharing a common sense of loss. We made small talk. She was drinking Chablis, and not her first glass of the evening as I surmised from her speech. She offered me a glass. I declined. I was neither recording our conversation, nor making notes. But there were things I needed to learn from Heidi, and I couldn't afford to let any critical details slip through the cracks this late in the game.

She told me that she had spoken with Connie. Together they had made plans for a memorial service at a small community church in Tempe, not far from the university. It was scheduled for Monday night. I told her I'd be there.

"I'm going to leave Desert Diamond," Heidi said. There was something in the way she said it that sounded just a little strange, as though she were announcing that she was going to leave her lover, instead of just finding another job.

We were sitting on her sofa. She wore a pair of light blue shorts and a thin white blouse. "Sure you wouldn't like something to drink?" she asked again. I just shook my head no as she continued. "It just doesn't feel right being at Desert Diamond. I can't imagine that anyone there had anything to do with Charlie's murder, but even so, I think it's time to move on."

"Any idea what you'll do?" I asked.

"Got an old college friend, one of my sorority sisters down at the U of A. Married a guy who started a commuter airline in Las Vegas in the early '80s. Apparently they've done real well. They fly to a lot of the smaller cities in California like Fresno and Bakersfield. Guess those folks like to go to Vegas for the weekend, too. Anyway, they offered me a job and I'm going to take it. Won't pay quite as much as I make at Desert Diamond, but I don't care. I need to get away from here, to get out of Phoenix."

"Probably a good idea, Heidi," I said. "Do you mind if I ask you a few questions about Desert Diamond?"

Her expression changed. "You sound like a journalist now instead of a friend."

"Well, you got me there, Heidi," I replied. "I'm trying to be both. It puts me in a difficult position. So far, the police don't know about the files you copied. A few nights ago somebody broke into Charlie's apartment. I think those disks are what he was looking for. And I believe there's a connection between the disks and Charlie's murder. But I need more information before I can prove that."

There was a silence between us, a gulf that, until that moment, had been filled with mutual trust in the days since we first met. I considered the possibility that we could both walk away, leaving Charlie's murder as just another brutal, unsolved mystery. Heidi could go off to a new job and a new life in Las Vegas. But I had nowhere else to go, and no one waiting for me anywhere. It brought back the empty feeling, the one I had tried to wash away with large doses of tequila just a few days before.

Looking for Charlie had been a reprieve from the emptiness. Trying to solve his murder had become a mission. It was the kind of work I used to thrive on, the sort of job that had always heightened my senses, making me feel alive, not just going through the motions of life. By drawing me into the hunt for his killer, Charlie had somehow given me back my life, at least for a little while. I felt like I owed him one. I was going to make good on it.

"Heidi, three days ago, you asked me for my help. You came to me because Charlie said you should. He knew he was in some kind of danger. And he figured he could count on me to follow his trail of clues into that same danger, to find the answers that he was looking for. Yes, I think there's a story here, and yes, if I can, I'm going to write it. But that's not what got us here. Somebody somewhere did something terrible to Charlie. I owe it to Charlie to find out what happened. So I need you to cut me some slack. You needed my help. Now I'm asking for yours – as a friend."

I watched as her expression softened a little. "I'm sorry Travis. I don't have to tell you that it's been a horrible week. I guess I thought that with Charlie dead and the police involved after all, that you'd just go back to whatever you were doing before I showed up. I didn't realize that, well, that you would actually look for—" she paused, struggling to find less painful words than the ones she had, finally giving in to the phrase, "whoever killed Charlie." The words came with tears. After a few moments she said, "I don't get it. Why not just let the police do it?"

"In the end, Heidi, I'll tell the police everything they need to know, maybe even more than they really want to know. But for now, I'm just too close to back off. Maybe they'll find Charlie's killer before I do. I don't know. But I know I can't quit until this is finished."

"You mean that, don't you? You're going to risk your life looking for a killer just because you think you owe it to somebody?"

"I hadn't thought of it in those terms, but I guess that's what it comes down to."

She stared at me for a moment and then emptied her glass of wine. "I don't know people like you, Travis. The people I know go to work in the morning, put in their eight hours, take their pay check to the bank and go home to their families or their lovers. In their spare time they play a little racquetball or golf or take country swing lessons. They don't spend their days and nights out on the streets looking for, I don't know, whatever kind of people could have done that to Charlie."

"Sure you do, Heidi," I said. She looked bewildered. "You knew Charlie. Maybe he's not the kind of guy you dated in college or the type you see each day in the Desert Diamond office. But you've known him all your life. He went to bat for you when your step-dad was coming on to you. And he was out there, looking for something, something somebody didn't want found, when he was killed. It's not a pretty world, Heidi. Some people do some really awful things. You thought that wasn't part of your well groomed little life, but it is, and it's closer to all of us than we'd like to think. It's all tied together in a tangled web covered with illusion so thick you'd need a chain saw to cut through it. That's what Charlie was doing, trying to cut through the illusion, trying to shine a light on some of the dark, dirty little secrets in this town."

I paused for a moment. I didn't really know how well she knew her brother or the work he did. I wanted to give it time to sink in.

She looked at her empty wine glass, stood up, walked to the counter, and poured herself some more Chablis. "And that's what you're doing now, too, isn't it? Looking for those dirty little secrets." She took a sip, looking at me without returning to the couch.

"Maybe they're big secrets, Heidi. I don't know for sure, yet. Maybe Charlie was looking for one thing and stumbled into something else. I guess that's the difference between me and the police. They just want to find Charlie's killer. I want to find the whole story—not only what Charlie was looking for, but whatever it was that he found."

"And what is it you want me to do?" she asked.

"Two things, Heidi. I need you to tell me a little bit about the files you copied. And then I need you to help me talk to somebody."

"Who?"

"Does Desert Diamond have a system administrator, somebody who keeps the computers running?"

"Yes. His name is Ted Humphries. Why?"

"He's the guy I need to talk to."

CHAPTER 33

Merritt Donavon and I were about 20 minutes into our run. It was early enough that the heat wouldn't kill us. But the sweat was pouring off of me as I tried to keep up with a young man ten years my junior and twenty pounds lighter. We ran along the hard-packed bank of the Arizona Canal a few miles west of where Charlie's body had been found.

I'd known Merritt since he was a second lieutenant right out of Texas A&M and the Officer Basic Course. His dad served in the 1st Marine Raider Battalion in the Pacific during World War II. Merritt had been named for the battalion's legendary commander, Merritt A. "Red Mike" Edson. Somehow, perhaps from the stories of the Raiders he'd heard as a boy from his father, he had developed into an exceptional leader. He valued the council of his sergeants, but understood that the responsibility for decisions was on his shoulders. Despite his lack of active duty experience, old soldiers like Joe Diaz and I had come to respect him and enjoyed serving with him.

"So," Merritt asked me, "you want to talk about the banking business?"

We had been running almost long enough for me to overcome my oxygen deficit, but in keeping up with Merritt, anything I said had to fit with my hard breathing. "Not banks, so much. S&Ls. And one, in particular."

"Yeah? Which one?"

"Eldon Geetus owns one in Texas. Know anything about it?"

"A little. You hear some things when you're in the business."

"Like what?" I asked.

"His S&L in Texas loans money to his development company in Arizona."

"Anything wrong with that?" I asked.

"The president of an S&L, just like the president of a bank, has three basic responsibilities. He's responsible to the ownership, usually stockholders, to make them a reasonable profit on their investment. He's responsible to his clientele, to see that they get a fair return on the savings they deposit. And, he's responsible to the public, meaning he has to operate in accordance with the laws that govern his institution. I'm no expert on the law when it comes to S&Ls. On the one hand, it could be a good deal for everybody concerned. But, it sounds like he's putting all the eggs from his S&L in one basket, if you know what I mean."

I grunted acknowledgement, not wanting to waste oxygen. South of the canal were lush back yards of homes that were built in the fifties and early sixties on what were once date and citrus groves. Most of the trees from the groves had been preserved during construction. Those homes came with the rights to irrigation water from the canal, so once each week their owners got to flood the yards at a fraction of what it cost other city residents to water their lawns.

It was an economic reality that had spread throughout the Valley for half a century. The land became more valuable than the crops that grew there. So farmers sold out to developers. It had started near the center of Phoenix in the 1940s, and by the 1990s it had spread to little farming and ranching communities like Gilbert on the east side and Tolleson to the west.

I was beginning to feel a little stronger, as though my legs and lungs were making a comeback. I was able to open up my stride a little, taking slightly longer steps so I wasn't fighting so hard just to keep up with Donavon's pace.

"So, what's the worst thing that could happen to all those eggs?" I asked.

"Well, if Desert Diamond Development goes tits up, it'll probably take the S&L with it. Not likely to happen. They're doing a lot of business from what I hear. Got developments all over the Valley."

"So," I wondered, "as long as thousands of people move here every year, Geetus keeps building homes, and he's got no problems?"

"That's my guess," Donavon replied, "unless we get some major blip in the economy that would cause housing sales to plunge. It happens from time to time in markets all across the country. Hardly ever happens here. But it could. The fact is the economy in this town is based on the housing industry. We build homes. Tens of thousands of people move here every year and buy them. If that slows down, even a little, we're in big trouble, 'cause there really isn't another industry here to keep things going."

We ran east along the canal bank, all the way into Scottsdale. At 68th street we turned around and headed west, retracing our route.

"Joe Diaz says I should give up on trying to get you back into the unit," Merritt remarked as we crossed 64th. To our right Camelback Mountain dominated the landscape, rising up out of a sea of luxury homes. The construction of a big, new resort was visible on the southern slope, just above the old golf course.

"I'll tell you the truth, Merritt. I've enjoyed my years in the unit. The Reserves turned out to be a lot better than I thought it would when I left active duty. But Special Ops is a young man's profession. And hell, I'm over forty, and frankly I just can't keep up with those young Rangers just off active duty. And if I can't keep up with them, I sure as hell can't lead them. Besides, these days I end up working most weekends anyway. So, when I got my 20-year letter*, I figured it was a good time to do a graceful exit. Better to go out while people like you are still saying good things about me. We've both seen too many guys who stayed too long, holding down a slot and getting a check each month, but not really pulling their weight. I don't want to do that."

"Sounds like Diaz was right. I should have known. He usually is." There was a half chuckle in Merritt's voice as he

---

* A statement from the Army Reserve personnel center that a soldier has completed 20 years of combined active duty and reserve service, and therefore qualifies for some retirement pay upon reaching age 60.

said it. "Even so," he continued, "you ever change your mind, call me. I will find you a slot in the unit."

"Fair enough, *Dai Ûy.*"

By the time we'd gone five miles I was actually starting to feel good. Maybe I had managed to sweat all of the booze and pain pills out of my system. Perhaps it was just the endorphins finally kicking in. Whatever the reason, I was enjoy matching Merritt Donavon stride for stride as we picked up the pace a notch for the last mile. We opened it up for the last few hundred yards, running hard, breathing hard, hearts pounding, each one pushing the other to put out just a little bit more, and finishing side by side.

After we'd stopped and caught our breath, walking it out so as not to let the muscles tighten up, Merritt looked up at me and remarked, "You know, that was a crock of shit about you not being able to keep up with the younger guys. You just proved that."

"Must have caught me on a good day, *Dai Ûy.*"

"Yeah, right," he replied.

"No, honestly," I said, "I haven't felt this good in weeks."

We'd been running for a little less than an hour. I had time for a quick shower before I drove out to the east valley for a meeting at a soccer game.

CHAPTER 34

Thirty minutes later I was driving out toward Gilbert. The run with Merritt Donavon had left me feeling strong and resilient, reminding me that I had once been a very good soldier. It was as though I had somehow made my way out of a bad dream, and was no longer being held down by the booze, pills, pain and self-pity. I was ready to take care of business.

There was only minimal traffic on the eastbound freeway early Saturday morning. I took the time to think over what Heidi had told me the previous night. She had agreed to call Ted Humphries, the guy who kept Desert Diamond's computers running, to see if he would meet with me sometime Saturday.

I asked her about copying the files. I wanted to know the details. She told me that she had stayed late one evening, under the pretext of working on her piece of the company's quarterly financial report. While she could access much of what Charlie wanted from her own computer, she knew that she could copy more information by logging into the system as Delbert Geetus, Desert Diamond's chief financial officer and the son of Eldon Geetus. She had his login and password. He'd given them to her several weeks before. He'd called from Houston and needed some information that was on his computer. He told her how to access his files, and never changed his password when he returned.

So with no one else in the office, she walked from the accounting department into Delbert's office with a box of blank disks. She logged in using Delbert's password. Heidi didn't bother to look at each file. She just copied every file in every directory that Delbert had stored under his account. They filled six black three and a half inch double-sided double-density computer disks. Then she logged out, placed the disks in her purse and left the office. I didn't ask Heidi if Delbert gave his password to all the girls in the accounting department.

The thought had crossed my mind that if Charlie was killed because of those computer disks, then Heidi was in danger, too. When I mentioned that possibility to her, she told me my fears were highly unfounded. "There's no way anyone would make a connection between Charlie and me," she insisted. "No one at the company suspects that I copied that information. And no one knows that Charlie was my brother. Our names are even different."

I asked her about the names.

"I didn't have much of a connection with my birth father," she replied. "I was pretty young when he died. When my mother remarried she changed her last name. Mine got changed as part of the package, I guess. But once I had a choice, I wanted to sever all connections to my stepfather. I'm sure you can understand that. So once I finished college, I dropped his name altogether. Charlayne was my middle name. I just started using it as my last name. After a few years I submitted paperwork to the court and had my name legally changed."

I got to the soccer field and walked in front of the small set of bleachers where parents were sitting to cheer for their daughters. The morning air was filled with the green scent of alfalfa and just a hint of steer manure. Despite the many new housing developments, Gilbert was still a farming community.

I heard a guy call out, "Travis, up here." I walked to the top row of the bleachers and shook hands with Alan Davies. He was a fit looking guy who I guessed to be in his early thirties. He wore khaki shorts, a pink golf shirt, and brown penny loafers that all looked like they were fresh out of a J. Crew catalog.

I took a seat next to Davies and asked him which of the girls on the soccer field was his daughter. "Number seven in the red jersey," he said, pointing out a slender young girl with a blond ponytail.

We sat for a moment or two just watching the game. There were other parents in the bleachers, but none sitting near us. The referee blew her whistle as the ball went out of bounds. Without turning to face me Davies said, "So, Janie said you want to know about water issues."

"That's right. Orme Dam, in particular. There seems to be some question about whether or not it is a viable alternative. Since you're actually in the business, I'm hoping you can shed a little light on the subject."

"Fair enough," Davies replied. "Let's start with a little history."

"Okay. Do you mind if I record this?" I held up my micro-cassette recorder.

Davies thought for a moment. Then he said softly, "Let's say it this way. Since I'm doing this as a favor to Janie, and not in my official capacity as a community relations representative of Central Arizona Water and Power, I don't want my name to appear in print. I don't mind if you record this. If we start talking about something that I don't want recorded, I'll ask you to turn the recorder off."

Davies looked at me. I nodded. "Okay Alan, that'll work."

"For some reason," he said, "and nobody really knows why, the state began to experience some very unusual precipitation patterns beginning in 1965. Maybe it was an El Niño thing. We didn't have infrared satellite photos of the oceans back then, so nobody knows for sure. But for several years, from '65 through '81, Arizona experienced several of what we used to call 50 and 100-year floods. These were weather events that, based on what the scientists had deduced from various geologic and botanical sources, should have only occurred once or twice each century. And yet, during that 16-year period, we got one right after the other.

"Well, needless to say, all that rain caused some problems. CAWAP had based its capacity, that is, how much water it can hold behind the two dams on the Verde and the four dams on the Salt, on the historic flood data we got from the scientists. So when the rain started to fall in late '65, we had to start releasing water from the dams. By that I mean we dumped through the spillways, rather than the usual route that turns the big turbines and generates electricity. I say we. Actually that was way before my time. Anyway, there was lots of runoff coming into the lakes. CAWAP had to dump water in an orderly fashion, 'cause if you let it spill over the top of the dam, well, you run the risk of losing the dam altogether. If that happened to a big dam upstream, Roosevelt, for instance, it could have a domino effect and we'd lose the downstream dams, too. Wouldn't be pretty."

"I remember that first release," I said. "It was December and I was a maybe a freshman or sophomore in high school. A whole bunch of us went to the riverbank, down stream from the Tempe Bridge, just to watch the river run. It was quite an event. I grew up in Phoenix, and I'd never seen the river run before. And suddenly there it was, rushing past all brown and foamy. Having spent my whole life in the Valley, I'd never seen anything like it."

"Yeah, and you weren't the only one. Really, nobody in the Valley had seen the river run since the dams were built and we started routing the water into the irrigation canals. Anyway, as I said, this continued for about 16 years. Lots of new bridges got built during that time. Then along came the 80s and we went into a drought. No more big rains. No more big snows in the mountains. But Phoenix and the surrounding communities continued to grow like crazy. And there was a genuine concern that water scarcity could become a problem in the not-too-distant future.

"Well, people remember quite vividly, just like you do, the sight of all those millions of acre feet of water rushing down the river bed during the flood years. And in light of the current drought and potential for water shortages, they started to think that it was a shame we couldn't have held on to that water somehow instead of just sending it down the river.

"Now that sounds great in theory, but there are serious physical limitations that come into play in terms of water storage. The first is that the six dams in the system can only store so much water at their maximum capacity. And the second is that in prudence, CAWAP has to keep them somewhat below capacity at the beginning of each rainy season, just to ensure there is a cushion in case runoff is suddenly coming into the system faster than we can release water through the spillways. So the logical alternative, at least in the mind of some people, is to increase storage capacity by building one more dam."

"And that 'one more dam' would be Orme Dam?" I asked.

"Yes. If a dam were to be built, it would be Orme Dam." Then, with a nod toward my tape recorder Davies said, "Why don't you turn that off for a moment?"

"Okay," I replied as I held the recorder up high enough so that Davies could see me push the OFF button.

On the field, the official blew her whistle, indicating the end of the period. Parents below us stood to cheer for their girls, who gathered together on the sidelines, drank from their water bottles, and listened to their coach's guidance for the second half of the game.

"Here's the thing," Davies continued, speaking in soft, hushed tones, "and this is completely off the record and I'll deny ever saying it. Nobody at CAWAP wants any part of Orme Dam."

"That's real interesting," I said softly. "Want to tell me why? I mean, it sounds like a perfect fit. CAWAP is in the business of storing water in man-made lakes and then selling the electricity that's generated when that water goes through the turbines at each of the dams. Why wouldn't you want one more?"

"Three reasons. First, if the dam were built, at full capacity it would put more than half of the Fort McDowell Yavapai Indian Reservation under water. That's a tiny little reservation by Arizona standards, barely four miles by ten miles. Trying to force something like that on the tribe would be a public relations nightmare for CAWAP. I like my job. It pays me a decent salary, provides good benefits for me and my family, and affords me a reasonable amount of respect in the business community. Even so, I don't think I'd want to stick around for that one."

"Okay," I said. "What's number two?"

"Simple economics. The two dams on the Verde River and the four dams on the Salt were built in canyons. They are capable of storing enough water to generate a significant amount of electricity. That electricity has paid for the dams many times over. If the proposed Orme Dam site, at the confluence of the Salt and the Verde, were a good place to build a dam, we would have put one there back when the others were built. So while it could, perhaps, be useful for storing a little more water, it would not be a moneymaker from the standpoint of generating power."

"That makes sense. And number three?"

"CAWAP doesn't build a dam based on a freak weather pattern. All that flooding between '65 and '81 was just a blip in the historic record. When we pointed that out to the early proponents of the dam, things really got weird. They came up with this hair-brained scheme that involved cloud seeding to produce more rain and snow each year, then cutting down millions of acres of ponderosa pine forests up on the Mogollon Rim so the trees wouldn't be sucking up all that precipitation. Thus, they reasoned, the increased run-off could feed right into the CAWAP reservoir system, ensuring plenty of water for future growth in the Valley."

"Interesting," I said. "I don't know much about cloud seeding, but cutting down the trees on the rim sounds like the leading edge of an environmental disaster."

"Disaster is the correct word, Travis. The erosion alone would be horrendous. So would the destruction of wildlife habitat. I find it real scary when people with no scientific standing whatsoever start advocating radical environmental changes like that. Which brings to mind another thing. Cloud seeding during a drought doesn't work."

"Really? Why is that?"

"Just a little meteorological science. Clouds are made from tiny, cold water droplets that form ice crystals around little particles of dust and other particulates. When those crystals get heavy enough, it rains. All cloud seeding does is provide a few more particulates around which crystals can form. But if there is insufficient moisture in the air to begin with, cloud seeding doesn't help. It doesn't matter how many extra particulates you throw up there. If there are no water droplets already there to form crystals, it's not going to rain. Drought equals drought."

I nodded my head, thinking over what Davies had told me. CAWAP's reasons for not wanting Orme Dam built seemed very sound. That raised a question. "Alan, given those three, very sensible reasons against the dam, why are we talking off the record right now?"

Davies thought for a moment. "Central Arizona Water and Power is subject to three different governing bodies. First is Congress, which created it, and which, periodically, enacts legislation that will impact it. For instance, there was some federal legislation a few years ago that actually mentioned Orme Dam by name, and envisioned it and the lake it would create as a sort of storage facility for water from the Colorado River that is brought into the interior of Arizona via the Central Arizona Project Canal. Fortunately, that bill said 'Orme Dam or a suitable alternative.' Then there is the Arizona Corporation Commission, which reviews CAWAP's operations and what we charge customers for electricity. Since CAWAP has been granted a monopoly in terms of providing electricity to the citizens who reside within the various irrigation districts served by CAWAP, state law mandates that the Corporation Commission must approve the rates we charge for electricity. And finally, CAWAP's board of directors is elected by the Water Users Association, which is composed of everybody that uses water from the CAWAP irrigation canals.

"Since all three of those governing bodies are elected, there is, I'm sorry to say, a certain amount of politics that gets in the way of good policy and management. I tell you all this just to point out that the reason we are talking off the record right now is that all CAWAP employees have been instructed to not say anything about Orme Dam, lest our statements should be construed as an official position of CAWAP. In short, we don't want to piss off any politicians. Most of us, especially those of us who deal with the public on a regular basis, don't much care for that policy. It ties our hands when we could be providing good information for rational decisions by policy makers and the electorate. Even so, that's how it is."

"Alan, I appreciate your candor. Since we're off the record, let me ask your opinion. Let's say there's somebody running for Congress—no need to name names at the moment—who says that Orme Dam ought to be built. What's his motivation?"

"Oh, gee," Davies grinned, "running for Congress. I wonder who that could be? Here's my best guess. Running for Congress costs a lot of money these days. So he's got to go out and get some. There are two sources of money that come to mind in this instance. One is the construction unions that could put a lot of their people to work for several years building a dam that would be, conveniently, commuting distance from the Valley. And the other would be anybody who has some desert land that would, if the dam were built, become lake front property. Now that would be a handy return on an investment, wouldn't it?"

CHAPTER 35

With more than an hour before my interview with Sandy Dominguez, I went to my office. The fax of Dominguez's campaign positions had arrived. I read through it quickly, looking for anything interesting, making a few notes on a legal pad. There was some biographical information. Then there was the usual stuff about representing the people of his district, not the special interests in Washington.

It said Dominguez favors fiscal responsibility through a balanced federal budget that eliminates government waste and inefficiency, without sacrificing a strong national defense or the quality of life of Arizona's working families. Well there was an original position! And he intends to improve the Arizona economy by supporting initiatives that will create jobs in the private sector and ensure continued growth and prosperity in the Valley of the Sun. Sounded like Orme Dam to me.

Once I had finished, I checked my voice mail. Heidi had called. She said Ted Humphries, Desert Diamond's system administrator, had agreed to meet with me. He'd be at the Indian Bend Bar and Grill at five that afternoon.

I took a few minutes to add some of what Alan Davies had told me about Orme Dam into my computer. That made me think of something I had seen in files in Charlie's apartment. So I went into the database, found Rafer Malone's phone number, and called his apartment. Rafer's grandfather, Arthur Davis, answered the phone. He said Rafer was showing some people an apartment at one of his other properties. I told him there was something in Charlie's apartment I wanted to take another look at, and that I knew Rafer had changed the lock.

"No problem," he said. "Rafer should be back in a little while. But if he's not here when you come by, I can let you in." I thanked him and told him I'd be by between noon and one.

I decided to make one more call before heading for my meeting with Sandy Dominguez. I figured that it wasn't too early to call Joe Diaz at home on a Saturday morning.

Shelly answered. "Hi, Shelly. It's Travis." I was trying to remember what Joe had said while we were drinking beer at Brandy's—something about Shelly finding out about one of his girl friends.

I'm not very good with small talk, and it felt especially awkward because I knew they weren't getting along very well. I'd known Shelly socially for several years, ever since Joe and I became friends. So I knew I should make a little friendly conversation before asking if Joe was around. Fortunately, Shelly was good enough for both of us.

"Hey, Travis. I never get to see you anymore since you left the unit. What have you been doing with all your free weekends?"

"Well mostly I just try to stay out of trouble, Shelly. Though it doesn't seem like I'm very good at that lately."

"Oh yeah, right, you wild and crazy journalist." It was no secret that, compared to her husband, Shelly thought I was somewhat saintly. "Mike has the boys at a little league game this morning. They just left, so they won't be back for a couple of hours. Maybe you should come over. You could show me how you try to stay out of trouble, and I'll show you some things that will make it hard for you."

Shelly was a blond with big tits and big lips. She wasn't my type at all, but she was exactly the kind of girl that Joe was attracted to. And sometimes, when she was really pissed at Joe, she would do what she was doing, flirting with me using suggestive language, hinting that if I were to come over for a visit, she just might have to release all of her pent up sexual frustration and do me like I'd never been done before. "Shelly," I said, "it's not nice to tease a man who's down on his luck."

"That's what I love about you, Travis. You make me believe that you're only turning me down because you think I'm just teasing you."

"Actually Shelly, I'm turning you down because I've got enough people pissed off at me right now. I don't need to add one very bad Chicano cop to the list. But I still think you're just teasing me."

"Well, you got the 'very bad' part right, Travis. Can I give him a message for you?"

"Well, later may be too late. I'm doing an interview with Sandy Dominguez in about thirty minutes. I was just wondering if Joe had heard any gossip from the Mexican grapevine about him."

"Joe could probably tell you a few things. But I could tell you more. And I'd love to tell you some stories about Sandy Dominguez. In my office we hear everything that happens at the capital. There's stuff that goes down that you wouldn't believe, Travis." I'd forgotten Shelly had worked in the state government, in various offices, for several years. She had started out in a lowly clerical job, and had worked her way up to a mid-level manager position. I didn't know what role her good looks played in getting promoted. But there was no doubt that they helped her get noticed. Shelly had a body that a supervisor could never ignore. "How much time did you say you have?" she asked.

"I've got to be at his campaign headquarters in a half an hour. Can you give me the short version now, and leave an option for some follow-up later?"

"So, you only have time for a quickie right now, but you promise later we can do it real long and slow?" She was absolutely dangerous when she talked like that. I had to be careful, but I also needed to hear what she had to say about Dominguez.

"That sounds good, Shelly. Give me something hot and juicy right now. Later on we can take our time and go over all the intimate parts in great detail. How does that sound?"

"Oh, that sounds very nice, Travis. And I guarantee you're going to like it."

With our little verbal foreplay out of the way we got down to business. "A few years ago, must have been '89, because it was after I moved from DPS* to the Department of Administration, there was a big drug bust at an upscale strip club over by the airport. At the time it was called Danielle's, I think. It's called something else now. Anyway, there was a lot of coke going though there. The girls were using it, of course, to kind of get themselves up before going out to perform. But there was also a lot of distribution going on from there, as well."

"What's this have to do with Dominguez?" I asked, wondering if I was wasting my time. Shelly loved to share gossip from work.

"I'm getting there, dear. Give me a minute to put the picture together for you. The bust was a combined operation. State agents had the lead, with assistance from Phoenix PD and the Sheriff's Office, about 20 officers in all plus a team from the Attorney General's office, with more officers outside to move all the suspects to the jail. Now, who do you suppose happened to be one of the patrons, who, as I recall, was on the receiving end of a little lap dance when the cops crashed the party?"

"Let me guess. Sandy Dominguez?"

"That's right. Now, as far as anyone knows, he wasn't involved with the coke thing. But he knew it would look real bad if his name showed up, either in an official report, or in the newspaper story about the bust. So he immediately started doing damage control. First he determined who was there from the Attorney General's office. At the time Sandy was running the Governor's Office of Community Development, so he was well known around the capital, and well connected."

"So the guy from the AG's office let him slip out the back way?" I asked.

---

* Department of Public Safety, the state's law enforcement agency, which includes the Highway Patrol and the Criminal Investigation Division.

"Yes, but that's not all. Sandy realized that he knew one of the other patrons who were being rounded up and questioned. They had met at a community development meeting Sandy had put together for some big commercial developers, a few large-scale homebuilders, and some bankers and other financiers. So Sandy tells the cops that this guy was with him, and they let them both go."

"Let me take another wild guess, Shelly. The other guy was Eldon Geetus?"

"Wow, sugar. You're psychic. The other guy was his son, Delbert Geetus."

"Delbert, eh? Interesting. Okay, so we've got a couple of guys who go to a strip club. That's not exactly news, Shelly. Even if one of them is running for Congress."

"We're not done yet, sweetie."

I glanced at my watch. I had fifteen minutes, at the most, before I had to be on my way to my appointment with Sandy Dominguez. "Okay Shelly," I said, "I'm going to switch you to the speaker phone so I can type while we talk." With that I pushed a button on my phone and put down the receiver. Then I opened the computer file for Sandy Dominguez and frantically began typing as Shelly continued with her story.

"It was a few months after that, I think, that three women who worked in Dominguez's office filed a sexual harassment complaint against him. It started out with just one woman who said that Dominguez kept hitting on her in the office, putting his hand on her ass and implying that, with a little encouragement, he could help her move up into a better paying position. Then a couple of other women came forward with similar stories. Any complaints like that come through the Department of Administration, which is how I found out about them."

"That's interesting," I said. "I don't remember hearing anything about that. Was it ever in the press?"

"No baby, that's the interesting part. All three ladies agreed to retract their charges. Sandy Dominguez was reassigned as the new director of the Water Resources Board, and nobody ever said another word about it."

"But there must be more to that story, right Shelly?"

"Of course there is, dear. I was sufficiently curious that I arranged to have a few drinks with one of those girls one Friday after work. Now keep in mind, all three of those girls were just admin-clerical staff, pulling down six dollars an hour if they were lucky. And believe me, I know what that's like, 'cause I've been there. She told me it went down just like this. She gets a call asking her to come up to see James Glassmoyer, the director of the Department of Administration. Glassmoyer, by the way, had announced that he was planning to run for Secretary of State in 1990. And there's somebody else in the office. He's a guy in a suit she's never seen around the capital. He's got a cashier's check for $100,000.00 made out to her and a piece of paper she needs to sign to get that check. All she has to do is retract the allegations and agree to never speak of the matter again. She told me that she believes that the other two girls got the same offer. None of them were in a position to turn it down."

"That's good stuff, Shelly. I don't suppose you happen to know who wrote the check?"

"There wasn't a name on the check. But the girl was no dummy. She made a photocopy of it before she cashed it. It was issued by Diamond Savings and Loan in Houston, Texas."

"Shelly, would it surprise you to learn that Diamond Savings and Loan is owned by the Geetus family?"

"Wouldn't surprise me a bit, sugar. I just wish I had a hundred grand for every time somebody grabbed *my* ass."

"I'm sure it would be worth every penny, Shelly. Is there anything more you can tell me about the relationship between Dominguez and Geetus?"

"What I hear is that the elder Geetus is bankrolling Dominguez's run for Congress, with some help from the construction unions. The agreement is that if Sandy wins, key people from his campaign staff will start work on running Delbert for Congress in an adjacent district two years from now. And, Sandy, of course, will be more than happy to campaign for his asshole buddy Delbert, 'cause his own re-election campaign will be funded by Delbert's old man."

"Shelly, you give good story, maybe the best in town. I owe you."

"Yes you do, Travis. And I expect to be repaid with personal services at a date to be determined. I know you've got to run now, but just remember who butters your bread for you."

"Thanks Shelly. I'll be in touch."

I was due to meet Dominguez in ten minutes. On a Saturday morning, with little or no traffic on the streets, I could get there in five. I closed the Dominguez file, then found the phone number for Connie Torelli. I got her voice mail. "Connie, it's Travis. If you wouldn't mind, could you check for a couple of things on that printout. First, there were three cashier's checks, each for $100,000.00, paid by Diamond Savings and Loan, probably in 1990. The other thing is contributions made to candidates for secretary of state in the 1990 election. I'll tell you more when we can talk. Thanks."

Ten minutes later I walked into the storefront campaign headquarters of Sandy Dominguez for Congress. Between Alan Davies and Shelly Diaz, I had learned more than I was likely to get from interviewing Sandy Dominguez. But I had an appointment with him, so I figured I'd see if I could shake his tree just enough to see if anything good tumbled out.

I was welcomed at the door by a perky co-ed. I told her my name, handed her my business card, and said I had an appointment with Sandy. "Yes, Mr. Jefferson." She called across the room, which was occupied by a half dozen people busy making phone calls or typing away at computers, "Cecilia, Travis Jefferson is here."

A woman in a navy blue pants suit with a red and orange scarf around her neck walked over to me and introduced herself as Cecilia Montoya, Dominguez's campaign manager. "We're glad that you could meet with Sandy today," she said and she asked me to follow her. I grabbed a couple campaign pamphlets before Montoya hustled me through a doorway, down a short hallway, and into a small meeting room.

Sandy Dominguez wore black slacks, a light blue long sleeve shirt with a red tie. He raised his considerable bulk up from his chair as we entered. He was easily six feet two inches tall, maybe six three. He weighed in the neighborhood of two hundred fifty pounds. He smiled, reaching across the table with a large right hand to shake mine, "Travis, I'm Sandy Dominguez. Thank you for coming. Please, have a seat."

I slipped into a chair opposite Dominguez, and Cecilia Montoya sat next to me, closer to the door. I placed my mini-cassette recorder on the table along with my yellow legal pad. "First," I asked, "I should ask if you mind if I record this interview?"

"Not at all, my friend," Dominguez grinned. "That's the best way to make sure you don't misquote me."

I asked him the usual stuff, why he was running, why the voters of the new district should choose him, giving him a chance to spout campaign rhetoric. Dominguez described how he could connect with voters across the socio-economic spectrum. His grandparents, he said, were immigrants. His parents were working class citizens with a strong belief in the American Dream. He and his siblings were the first generation in his family to go to college.

In terms of the issues, Dominguez stressed that what was really important was the economy. "This recession has been especially hard on the working poor, the families with no safety net. I believe," he said with religious-like fervor, "that if we have the means to create jobs that will put people to work, then we have a moral obligation to do so."

"Jobs like those that would be created building Orme Dam, for instance?" I asked.

"That's certainly one possibility," he replied. "Orme Dam is important not only in terms of creating jobs now, but in securing the kinds of continued growth that the Valley needs to sustain economic prosperity into the future. As director of the Water Resources Board, I understand how vital it is for the Valley to have a dependable water supply. Orme Dam would help ensure that the water will be there when we need it."

He talked about other things he would fight for in Congress, things like federal highway money to help build the Valley's freeway system, and HUD money for redevelopment in downtown Phoenix, Education money to refurbish Phoenix's inner-city schools.

"Sandy," I said, "let's talk a little more about your experience in public service. You're currently the head of the Water Resources Board. Before that you headed up the Governor's Office of Community Development. Would you talk about your responsibilities in each of those positions and how they've helped prepare you for higher office?"

His response was the usual horseshit about a deep appreciation of how the issues impact working families and an understanding of how government really works.

I knew that it was time to cut to the chase. "Speaking of how government really works Sandy, I understand that it was your decision to not release the results of the Water Board study."

Dominguez glanced down at the tape recorder. It was not a question he was expecting, and it was clear that we were now off his prepared campaign script. I felt Cecilia Montoya flash me a caustic look, then she and Sandy exchanged glances.

"Well," he replied, "it would not have been prudent to release the results of a study that was not complete. In disregarding the potential storage that would be gained with an additional dam in the equation, the study produced results that have questionable validity. I felt it would be irresponsible to release the study until that flaw has been rectified."

"So once data that includes the potential storage Orme Dam could provide is added to the analysis, you'll release the results?"

"Based on what I've seen of the study so far, I believe we should be able to at least produce a preliminary report once that is accomplished, yes."

"And in order for the report to be as accurate as possible, will you include the potential gain from cloud seeding and the removal of large tracts of timber on the Mogollon Rim?"

"Well," he frowned, "I think we might want to look at presenting two possible result sets, one with just the dam, and the other that included the runoff enhancements that you mentioned. That could form the basis for a useful cost/benefit analysis as we consider the Valley's future water needs."

"Well, thank you for coming to talk with us today, Travis," Cecelia Montoya said as she stood up.

"Just one more question, Sandy." I remained sitting. Dominguez was halfway out of his chair, frozen for a moment in a semi-stooped position. "For the record, is there any connection between your support for Orme Dam, the presence of you and Delbert Geetus at a topless bar during a major cocaine bust, and the large cash payouts to three state employees who accused you of sexual harassment?"

Cecelia extended her arm with the palm face out toward Dominguez like a traffic cop telling a driver to stop. "This interview is over Mr. Jefferson," she said in a voice that was fire and ice. "Sandy, we don't want to be late for our next appointment."

I picked up my notepad and tape recorder, but I didn't shut the recorder off. I was hoping I might get one candid remark from Dominguez. He didn't let me down. He followed Cecelia Montoya toward the conference room door. As he got to the door he turned back to me as though he were blocking my exit and said in a menacing whisper, "You print that shit about me being at Danielle's when it got busted, and it will be the last thing you ever write in this town."

"Well, Sandy," I said with a half smile, holding up the tape recorder so he could see that it was still rolling, "it just goes to show you that history does repeat itself." He looked at me with his mouth open, for once at a loss for words. "That's very similar to what Ace Martin said to me when I asked him about his bogus military career. Have a nice day, Sandy." I pushed my way passed him and walked through the campaign office, clicking the recorder to the OFF position as I stepped out into the heat along Central Avenue.

CHAPTER 36

Arthur Davis answered when I knocked.

"Hello, Travis," he said. "Rafer's not back yet." He pulled a ring of keys out of his pocket. "Come on up, and I'll let you in." As we headed up the stairs he turned to me, "Rafer told me you were the one that had to identify Charlie's body down at the morgue."

"Yeah, that's true," I paused. "Then I brought his sister down there. They needed next of kin to make it official, I guess."

"That's just a damn shame that somebody would do something like that to Charlie," Arthur Davis said. "He never did nothing bad to anyone in his whole life." As we reached the top of the stairs he added, "I've tried to live my life as a Christian, but there are times when forgiveness escapes me."

"I know what you mean," I said. "Certainly seems like somebody ought to pay for what happened to Charlie. There's going to be a memorial service on Monday night."

"Yeah, Charlie's sister called yesterday to invite Rafer and me. It was very thoughtful of her."

Arthur Davis unlocked the door to Charlie's apartment and let me in. "J. R. Ragsdale was here yesterday with another detective. He was asking Rafer why he never reported the break-in to the Phoenix police."

"Yeah? What'd Rafer say?"

"Rafer told him that, near as he could tell, nothing was missing, so it didn't make much sense to have the police come out and file a report." Then after a short pause he continued, "Though I imagine it may've had just as much to do with Rafer not wanting the police going through Charlie's business, if you know what I mean." Another pause, "Not that I think Charlie was doin' anything wrong, you understand. But the police start pokin' around in your business, no tellin' what they might find." He handed me the key. "Just lock up when you're through, Travis. I'll be down stairs when you're done."

The inside of Charlie's apartment didn't look much different than the way it had the last time I was there. Elena

Sanchez had stacked the folders that we had found strewn upon the floor. They were still there in neat piles. I suspected that Ragsdale probably took a look at them, and didn't find anything much of significance.

I squatted down next to one of the piles and began looking at the folder labels. Half way into the second pile I found what I was looking for. It was the folder labeled Orme Dam. I sat down on the nearby couch, laid the folder on the coffee table, and opened it up.

There were a number of reports, some environmental, others more political in nature. They covered the whole spectrum from the destruction of habitat of a few birds, to the projected need for a new bridge to replace the one that now stood where the Beeline Highway crossed the Verde River. I didn't understand all of them. But others seemed to corroborate the things that Alan Davies had told me earlier that morning.

Then I found what I was looking for. Somehow I knew that, if it existed, Charlie would have had it. It was a map that showed the lake on the lower Verde River that Orme Dam would create. Somebody, probably Charlie, had used colored highlighters to outline various tracts of land around the lake. Nearest the dam, outlined in orange, was the Salt River Indian Reservation. The Verde River cut across the eastern tip of that reservation. Just two miles upstream was the southern edge of the Fort McDowell Reservation, its boundary highlighted in pink. The land that would be flooded by the lake had been marked using diagonal blue lines. They covered over more than half of the small Fort McDowell Reservation. Then just to the north of that, surrounded on the other three sides by the Tonto National Forest which was outlined in green, was a tract of private land along what would be the western shore of the upper reaches of the lake. It was outlined in yellow. The words *Diamond Rio Estates* in Charlie's handwriting were written inside the yellow rectangle.

Diamond Rio Estates was the gated community in the desert northeast of Scottsdale that Desert Diamond

Development was building. So Geetus was hoping Orme Dam would turn his high-end desert development into a lakefront paradise. And that would undoubtedly enable him to jack up the price of his lots considerably.

It was not exactly a smoking gun, just an obscene reminder of what happens when business and politics get in bed together. Dominguez would push for the construction of the dam. The dam would turn some relatively cheap desert land into lakefront properties. Geetus would make a bundle selling the lots, thus recovering what it cost to bankroll Dominguez into Congress where he would be in a position to help Delbert Geetus get elected in an adjacent district two years later. And he'd probably have a big chunk of change left over.

I now had a few pieces of the puzzle that fit together. It wasn't nearly enough to solve it. And I knew that I didn't have much time to get the rest of it. But it was something to work from, and that was more than I had the day before when Ragsdale gave me 48 hours to come up with some answers. I had 22 hours left.

CHAPTER 37

It was close to two that afternoon when I got back to my office. Having skipped breakfast for my run with Merritt Donavon, I was overdue for lunch by the time I left Charlie's apartment and returned the key to Arthur Davis. So I stopped at a Mexican take-out place called El Gallo, and arrived at my office armed with a huge California Burro (black beans, Spanish rice, cheese, onions, cilantro, guacamole, lettuce, and salsa, all wrapped in a large, whole wheat tortilla) and an extra large Dr. Pepper. I had a few hours before I was supposed to meet with Ted Humphries, the Desert Diamond system administrator, so I settled in to do some serious work on my computer.

I'd been there about ten minutes when the phone rang. It was Joe Diaz. "Hey Travis, Shelly said you called. What's up?"

"Joe, thanks for getting back to me. You were right about that John Doe they pulled out of the canal. I went to the morgue. It was the guy I was looking for."

"Really. Well I'm sorry to hear that, man. You got any idea how he ended up that way?"

"Nothing solid yet. The M.E. says he was probably dead before his body hit the water. Beat up pretty bad, too. J.R. Ragsdale's got the case. We've talked some, but he's not telling me much. He was actually treating me like a suspect for a while."

"No shit, Sherlock. He called me at work and asked me about you."

"I'm not surprised, Joe. He seems pretty thorough. What did you tell him?"

"Not much. I said that you were a long-haired, commie drug dealer, but to the best of my knowledge, you'd never actually kill anybody."

"Thanks, pal." I replied. "It's always good to know I can count on a buddy like you."

"It was the least I could do for an old friend. But seriously, I told him I'd known you for 10 years, both socially and in the military, that he should not consider you a suspect, and that if I was him, I'd definitely want your help in solving the crime because you are very good analyst."

"Thanks, Joe. I appreciate that."

"Hey, no problem man. But you should keep in mind that the Scottsdale PD thinks that everybody on the Phoenix PD is an ignorant scumbag who shouldn't be allowed east of 56th Street, so there's no telling how much credibility Ragsdale is going to give my assessment of you. If he thinks you're dirty, it's not much of a leap for him to assume that I'm dirty, too."

"Well, that's real encouraging. But I appreciate you saying good things about me anyway. Hey, on another note, Shelly and I were talking about Sandy Dominguez. Can you verify the story about him being at a strip club called Danielle's when a drug bust went down?"

"You asking officially, or off the record?"

"Does it make a difference?"

"Yeah. Let's say it does, for the moment."

"Okay, Joe. We're off the record. Tell me about it."

"I was there, man. But my name doesn't show up on the report. I was undercover—gold chain, gold earring, the whole nine yards. We were looking for links to organized crime, any solid connection between the mob, Danielle's, and the cocaine deals that seemed to be going down there. So we had three teams of two guys each, with a team covering the place every night. My partner and I, a guy from the Attorney General's office, were there the night the bust went down. We knew that it was coming, but we wanted to maintain the surveillance without blowing our covers. So, the teams that did the bust were advised that we were on site, and my partner and I were treated just like everybody else."

"So you saw Dominguez pull some strings so he and Delbert Geetus could get shuffled out the back door?"

"That's the way it happened, man. My partner knew the guy who let them go."

"And, as far as you know, they were not involved with the cocaine deals. Is that right?"

"Right. Nothing connecting them to the drug deals. I think they were just there to drink and drool."

"Fair enough. Had you seen either of them there before?"

"Yeah, I'm pretty sure I'd seen the Geetus guy there at least a few times before, though at the time I didn't know who he was. It wasn't until the night of the bust that I found out who he was, and only then because I was curious, since Dominguez seemed to know him well enough to try to save him some embarrassment. So I had my partner check later with the guy who let them go. He had looked at both of their driver's licenses before he let them slip away. That's how I got his name."

"Alright Joe, I appreciate you telling me that. I've got to talk with Ragsdale tomorrow. Hopefully I'll know some more by then. I'll let you know how it goes."

"Yeah, keep me posted. I never liked Dominguez much anyway. If you get some real dirt about him, I'd like to hear."

"I'll do my best, pal. Talk to you later."

I spent the rest of the afternoon on the computer, making sure that I had every piece of usable information logged in, then poring over the name, dates, and locations, trying as hard as I could to find a pattern, some thin thread that might tie it all together so it made sense. I read over my notes, again and again, looking for anything I might have overlooked. Then I reviewed each of the tape recorded interviews I had done. Experience had taught me that the information all had some connection, that nothing happened in a vacuum. But how it all fit together was eluding me.

The event matrix, which matched up people with events, wasn't showing me much. There were just too few events to produce any kind of analysis. Sandy Dominguez and Delbert Geetus are both at a strip club when it got busted, but apparently didn't actually connect until the bust went down. And they had met some time before that at a meeting for developers and financiers that Dominguez had put together. Hard to see how their relationship might be connected to Charlie Gonnerman's murder.

Just before he had disappeared, Charlie was seen at Ragtime Cowboy Joe with the big guy with curly blond hair who used the name Larry. He was probably the same guy who nearly broke my jaw then ran out the door the night I went back to Charlie's apartment. Certainly Larry, or whatever his name was, probably was connected to Charlie's murder, but the how and more importantly the why of that connection remained a mystery.

It was around four when Connie Torelli returned my call. "Hi Travis. It's Connie."

"Hey Connie. How're you doing?"

"Not real well. I'm grateful that I've got my work to keep my mind occupied, but that's been real hard, too. You know, I try to get something done, and then I think about Charlie, and then I just can't focus on anything. And I end up just sitting at my desk sobbing, and I'm angry and sad and heartbroken. And I know that if they find whoever killed Charlie, it's still not going to bring him back, not ever."

It took me a couple moments to reply. What do you say to someone who has lost the person they love? "Connie, if there is anything I can do, anything at all."

"Come to the memorial service on Monday, Travis. You've known Charlie longer than anyone other than his family. I'd really appreciate it if you could say a few words."

"Sure, Connie. I'd be happy to. Anything else?"

"Yes. Keep doing what you're doing," she replied, a firmer tone in her voice, the street-smart girl from Philly. "Find out who the hell did this to him." And then her voice broke again. She didn't sob into the phone, but I could almost hear the tears start to fall down her face. "Don't let 'em get away with it, Travis. It's just not right."

"I won't, Connie. We're going to find them. And when we do, they're going down."

"Thanks, Travis," she said. "I think I've got the information you were looking for. Here goes."

For all its somewhat incestuous banking and development deals, Desert Diamond Development kept quite meticulous books. Connie had found an entry in the Desert Diamond check register for a check for three hundred thousand dollars payable to Diamond Savings and Loan. The explanation for the expenditure was listed as "three cashiers checks." Connie then cross-checked the entry from the check register against the double entry expenditures for the same day. The $300K was listed under the column of miscellaneous expenses.

"Thanks, Connie. I appreciate you digging that out. You do good work."

"Like I said, I just hope it helps."

"I think it will. Thanks again. I'll see you on Monday night."

With about a half an hour left before I had to leave to meet with Ted Humphries at the Indian Bend Bar and Grill, I took a look at the time event chart on the computer. I had not been as diligent in getting all the information into the chart as I should have. I reviewed the chronology of events, earliest at the top of the screen, most recent at the bottom. Events that were in close proximity to one another had significant importance if two or more key individuals were also involved in those events. But there just weren't enough key people and events coinciding to create a pattern.

With nothing else to go with, I focused on Charlie, highlighting each event in which his name appeared and the name of anyone else associated with the events. Then I went back to the event matrix, highlighting each instance of Charlie's name, and the name of anyone whose name was now highlighted on the time event chart. And then I thought I saw something. On the event matrix I highlighted the next two events in which any of those names appeared. Then I highlighted those events on the time event chart, too. I moved back and forth between the screens once again, getting a better sense of the time that had transpired over the course of a handful of events. It didn't provide the complete picture. But for the first time, some disparate pieces of the puzzle began to fall into place. And I began to think I knew what had happened to Charlie Gonnerman. And maybe, just maybe, why.

CHAPTER 38

I arrived at the Indian Bend Bar and Grill a little before five. It was on Indian School Road, just east of 48th Street, in a nondescript strip mall that also housed a convenience market, a laundromat, and a television repair shop. Merritt Donavon and I had been just a block or two north of it on our run along the canal bank that morning.

The small tavern took its name from the Indian Bend Wash, which begins near the base of the McDowell Mountains northeast of Scottsdale. From there the wash heads south through the middle of Scottsdale, eventually emptying into the Salt River bed just south of McKellips Road which separates south Scottsdale from north Tempe. The wash itself was named for a ninety degree turn that the Arizona Canal makes near the boundary between Scottsdale and the Salt River Indian Reservation. The wash crosses the canal near that bend.

There are thousands of washes in Arizona, and most of them don't have names. But Indian Bend Wash created a small engineering challenge for the builders of the Arizona Canal when it was constructed in the 1880s. Although the wash is dry most of the year, during a heavy rain the runoff from the McDowell Mountains can be significant. They don't call them gully washers for nothing. So at the point where the wash crosses the canal, a gate was created on the north bank of the canal to allow the runoff to flow in. But the flow of a serious gully washer could occasionally be enough to cause the canal to exceed its capacity and overflow, causing damage to nearby homes and the canal, itself. So the engineers had to include an out-flow gate on the south bank of the canal.

Since the wash was creating the need for additional engineering, the builders of the Arizona Canal had to call it something. So they named it for the nearest reference point on the canal, that big bend the canal makes just as it leaves the Indian reservation. The name stuck. During that series of fifty and hundred year floods Alan Davies had talked about, the flooded Indian Bend Wash had literally cut Scottsdale in half on several occasions. Beginning in the mid-1970s, the City of Scottsdale built bridges over the wash, and turned the wash itself into a greenbelt, complete with parks, lakes and golf courses. Why the little tavern four miles west of the wash was called the Indian Bend Bar and Grill was anybody's guess.

It was dark inside. My eyes took a few seconds to adjust. The place smelled of beer and the burgers a bartender was cooking on a grill behind the bar. The room was narrow but deep, with the bar on the right and a row of small tables on the left. At the back of the room was a jukebox. As my eyes adjusted to the dim light, I could see another room in the back, past the end of the bar, where a couple of girls were shooting pool. There were three guys sitting at the bar, drinking alone. The tables were empty except for the one furthest back. The guy sitting at the table raised his glass of beer and nodded at me when I looked his way. I walked back to his table and asked, "Ted Humphries?"

"You must be Travis Jefferson," he replied. "Go ahead and order something from Buddha, and bring it back here."

There was a menu of offerings from the grill posted on a sign behind the bar. In addition to various styles of burgers, they had grilled quesadillas. Buddha was the bartender. He was big and round. There was a brass Buddha, about eight inches tall, sitting on a little stand next to the cash register. I asked the human Buddha for a green chile quesadilla and a glass of draft beer. Buddha brought me the glass of beer. I put some cash on the bar, and walked back to Ted Humphries' table.

I knew going in, my talk with Humphries wasn't going to be a typical interview. My interests were no longer purely journalistic. I had started a few days before, working on a story about a possible cover-up of the results of a study done by the state Water Resources Board, and trying to find Charlie Gonnerman for his sister Heidi. The water story seemed to be full of lots of plausible deniability with no hot, smoking gun. And I had found Charlie Gonnerman lying cold and discolored in the coroner's icebox.

I needed information from Humphries, information he probably wouldn't be giving out to just any reporter who wanted to ask him some questions. I needed to get him talking and keep him talking, while at the same time keeping him off balance just enough to have him be afraid, and make him believe that I was the one who could save him when he felt himself start to fall.

"Heidi said you wanted to talk about our computer system," he said as I sat down at the table with the cold glass of beer in hand.

"Yeah. Heidi told me you're the system administrator for Desert Diamond. I guess first I'd like to hear about what that entails."

"You known Heidi long?" he asked. I couldn't tell if he was just making small talk. I wondered if he was really asking me if I was sleeping with Heidi.

Humphries' physical appearance was not impressive. He was of medium height, a tad on the chubby side, and his red Bermuda shorts, black socks and sandals said he was not a slave to fashion. He wore his dark hair somewhere between short and long, as though making a decision about its appearance had been indefinitely put on hold. I figured it was a good bet that all those beautiful girls who worked for Delbert Geetus were not coming on to him around the water cooler in the office each day. I guess he naturally wondered who they were wrapping those beautiful long legs around each night, since it sure wasn't him.

"A while," I replied ambiguously. "You like your job, Ted?"

"Yeah, I guess," he replied. "Good pay and benefits. I've got a lot of responsibility. If I say we need something for the system, I usually get it without a lot of questions asked. So, yeah, I like it. No complaints, really. Why do you ask?"

"I'm guessing that you must be pretty good at what you do. If you had to go out tomorrow and find another job, you wouldn't have much trouble, would you?"

"Well, no. I don't suppose I'd have much trouble. I mean, from what I hear, the job market in general isn't real great

174

right now, you know, with the recession and all. But things seem to be growing real fast in the computer field, so I'm guessing that I could find something else without too much trouble. But like I said, I'm pretty happy doing what I'm doing. So, I don't think I'm going to be poring over the ads in the help wanted section of the paper tomorrow."

"Well, Ted, at the risk of saying more than I should, and because Heidi tells me that you're a pretty good guy, I'm going to recommend that you do just that tomorrow. Get yourself a copy of the Sunday paper, read the want ads real good, and then polish up your résumé. That way you'll be a couple of steps ahead of the game when the shit hits the fan on Monday morning."

The bartender called out, "Quesadilla." I asked Humphries to excuse me for a moment, then returned a few seconds later with my quesadilla and a cup of salsa.

Humphries looked at me as I dipped the quesadilla into the salsa and took a bite. The bartender had fried it in some sort of buttery liquid he had spread on the grill with a brush. It was probably an artery-blocking heart killer. It was also delicious. I chased the bite with a sip of cold beer.

"I'm not sure I know what we're talking about," Humphries said, looking a little flustered that I would just leave him hanging while I focused on my quesadilla and beer. "When what shit hits what fan?"

"You're the system administrator for Desert Diamond, right Ted? That means that, among other things, you bear a great deal of responsibility for the files on the Desert Diamond computers. Some time very soon, I'm guessing early Monday morning, the police are going to come to Desert Diamond with a search warrant. It will include a search of Desert Diamond's computer files. They will have probable cause to believe that state and federal laws have been broken, and they will take your hard drives into evidence."

Humphries stared at me with his mouth open.

"As you can imagine, this is going to put you in a very precarious position. While you probably can't be expected to have knowledge of the contents of every single file on the system, you do have a responsibility to see that, in general, the system you administer is not being used for any illegal activities. So it's quite likely that the police are going to ask you an awful lot of questions." I took another bite of quesadilla and a sip of beer as I watched Humphries' fat fingers tighten their grip on the glass of beer he was holding.

"Now Ted, since I've told you this, if you were to go back to the office and start deleting files, well, then you'd be charged with destroying evidence and probably obstruction of justice, too, since, when the police talk to me, I'd have to tell them about our little conversation. And besides, you and I both know that when you delete a file, it doesn't really go away. So when they come to get your hard drives, they're going to find those files anyway."

"Shit!" Humphries brought his beer glass down hard on the table top, spilling some in the process. I could tell that there was more he needed to say. I pulled a couple of napkins out of the dispenser on the table and tossed them on top of the spilled beer.

"And I can appreciate that you'd feel a certain loyalty to your employers. Like you said, you've got a good job with good pay and benefits. So maybe you'd be inclined to cover for them, not tell the police everything you know, hoping maybe this will all just go away." I let him chew on that prospect for a few moments while I had some more quesadilla. "But I think you've got to ask yourself a couple of questions," I continued after another sip of beer. "Would they do the same? Are Eldon and Delbert going to cover for you? Or would they sacrifice their computer guy to save their own rich asses? What do you think, Ted?"

"Fuck!" he said, his fingers still mercilessly squeezing the life out of his beer glass. His tone had moved from shock to anger. That was good. I wanted him to be so fucking mad at Geetus and son for leaving him in the scenario I had painted for him that he'd tell me everything I needed to know.

"Fuck!" he whispered. He looked up at me as I took another sip of beer. "Mr. Jefferson," he said, "I don't think they'd hesitate for a moment to sacrifice me if they thought it would save the company." I let that hang in the air a bit longer. I wanted to let him hear it echo inside his own head so he wouldn't forget it. "What should I do?"

"Well, Ted, I'd say first off, we should both get another beer."

CHAPTER 39

It was after seven when I excused myself to go to the restroom. There was a pay phone near the door. I called Allison Rowe's home number, got her answering machine, and left a message, telling her I had something she was going to want. I left both my home and office numbers.

I took a leak, then went back to Humphries. I had asked him if Delbert Geetus had access to the internet or any electronic bulletin board systems. Humphries told me Delbert Geetus had called him into his office the previous winter, said he had been reading about something called electronic bulletin board systems, or BBSs, in some computer magazines. He asked Humphries if his office computer could be set up to access some BBSs. Humphries was familiar with BBSs.

Desert Diamond had one modem installed on its system. It was wired to a dedicated computer, what Humphries called the main server, which would connect to the savings and loan in Texas each night to exchange financial information. The server also handled in-house communications for all of Desert Diamond.

Humphries knew it wouldn't be much trouble to install another modem on Delbert's office computer. He bought the fastest modem available and the best software to support it. Once it was installed, Humphries showed Delbert how to use the software to have his computer dial the phone number of a BBS, build a list of phone numbers for any BBSs he wanted to visit, and store any files he might download. And that was that. Humphries said that he never thought much about it again, and never wondered where Delbert might be hanging out when he was online.

"You know, Ted,' I said, "there's a story I hear about some disks that supposedly have a bunch of files from Desert Diamond on them. From what I understand, that's why the police are very interested in the files on your system."

"Yeah," Humphries replied. "Mr. Welty called me into his office last week. He said he'd been talking to some guy who says he had some disks with our files on them. I guess the guy was offering his services as some sort of computer security consultant or something, telling Welty our security must be real weak if our files are showing up places where they shouldn't be."

"Interesting. Did you catch the guy's name?"

"No. Mr. Welty didn't say."

"Any idea how he got the files?"

"Not really. I guess, theoretically, some hacker could have gotten into our system, especially if Delbert is spending a lot of time online. He's the Financial Officer, so the consolidated books are on his computer. But the girls in his office do the bulk of the work. Each of them has a piece of the books that they're responsible for. Then it gets consolidated on Delbert's computer."

"Who's Mr. Welty?"

"He's the head of security for Desert Diamond. From what I hear, he and Eldon Geetus go way back. Anyway, Welty tells me we've got a leak and he wants to know where. Said he wanted to know if I hear or see anything unusual, anything at all. He was real serious about it, and he can come across like a pretty mean son of a bitch sometimes."

"What's Welty's first name?"

"George."

"Just out of curiosity, what does he look like?"

"Oh, let's see. He's about six feet tall. A little bit heavy set, I guess. Gray hair, long enough to comb. I guess he's in his late-fifties, maybe." As Humphries said that, his expression changed. "Shit, Travis. I left him a message this morning, telling him that Heidi had called asking me if I would meet with you. I'm sorry. I should have told you sooner, but with all that talk about the police and stuff, I completely forgot about it."

I was already getting up from my chair. "How can I reach you if I need to, Ted?"

He took a business card from his wallet. "My pager number is on there. Just put in your phone number and I'll get right back to you. You think it's a problem that I told Welty about you?"

"I don't know, Ted. But if I were you, I wouldn't go home tonight. Go find yourself a cheap hotel. Hell, they're all cheap this time of year. You might even want to call in sick on Monday morning. I'll be in touch." And I was out the door.

I wasn't concerned that Humphries had told Welty he was meeting with me. I realized that sooner or later I was going to have to talk with Welty anyway. But the fact that Welty knew that Heidi was involved made alarms go off in my brain. Welty wouldn't have to be a rocket scientist to link Heidi to the leak. And Humphries had said Welty could be a real mean son of a bitch. In my experience, mean sons of bitches tended to do very bad things.

Darkness was just beginning to set in. The air was still hot, and even with the windows down, I was sweating as I drove east toward Heidi's apartment. I could see the flashing red lights as I approached 68th Street. There was an ambulance, three patrol cars, and a couple of unmarked detective's cars in the parking lot. I felt a wave of nausea, brought on by a surge of adrenaline mixed with the fear that for the second time that week I was arriving too late to do any good.

I parked in the first space I could find and ran toward the walkway that led to Heidi's apartment. A uniformed Scottsdale Police officer blocked my path. "Please wait just a minute, sir. We need to keep this clear for medical personnel."

"What happened?"

"I can't provide details, sir. The detectives are trying to determine that now."

I could see another uniformed officer coming toward us from within the maze of apartments. Behind him two paramedics were carrying a stretcher.

"Is Ragsdale here?" I asked, my voice louder than it should have been.

The officer gave me a curious look. "Yes, Detective Ragsdale is on the scene."

The officer in front of the paramedics called out "Coming through, Ken." I backed up a couple of steps, more out of reflex than anticipation of Officer Ken's next request. I moved sideways toward the ambulance, while trying to get a look at the body on the stretcher. The glimpse I got told me there was no more point in looking. A sheet covered the body, including the face. The sheet was stained with blood. All that was visible were her feet. She was wearing brown sandals, the same brown sandals she wore the night we went to Charlie's apartment.

CHAPTER 40

I waited, sweating in the hundred-degree heat and flashing red lights for a half an hour before J. R. Ragsdale emerged from the apartment. He gave me a look, something between annoyance and disgust, said something I could not hear to one of the uniformed officers, then spoke to the paramedics.

As the ambulance departed, Ragsdale and the uniformed officer he had just talked to approached me. "Mr. Jefferson, how nice of you to save me the trouble of having to send someone to find you." He nodded to the officer, "Search him, cuff him, read him his rights, and put him in the car."

"Damn it, Detective, don't do this. We need to talk."

Ragsdale acted as though he didn't even hear me. "Get him out of my sight."

"Sir, place your hands on the car, spread your hands and feet apart."

I tried to get my emotions in check and assess my situation. For a fraction of a second I considered taking the officer down. I could probably do it with a side kick to his knee cap. He was young, but with all the cop paraphernalia on his belt, I figured I could out run him. I let the wisdom of my experience chime in. Maybe I could take him in a foot race, but I couldn't out run the radios, the helicopters, and the bullets. I had a good alibi. Eventually I would walk. So I put up with the indignity of the search, the handcuffs, and listening to the young officer begin to recite, "You have the right to remain silent..."

Twenty minutes later, having been duly transported to the Downtown Precinct of the Scottsdale Police Department, photographed and fingerprinted, I sat in the interview room, awaiting my audience with detective J. R. Ragsdale. The handcuffs, which had been removed during fingerprinting, were back on my wrists with my arms behind me. Not my favorite position.

I was still seething in anger at Ragsdale, but I was trying my best to keep it in check. I needed his help. I couldn't do what I had to do without being on the street. As long as Ragsdale was focusing on me, he wouldn't be looking for the person who murdered Heidi.

When the door opened and Ragsdale walked in, I stifled my urge to tell him what an incredibly stupid motherfucker he was. I knew it would not serve my needs to embarrass him in front of any other cops who might have been watching from outside the room. But I could not bring myself to be a docile suspect, either.

"Let's get this over with, Detective. You and I both have more important things to do tonight."

Ragsdale acted as though I had not even spoken. He had a file folder with him, which he appeared to read over before speaking. "Mr. Jefferson, you are being charged with the murder of Ms. Heidi Charlayne. This is a very serious charge that could cause you to face the death penalty. I understand that you have waived your right to counsel and are willing to speak with me regarding the charge against you. Is that correct?"

"Cut the shit, Detective. Whoever killed Heidi is still out there, and we both know it. You're wasting your time with these theatrics. You and I do have things to talk about. But that's not going to happen until you knock off the bullshit, get these cuffs off of me, and start asking the right questions."

Ragsdale hesitated. I was guessing that he did not really consider me a murder suspect. More likely he was tired of playing games with me and thought if he could scare the shit out of me I would tell him everything and expect nothing in return. I knew it was time to put all the cards on the table. But I wasn't going to do it wearing handcuffs.

"I suppose you can account for your whereabouts and activities earlier this evening. Is that right, Mr. Jefferson?"

"If you ask the nice man who took my wallet and car keys and placed them in a baggie for safe keeping if I can have them back, I will give you the pager number of Ted Humphries, the guy I was talking with from five this afternoon until around seven thirty this evening. He is someone you should talk with anyway, Detective, so I suggest you get in touch with him."

"And where were you and this Mr. Humphries from, what did you say, five until seven thirty?"

"A little place called the Indian Bend Bar and Grill. It's on Indian School, just east of 48th Street. I would imagine that if we could catch the bartender, a big guy they call Buddha, while his memory was still fresh, he would also verify that I was there. I was the guy who ate a really great green chile quesadilla and drank Heineken draft."

Ragsdale wrote down what I told him. It was the sort of detail a good cop would appreciate. Without saying anything more to me, he walked to the door and stepped out of the room. I waited, knowing that I'd scored whatever points I was going to score in that round. Either the cuffs would come off and we would talk some more, or I would spend an unpleasant night among less than desirable company at the county jail.

My anger had subsided enough to allow me to feel sorrow over the death of Heidi Charlayne. I had known her less than a week. But I had held her as she cried, mourning the loss of her brother. She was warm flesh and blood who had counted on me to do the right thing. I had let her down by not finding Charlie in time. Now I couldn't help but think that I had failed her again. And maybe, because of that failing, she was now lying in a cold drawer at the county morgue, covered by a sheet stained with her own blood, waiting for Doctor Suroop to carve out the details of her brutal death.

I had to focus on something else. If I continued to think of Heidi, and whatever responsibility I had in her murder, I would be immobilized, unable to do what was necessary to find Charlie's killer and hers. I knew I now had nearly all the pieces to the puzzle. But I still had to put them all together in the right order to see the picture. And once I could see the picture, I would have to recognize it for what it was.

Ragsdale walked back into the room. He took a seat across the table from me, placing a cassette recorder with a small microphone between us on the table. His folder was open on the table. He placed a yellow legal pad next to it. A uniformed officer who had come in with him inserted a metal key into each of the handcuffs and opened them up. He took the cuffs with him as he walked out, leaving Ragsdale and me alone.

"Travis," Ragsdale began. It was the first time he called me by my first name. "It's time for us to have ourselves a little 'Come to Jesus' meeting. This is where I convince you that we are on the same side and you should be helping me before anybody else gets killed. As you said earlier, we have things to talk about. The handcuffs are off. You are no longer being charged in the death of Heidi Charlayne. You are not a suspect. So, let's talk."

There was something compelling in his sincerity. I had to remind myself that Ragsdale could very well be playing good cop in contrast to his previous role as bad cop. Even so, I knew he was right. We had to work together. I had no need to protect Heidi as a source anymore. She was dead. So I was free to tell Ragsdale just about everything I knew.

"Alright, Detective. How do you want to do this?"

"Start at the beginning," he said. He wasn't being funny, just methodical.

"Okay," I began. "This story has several beginnings."

CHAPTER 41

I gave Ragsdale the story as well as I could, starting with Heidi tracking me down at Lucinda's. I told him how that had led to me contacting Mike Layton at the Valley Views, and to my conversation with Joe Diaz at Brandi's Cantina. It was just coincidental, I told him, that Layton also handed me the water study assignment. The two projects seemed to weave in and out of one another, though their connection to one another was obscure. The link between them was a dead man named Charlie Gonnerman.

Ragsdale wasn't that interested in the water study, goings on in state government, or the political ambitions of Sandy Dominguez. He had three homicides in one week, and that was three too many for a resort destination like Scottsdale. Though he didn't tell me in so many words, I imagined he was under tremendous pressure from city hall, which in turn was feeling the heat from the local business community, to end the killings and get somebody behind bars. People had to know that Scottsdale was once again a safe place to vacation, play golf, do business, spend money, and even raise a family.

What Ragsdale wanted from me were facts, not analysis. He was a seasoned homicide detective with two decades of police work under his belt. He didn't need some mangy looking journalist with no background in law enforcement trying to tell him what it all meant.

After a couple hours, I had brought him up to the point where I arrived at Heidi's apartment that night. I had left out one thing. While I had told him about the computer disks that Heidi gave to Charlie, I didn't mention the images that Jay Fujiwara had discovered on them. Jay was certain that possession of such images was illegal. Admitting to a police detective that I was in possession of them could get the handcuffs put right back on. That seemed like a bad idea.

Ragsdale showed only a mild interest in George Welty, Desert Diamond's head of security. "I thought we were supposed to be looking for Larry, the tall, blond mystery man," Ragsdale said. He was starting to look tired. "Now you're telling me you think this guy Welty should be a suspect, just because he shows an understandable concern for the theft of some files, which is exactly the sort of thing he gets paid to prevent. Where's the motive, Travis? Where's the motive in any of these murders? Where is the money, the sex, the jealousy, the drug habits, the things that usually provide us with some understanding as to why people kill each other? And what is their connection? What do they have in common? Is it possible that they are not related?" It was as though he were giving me an elementary lesson into the analytical process of a homicide detective.

"It's been a long day," Ragsdale said. "Go home. Get some sleep. Maybe you'll remember something we have overlooked this evening. Call me tomorrow, just to check in. Your 48 hours will be up at around noon."

"You'll be working tomorrow?" I asked. "It's Sunday."

Ragsdale looked at me as though he wanted to ask if I was truly as stupid as I appeared. "I have three open homicide cases on my desk, Mr. Jefferson. I am working until they are closed." He said no more, and arranged to have a patrolman drive me back to my car.

The night air was a little cooler as I headed home. It held just a hint of moisture—just enough to tease a rain-starved desert. I wondered if that meant that the summer monsoons would be arriving soon. Maybe it was just evaporation coming off of the Arizona Canal, then drifting slowly southward toward the slightly lower elevation of the dry, sandy bed of the Salt River.

I looked forward to a quick shower and falling into bed. It had been a long day. The early morning run had felt great at the time, but my joints and muscles were telling me that there was a price to pay for trying to keep up with young Merritt Donavon. Too much anger, too much sorrow had left me drained. All I wanted to do was get cleaned up, close my eyes and make it all go away, at least for a little while.

At 16th Street I turned north and went a couple of blocks, turning into the dirt parking lot of the little place I called home. My house was actually more of an apartment. It was the second story of an over-under duplex. Back in the fifties, the owners had lived upstairs and operated a hairdresser's shop downstairs. The building was set back about eighty feet from 16th Street. What should have been a spacious, grassy lawn was a parking lot for the patrons who used to come to get their hair done. In the sixties, the couple moved their shop to a new strip mall, and bought a house in the suburbs.

I knew something was wrong as soon as I pulled into the dirt driveway. Light came from the windows of my upstairs apartment. I knew I'd turned the lights off when I left that day. Lights generate heat, and my little apartment was already in the death grip of an Arizona summer.

I parked my Honda and resisted the urge to bound up the stairs to the small porch outside my front door. I made my way cautiously. I realized my headlights coming up the driveway should have announced my arrival to anyone inside who was paying attention. Even so, I had no intention of being caught off guard as I had at Charlie's apartment a few nights before.

I moved up the stairs as stealthily as I could, hunting for any sight or sound that might give me a clue as to what was going on. The spring on the screen door held it shut, but the wooden door behind it was wide open. The door jamb was torn and splintered at the lock. The door had been kicked hard, the force ripping the bolt through the door jamb.

I stepped carefully through the doorway into my living room, and began to survey the damage. The walls, windows and ceiling remained intact, but the rest of my home was damn near destroyed. The sofa and reclining chair had been torn apart. Tables were overturned. My modest 16-inch television was smashed. All my books were dumped off the shelves. Photographs had been pulled from their frames and tossed on the floor.

Everything in the kitchen – whether food, dishes, soap, or utensils – was thrown on the floor. My little microwave oven lay in pieces among the shards of plates and glasses. In the bathroom the contents of the medicine chest were on the floor, the shower curtain and rod pulled down, and the top of the toilet tank was dumped into the bathtub. Cleaning supplies and extra rolls of toilet paper had been pulled out from the cabinet under the sink and thrown around.

In the bedroom my mattress and box springs had been slit open and ripped apart. My clothes lay in shambles all over the floor. My stereo was in pieces as though someone very large had stomped on it several times. Every vinyl record was pulled out of its cover, every cover ripped apart. Cassette tapes were all smashed. There was nothing unopened. Nothing left untouched or unspoiled.

One stark fact stood out. Nothing, absolutely nothing, was missing.

CHAPTER 42

I was exhausted, emotionally drained, and my home had been violated. I felt deeply confused and disoriented. I needed to rest and I felt like crying, if not for myself then for Heidi and Charlie, and for the people who had loved them. But I was also angry, and I needed something that would keep me going a little longer, so I let the anger come to the surface, let it give me the energy I would need. Looking for Charlie and then for his killer had engaged me intellectually and professionally. But I had managed to keep my feelings about it at a distance. Heidi's murder had shocked me, but whatever pain I might have felt over her death had been mostly sublimated by the humiliation and confusion of being arrested and interrogated.

Through it all I had tried to remain emotionally detached. It was a survival mechanism left over from the war. People die, and you just try not to think about it. If you do you become frozen in an emotional gridlock, unable to complete the mission or save the lives of your friends. But I couldn't remain detached anymore. Now the war had come into my home. My interests were no longer just professional. Now it was personal.

Whoever invaded my home hadn't found what they were looking for. That meant there was one more place they would have to go. I had no choice but to go there myself. So I headed back down the stairs, got in my Civic, and started to drive toward my office.

I had only gone a couple of blocks on 16th Street when I realized that whoever had trashed my house might not know where my office was. My name and address were in the phone book, but my business card only had my post office box number for an address. I glanced in my rearview mirror, wondering if any of the dozen or so cars behind me were watching to see where I might go.

I crossed Indian School Road going south and continued for about a quarter mile, keeping an eye on my rear view mirror. Some streets have traffic on them on Saturday night.

Some don't. Having grown up in the Valley, I knew of several quiet little residential neighborhoods. I turned into one of those neighborhoods, continuing to glance in the rear view mirror. Another pair of headlights turned too. I tried to make out the type of vehicle, but it was too dark to tell.

I drove slow enough to make it easy to follow me, as I turned right and then left through the residential neighborhood. The headlights in the mirror stayed with me, pulling a little closer so as not to lose me. Those lights were high off the ground. It was most likely a full-size pick up truck.

I took a gamble. I knew the street I was on would dead end at a canal bank. I down shifted and stomped on the accelerator, increasing the distance between my Honda and the big vehicle that was trailing me. I was counting on it taking the other driver a few seconds to react.

I could hear the roar of a big engine accelerating hard as the headlights started to gain on me. The driver was gunning it hard and picking up speed in a hurry. About thirty yards from the end of the street I turned off my lights, down shifted twice to cut my momentum without using my brakes, and threw the Honda into a hard U-turn, sliding over to the other side of the street with the engine idling, using the hand brake to bring my little Civic to a stop. The big truck had too many horses running. I could hear the big tires screeching. The shiny red, late model Chevy smashed through the wooden barricade, bounced into the air as it hit the earthen canal bank. It came down with a loud thud, nosing into four feet of water, the hot engine hissing as it turned canal water into a plume of steam.

I drove off as fast as I could, feeling my adrenaline surge. I turned on my lights and pulled out in to the Saturday night traffic on 16th Street. I wondered if Big Larry had been wearing his seatbelt.

Instead of parking in my usual spot in the covered space behind my office, I pulled into the big parking lot behind the Veterans Administration medical center across the street. I parked between a couple of other cars near a rear entrance to the sprawling medical complex. I took off, running first to the sidewalk along 7th Street, then to the intersection of 7th and Indian School Road.

The light was red when I got there, but within a couple of seconds I saw a break in the traffic just big enough to get through. I ran through the intersection, moved quickly past the corner, turned down the alley and ran the two blocks to the back of my office building. I unlocked the glass door, locking it behind me, and bounded up the stairs to the hallway, where I unlocked my office door and slipped inside. There was no sign of a break in. I turned on the lights. Everything was just as I had left it. I shut the door behind me. It locked automatically.

At first, all I could hear was my own hard breathing. I looked at my watch. It was after midnight. A long day was getting longer. I knew the adrenaline that had kept me going during the past hour would wear off soon, and exhaustion would be all that remained.

They hadn't found my office yet. Maybe they wouldn't. But that was not a chance I could take. I unlocked the big drawer in my desk and pulled out the newspaper to which Jay Fujiwara had taped the floppy disks. When they came, it would be the disks they would want. I wondered what it was about those disks that made them worth killing for, but I was too tired to ponder the question. It was much easier to reduce the issue to a simple economic principle, the old standby: supply and demand. They wanted them. I had them.

I took the box with the camera and lenses and placed them on the desk. Then I pulled out the bottom box, the one with my Colt .45 semi-automatic. I removed the gun from its holster and took two spare magazines out of the box. Then I put the holster back in the box, and placed the box, the camera gear, and the newspaper back in the drawer and locked it. I walked over and turned out the lights, then moved to a corner of the room and sat down facing the door with my back against the walls. I placed the spare magazines, each holding seven rounds, on the floor to my left. I held the gun with both hands. Anyone who came through the door would find out the price was going up.

CHAPTER 43

The cannon in my hands posed a small problem as I felt myself slipping from exhaustion to the edge of sleep. It was a powerful handgun, which could cause great damage, whether fired intentionally or by accident.

I pulled back on the slide and let it go forward. Then I placed my thumb on the hammer and slowly squeezed the trigger as I very carefully lowered the hammer out of the cocked position. That left a round in the chamber but the gun not cocked. If I should fall asleep, as I was certain that I soon would, I was not likely to blow my kneecap off with some uncontrolled twitch. And I was fairly certain that if anyone, big Larry for instance, should try to kick down my office door and barge into my office, I would have enough time to pull the hammer back and take aim. I knew from experience that I could do both at the same time.

Having prepared for whatever might come next, I let my back settle against the corner of the room. My mind put aside the memory Heidi's body, carried by the paramedics and covered with a sheet stained with her blood. I forgot about the disaster scene that used to be my home, and the red pickup truck that followed me into the dead end. I let it all go, let it fall away, and found myself thinking instead of Juliette Skye Valdez.

We had stopped at the house of one of her climbing friends to borrow some gear. All I'd brought with me from Phoenix were my harness and climbing shoes. They were all I would have needed if I decided to try out the routes in the Denver climbing gym. But Juliette had decided she wanted me to take her climbing on real rock. So her friend, a lanky, goateed young slacker named Jason, loaned us a rack of cams and stoppers and a half dozen nylon slings.

Jason looked at me with a combination of jealousy and mistrust, as though I was an old lecher trying to move in on his territory. Juliette explained that I was the guy who was doing the article about her for Outdoor West. Then he remembered his rock-jock manners and offered a rope. Juliette had her own, and a set of quick draws, short lengths of nylon webbing with carabiners attached to each end, standard equipment for sport climbers.

Sport climbers ascend routes that are bolted. Holes are drilled into the rock, and steel expansion bolts are pounded into the holes. The bolts secure a small piece of steel bent at a right angle called a hanger. The hanger has two holes, one on each side of the angle. The bolt goes through one of the holes, locking the hanger securely against the rock. A climber ascends to the bolt and clips a carabiner (at one end of a quick draw) through the other hole in the hanger. Then the climber clips the rope, which is tied to the climber's harness, into the carabiner that is at the other end of the quick draw. This provides protection for the climber. If the climber should fall, the climber's partner, who is below, feeding the rope out as the climber moves up, will hold the rope tight, and, ideally, the bolt, hanger, nylon webbing and carabiners will take the weight of the climber once any slack in the rope is taken up.

It works the same in a climbing gym, except that in the gym the holds are usually manufactured. They are bolted to the climbing walls of the gym. Nowadays, most beginning climbers learn to climb in a gym instead of at their local outdoor crag. Most of those who do venture beyond the walls of the climbing gym become sport climbers. Juliette was a sport climber.

Typically, sport climbers only climb routes that are bolted. They are concerned with the athleticism of the moves involved in moving up the rock. They don't want to have to spend time "placing protection." Putting in protection or "pro" while climbing routes that are not bolted is the province of the traditional or "trad" climber. It involves fitting a "piece of protection," usually a small mechanical camming device or a hexagon-shaped piece of aluminum alloy, into a crack in the rock. A carabiner is then clipped to the pro, and the rope runs through the carabiner. Learning to place protection, that is, seeing the crack in the rock and knowing the piece of gear that will fit into it snugly, and knowing how to place it so it will not pop out if you should fall, and doing it all with just one hand (since the other is holding on to the rock) is both art and science. It takes years to learn to do it well. I'd been doing it for twenty years.

We drove out of Denver, took an exit off the highway, followed the road up into the mountains, and took a turnoff that led to a meadow near the mouth of a small canyon. We parked the car, gathered gear, rope, climbing shoes, and water bottles and stuffed them in our packs, then hiked across the meadow to a lovely little canyon. At its mouth the canyon was about fifty yards across and covered with wild flowers. A trail, barely visible among the grass and flowers that thrive during the short, high-mountain growing season, followed a small stream.

As we walked the canyon narrowed and the walls grew higher on each side. Pine and fir trees covered the rocky cliffs above us. White clouds stood out against the blue sky. The mountain air was cool and sweet. It was a beautiful summer day in the mountains – the sort of day that is made for climbing.

The brisk, twenty-minute hike brought us to the wall. The canyon ended abruptly at a small pool. The canyon walls were sheer rock, beautifully polished by the water that had rushed over them each spring as the mountain snow above melted and found its way into the little canyon. The walls were broken by a series of cracks, most vertical, a few horizontal. It was these cracks that made the wall so attractive to climbers. They provided purchase for fingers and toes, just enough to make the climbs challenging, but possible. They also provided ample opportunity for putting in protection, thus making the canyon wall appealing to a trad climber like me.

Browne Canyon had been named after an early settler in the area. Climbing tradition holds that the first party to climb a route gets to name it. The guys who first climbed the walls above the pond in Browne Canyon back in the late 1970s happened to be Jackson Browne fans. They named each of the seven routes they pioneered after songs Jackson Browne had written and recorded: "Rock Me on the Water," "Something Fine," and "Running on Empty." The route I had chosen for my climb with Juliette was called "Late for the Sky."

We put on our climbing shoes and harnesses. The air in Browne Canyon turned cool as breezes high above us blew billowing clouds overhead, blocking out the direct rays of the sun. Looking up at the route, I tried to envision where and how I would place protection. Then I arranged the gear on a nylon sling and tossed it over my head so it hung from my right shoulder and down across my chest.

Strictly speaking, Juliette was the better climber. But she had zero experience lead climbing and placing the little nuts and cams that trad climbers use for protection. So it was understood from the first that I would lead the climb, placing protection as I ascended, while Juliette belayed me from below. Once I reached a good place from which to belay Juliette, she would follow up the route "cleaning" the protection I had placed and bringing it up with her as she climbed.

I tied the end of the rope to my harness with a figure-8 knot. Juliette checked my knot and harness. I, in turn, checked her belay device. Secure that we had not overlooked anything that could inadvertently get either of us killed if I should take a fall, I turned and faced the wall. "On belay?" I asked.

"Belay on."

I placed my hands against the rock wall, feeling the features of the crack, looking for the holds that would afford my hands the maximum leverage when my feet left the ground. "Climbing," I said, sliding my fingers into the crack above my head.

"Climb on," she said. I made the initial move and continued to work my hands and feet up along the crack, looking for the best place to put in a cam for a little protection. "Nice buns," she said.

I followed the crack, slowly working my way up 120 feet of good rock, placing pro as I ascended. A light rain began to fall just as I cleared the top of the climb. I used some of the rope to anchor myself to a large boulder, and chose a nice spot near the edge from which I could belay Juliette. The rain made the rock a little slicker, making the climb somewhat more difficult. But Juliette was such a good climber that it hardly mattered. After clearing the lip at the top of the climb she gave me a big hug and a kiss. "Thanks, Travis," she said as we held each other. "That was great. Thanks for bringing me here. What a beautiful place."

CHAPTER 44

The scream was loud and high-pitched. At first it was part of a dream. Heidi was backed into a corner in her living room as her pursuer moved toward her, a small caliber semiautomatic pistol in his hand. I came through the door, but I couldn't move fast enough, as though I were trying to run through water. The gun went off, but it made no sound. I saw the blood, but still Heidi continued to scream.

The gun fired silently again. As I struggled to save her I felt myself coming out of my dream, but the screaming didn't stop. It was there in the office. Without thinking, purely on old hard-wired reflexes, the .45 was up in both my hands and pointing across the room, my right thumb pulling back the hammer. As my eyes tried to focus they were also looking for the slightest sign of movement. My ears tried to zero in on the source of the intermittent screaming.

I was coming into consciousness, sitting up, eyes following the line from the rear sight to the front and beyond as my arms slowly moved the weapon, sweeping back and forth across the room. I felt my heart pounding as my aim locked onto my desk, the location of the high-pitched sound. Now fully awake, I realized Heidi's screams were the telephone, which continued to ring. I sprang up, my body now fully loaded with unneeded adrenaline, and leaped to the desk, picking up the phone with my left hand, the .45 still in my right.

"Hello," I said, louder than I should have, my body still not ready to believe that there was no life-threatening crisis.

"Travis, is that you? It's Allison. Are you okay?"

I slowly lowered the gun and placed it on my desk. "Yeah," I said, "more or less."

"Did I catch you at a bad time? I tried your home number first. I didn't think you'd be in the office on Sunday morning."

The events of the night came back to me—my conversation with Ted Humphries, the flashing lights at Heidi's apartment, Ragsdale and the Scottsdale police station, the scene of destruction at my house, the red truck that followed me.

"Allison, where are you?"

"My house. Why?"

"We need to talk"

"Sounds serious. You want to come over for some coffee? You sound like you could use some."

"Yeah. You're right." I glanced at my watch. It was a little after eight. The window shades had kept the office dark. "I'd love some coffee. Where do you live?"

"Do you know the condos at 7th Street and Van Buren. I'm in number 42. I'll tell the gate guard I'm expecting you."

It only took me a few minutes to drive to Allison Rowe's condo. Phoenix streets are quiet on Sunday morning. She lived in a slightly upscale enclave that had been carved out of a quarter of a city block in a decaying neighborhood in downtown Phoenix.

I felt just a little nervous as I approached the security gate at the entrance to the condos. My yellow legal pad was on the seat next to me. Under it was my .45, holstered with a round in the chamber.

"Travis Jefferson to see Allison Rowe," I said to the security guard as I pulled up.

"Thank you, Mr. Jefferson." He raised the gate without so much as a glance at the passenger seat.

The entire complex was painted a light shade of pink. The metal roofs, originally painted a reddish brown, had taken on touches of a turquoise stain. The condos were packed tightly together, interspersed with the usual well-watered tropical landscaping.

I found a parking space near the address Allison had given me. I wondered what to do with the gun. In light of the brutal events of the past few days, I had plenty of reason to want some fire power with me. But I had no reason to suspect I would need it at Allison's. Mostly, I didn't want to frighten her. So I placed the cannon under my seat.

Allison opened her door. "Hey Travis, come on in. How do you like your coffee?"

"With a little milk would be fine, or half and half, whatever you've got. Thanks for inviting me over." She led me through the living room to a counter next to the kitchen.

"Have a seat," She poured in hot coffee, and handed it to me across the counter and pushed some half and half my way.

"I was just about to make some breakfast," she said as she began breaking eggs into a bowl. "Can I offer you an omelet?"

"That would be great." I looked at the array of chopped ingredients she had spread out next to the stove—ham, onions, grated cheese, diced green chile, and sliced mushrooms. "Can I have mine with no ham?"

"Vegetarian? No trouble at all." She looked up from the eggs. "You have a rough night?"

"Started out okay. Then somebody got killed."

Allison looked up at me. After a moment she said, "You're not kidding, are you?"

"No. I wish I was. You remember that guy I mentioned, the environmentalist that Rafer and I both knew."

"The one they found floating in the canal?"

"Yeah. His sister worked at Desert Diamond. She'd been supplying him with Desert Diamond's financial information. Last night somebody put a bullet in her."

"Oh my God!" She stared at me. She was used to writing about land fraud, junk bonds, and the occasional embezzlement – not murder.

"There's a detective in Scottsdale named J.R. Ragsdale. He and I spent a few hours talking last night. He was curious about why people I know are getting killed. If it weren't for the fact that my alibis are air tight, I'd be having breakfast in the county jail this morning instead of here with you."

"Oh, Travis."

"That was just the start. While Ragsdale and I were having our little conversation, somebody trashed my house— literally tore it apart. Then after I left there, somebody followed me. That's why I ended up sleeping in my office last night."

"Oh, Travis. Did you and Ragsdale come up with any answers?"

"Not yet, Allison."

"What was going on when you called me yesterday?"

"I was in a bar, talking with a guy who works at Desert Diamond." I had to take a moment to remember the conversation and why it seemed so important to me at the time. "You ever hear the name Welty? George Welty, I think?"

Allison looked up from the omelet she was cooking for me. "That does sort of sound familiar, although I can't recall where I've heard it. Is he someone connected to Desert Diamond?"

"The guy I talked to said that Welty's the head of security at Desert Diamond."

She handed my omelet to me. "You want some salsa or catsup with this?"

"Salsa would be great."

She got a jar of salsa from the refrigerator. "I've got a few boxes of news clippings on the Geetus businesses that I've collected over the years. If I've got anything on anyone named Welty, that's where it would be. You're welcome to look through them if you want."

"Yeah, I would like to see what you've got."

Allison made an omelet for herself and refilled my coffee. I told her about my soccer game conversation with Alan Davies, my phone chat with Shelly Diaz, my interview with Sandy Dominguez, and finally the meeting with Ted Humphries. It was this last one that really got her attention. "So there's child pornography on the Desert Diamond computers? That's very interesting. Do the police know about it?"

"Not yet. Ragsdale's focused on the three homicides. The Desert Diamond offices are in Phoenix, and, so far at least, he doesn't have anything that ties Geetus and son to the murders." I took another sip of coffee. "I don't even know who would investigate something like files on a computer."

Allison looked thoughtful for a moment. "I think I know somebody who might."

"Who's that?"

"A woman in the County Attorney's office. Her name's Gail O'Halleran. She works white collar crime. I've talked with her about a couple of fraud investigations. But she's become sort of an expert on computer crime, too."

"What's computer crime?"

"Hacking mostly. You know, computer-savvy teenagers breaking into the networks of big companies. Sometimes they do it just so they can brag to their buddies that they did it. Sometimes they steal data like credit card numbers."

"She must be pretty sharp."

"Very. From what I hear, she's developing a national reputation as being one of the best people in the field. I can't imagine she'll be working for the County Attorney much longer."

"Do you know how to reach her?"

"Could be a little tricky on a Sunday, but I could give it a shot. But if I'm working on this then I guess I have to ask you, who's going to write this story, you or me?"

"Good question, and a fair one." We considered one another for a moment or two. "How about if we split the material. I'm already under contract to cover the murder of Charlie Gonnerman for the Valley Views. I'm happy to give you everything I have on Desert Diamond. That's your territory anyway and you've got plenty of material for background. Why not share everything, but work it from two different angles?"

"You know that I can't give you any credit when I publish mine, right? There's no way the publisher is going to let your name show up in the Gazette."

"That's okay, Allison. I don't need the credit. And I imagine that you don't want your name showing up in the Valley Views, either."

She smiled and held out her hand across the breakfast counter. "Sounds like we have a deal, Travis." We shook hands. "Now if you will excuse me, I'm going to try to reach Gail. Then I have to take a shower and get dressed for church."

CHAPTER 45

Research – going through stacks and stacks of paper, quickly scanning each one for any piece of pertinent information – can be agonizingly monotonous work. It would drive most people crazy. It was how I once earned my living as an intelligence analyst. I was very good at it then. As I sat on the floor in the little bedroom that Allison used as a home office, going over papers that filled four cardboard boxes, I hoped I still was.

Allison had amassed an impressive collection. She was good. Allison did her homework. Allison dug deep.

She had spent hours, days, probably weeks in libraries. She scoured microfiche copies of newspapers from Tallahassee, Ft. Walton Beach, Panama City, Mobile, Biloxi, Baton Rouge, Shreveport, Houston, Galveston, and Phoenix.

Anytime the name Geetus or one of his companies showed up in print, she'd burn a copy for her files. If other firms or individuals were mentioned with Geetus, she began to track them, too. More copies. More files.

They were arranged chronologically. No way to search on a single name. Cross-referencing was manual low-tech. She'd made hand written notes in the margins: *See Panama City News-Herald 4-18-85 and Mobile Register 4-21-85*.

Some files were actual newspaper clippings. Allison had cut them out of various Florida newspapers, then taped the clippings to sheets of paper, dutifully labeling the date and source of the article. After she landed a job with the Phoenix Gazette, she maintained a standing search criteria on stories that came over the news wires. If one or more of her key words showed up in a story, it would show up on her computer. If it was interesting, she would print out the article. If there were anything pertaining to Eldon Geetus, his business enterprises or his associates, she'd save it in her files.

Allison came into the room. She looked beautiful in her Sunday-go-to-meeting dress, thin and yellow, down to her knees, and with a hat to match. "Find anything you can use?" she asked.

"Not yet. But I've got a ways to go." I stood up to stretch.

"I'm off to church. Should be back in a couple of hours."

"Say a prayer for me please. I'm likely gonna need it."

"I'd be happy to." She gave me a hug and a kiss on the cheek just before she went out the door. I had to dodge the brim of her fancy yellow hat.

I'd been on the floor for an hour. My knees were aching, my back was getting stiff and I was just barely into the second box. A headline caught my attention:

Trial of Former Deputy Ends in Hung Jury

The jury foreman in the trial of former Bay County deputy sheriff George Welty told federal judge James Adair yesterday that the jury was unable to reach agreement as to whether Welty was guilty of violating the civil rights of Myron Lee Stott. Federal prosecutors claimed that Welty had beaten Stott after his arrest last year in Panama City for possession of marijuana, possession of drugs with intent to distribute, and possession of drug paraphernalia.

Deputy U.S. Attorney Steven Akins declined to say whether he would attempt to retry Welty. A source close to the case stated that it was unlikely that Akins would ask the court for another trial. "Frankly, the U.S. Attorney has bigger fish to fry right now. Bay County settled out of court with Mr. Stott, and it's likely that this will be the end of it."

Welty has been free on bond during the trial. He resigned from Bay County Sheriff's Department following his indictment by a federal grand jury in August, and since last fall has been employed by Gulf Coast Land & Development.

I continued through the second box and into the third. There were interesting tidbits, most reinforcing what I already knew about the Geetus empire, without adding anything new or significant. Eldon Geetus gives large check to local charity. Eldon Geetus with Senator Dowling on a big fishing boat off of Cabo San Lucas. Geetus makes a speech at the press conference where he announces the formation of the Citizens for Decency. Geetus breaks ground on new corporate headquarters on Camelback Road.

Two hours more of sitting, scanning articles, reading photo captions and my knees were screaming. My back chimed in, too. It was bad harmony. I got up to stretch.

Allison would be back soon. I stretched. I twisted. I reached up. I reached down. My knees were stiff. My back was sore. I walked into the kitchen. I opened Allison's refrigerator. I grabbed a cold beer. I went back to work.

Deep into box number four there was an article from 1991 with a photo. There had been some vandalism at the Diamond Rio development northeast of Scottsdale. Equipment had been damaged. A trailer was torched. The police suspected eco-sabotage. In the photo, Desert Diamond head of security George Welty surveyed the damage. There was another guy in the photo with Welty. He's in the background. He is not identified. But I recognized him. I stared at the picture while the puzzle pieces slowly began to fall into place.

CHAPTER 46

It was close to twelve thirty when Allison returned. "Gail O'Halleran paged me," she said. "I called her back from the church. She wants to meet this afternoon in her office. But she's concerned about evidence. She needs something to take to a judge if she's going to get a search warrant."

"I think I've got what she needs. I've got to get back to my office to take care of some things. Why don't you call Gail, tell her I've got the evidence she wants. Set up the meeting, then call me at the office and tell me when and where to meet you."

"Sounds good to me. Did you find what you were looking for in my Geetus files?"

"Yeah, I think so. I'll tell you about it later. Right now I've got to run." And with that I headed back out into the Phoenix heat.

I had an idea, but I wanted to do a little recon before committing to it. So instead of going straight back to my office, I drove to 16th Street, then headed north, past the small disaster area that had been my home, to Camelback Road.

The southeast corner of 16th and Camelback had once been a Pontiac dealership, the place for people who wanted big seats and a big engine, but didn't want to be lumped in with the geriatric crowd that drove Buicks and Oldsmobiles. Now it was an upscale blues club, part of the nightlife scene that stretched along Camelback. The club itself occupied the part of the property nearest the intersection. Behind it was a large parking lot surrounded by a six feet high concrete block wall. The entrance to the parking lot was on 16th Street toward the rear of the property. It was the only way for a car to get in or out of the parking lot.

I spent a few minutes in the parking lot, looking it over carefully. The main entrance to Suite 16, indicated by the neon sign above it, was at the back of the building, not far from the wall that bordered 16th Street. To the right of that, over at the other end of the back wall, was the service entrance. Next to that there was a wide roll-up door that served as the loading dock for food, booze, and amplifiers.

Security cameras covered the entrances. Another scanned the parking lot.

Back at my office everything still looked normal. I had work to do on the computer, putting pieces into their proper places in the association and event matrixes, but first I called Ted Humphries' pager number.

A few minutes later he called me back. The hard part was telling him about Heidi. "Oh fuck!" was his first reply. He said it over and over when I told him what I had seen after leaving him in the bar. There was fear and confusion in his voice. I did my best to calm him down. Then I asked him for what I needed.

"Ted, I was wondering if you have a number to reach Welty on weekends?"

"You want to talk to Welty?"

"Yeah, I do, Ted. I think I've found those disks he's looking for. I thought I'd see if he's offering a reward."

"You're shittin' me, aren't you Travis?"

"Give me his number, and I'll tell you about it in a couple of days, Ted."

"Okay, man. I'm gonna assume that you know what you're doing." He gave me two numbers – one for Welty's home number, the other for his pager."

"Anything else?" he asked.

"Just keep laying low, Ted. The shit's gonna start flying tomorrow. Do your best to stay out of the line of fire."

Two minutes later Allison called. "We're on with Gail O'Halleran at two. You got the evidence she needs?"

"I'll have it with me. Where's her office?"

Allison gave me directions. "Because it's Sunday, there won't be anyone there, so she'll meet us at the door right at two."

"I'll be there. And Allison, thanks for your help on this."

"Hey Travis, we've got a deal. I expect to get a story out of this that will make me the envy of business reporters everywhere."

"Not to mention a little payback for a land deal in Florida," I added. "I'll see you at two."

I opened the top drawer of my desk and took out the small tape recorder. It had a handy feature: a little microphone that connected to the telephone receiver with a small suction cup. I set it up to record, started it rolling, then dialed one of the numbers Humphries had just given me and got lucky.

"Hello," Welty answered at his home number. His voice was deep and gravelly.

"Mr. Welty?" I asked.

"Yes," he replied, "what is it?"

"Mr. George Welty?" I asked, just to make sure, not really wanting to talk with a brother or cousin.

"Who *is* this?" Now his impatience was coming on strong.

"Mr. Welty, my name is Travis Jefferson." I did my best to sound like a naïve rookie.

"Jefferson? Shit!"

"Mr. Welty I'm a journalist, and, well, in the course of a story I've been working on I've come across some computer disks that I understand may be of interest to you."

"You know damn well that I want those disks."

"Well, yes Mr. Welty, that's what I've been led to believe. And I understand that you're offering a rather substantial reward for their safe return."

"Reward? Jefferson, what the hell are you talking about?"

"Perhaps I was misinformed, Mr. Welty. Maybe I should just give these disks to the police, you know, as sort of a lost and found thing. I'm sure they would know what to do with them. I mean, if you're certain there is no reward."

"Hold on Jefferson." I thought I could hear his blood pressure go up a few points. "Wait, I do remember something about a reward, now that you mention it. Yeah, I remember now. A couple of hundred bucks, wasn't it?"

"Mr. Welty, the figure I heard was a thousand dollars."

"A grand? Jefferson what the fuck kind of scam are you trying to run on me, you little prick? I'll fucking turn your face into fucking hamburger if you try to pull some shit like that on me you fucking low life scum bag."

"Is that what you did to Charlie Gonnerman, George? Turn his face into hamburger before you tossed him into the canal? Well, really George that is terribly frightening, considering that I don't even like hamburger, so maybe the police station would be the best place for these disks."

"Damn it Jefferson! Wait, you smart ass son of a bitch." I waited a moment or two. I listened, wondering if I could hear him sweat on the other end, but there was just the noisy breathing of an old cop who hadn't taken very good care of himself over the years.

"There's a club on the corner of 16th Street and Camelback, George. Right down the street from your office. It's called Suite 16. I'm going to be there with these disks, in the parking lot behind the club, at 2 a.m. If you want them, that's where you should be, too. And you should also bring a thousand dollars in cash, as my reward for finding the disks and returning them to their rightful owner. See you at 2 a.m., George." I hit the disconnect button on my phone, heard the dial tone, and pushed the Stop button on the tape recorder. Then I got out my yellow pad and started making notes for my meeting at the county attorney's office.

CHAPTER 47

Gail O'Halleran met us at a side door of the county building. She looked like she was in her mid-40s, her short, reddish brown hair just beginning to show some streaks of gray. She wore khaki slacks and a light blue short sleeve blouse.

Allison introduced us, and Gail led us to the elevator. Once we were seated in her office, O'Halleran looked at me and said, "Okay, Travis, what do we have?"

"We have," I began as I placed the six computer disks on her desk, "computer disks that contain files copied from a computer in the office of Delbert Geetus, Vice President and Chief Financial Officer of Desert Diamond Development. They contain both financial and image files. The image files, I have been told, though I have not seen them myself, likely constitute child pornography.

"I came into possession of these disks during a search of the apartment of a man named Charlie Gonnerman at the request of his sister Heidi Charlayne who contacted me to help her find her brother. Ms. Charlayne and her brother are now both dead, as is another individual connected to this case, one Edward Pelosi. Detective J.R. Ragsdale has all three homicide cases, as the bodies were discovered within his jurisdiction."

"Interesting," said O'Halleran. She had not made any notes while I spoke. Now she began rapidly typing on the keyboard in front of her. Never looking down at her hands or her computer screen, she asked, "Do you have any idea how those disks came to be in Mr. Gonnerman's apartment?"

"They were given to him by his sister. Heidi worked in the accounting department of Desert Diamond, for Delbert Geetus. Charlie asked her for information on Desert Diamond's finances. She felt that she owed him for a big favor he had done for her several years ago. So she copied all of Delbert's files and gave the disks to Charlie."

"And how is it that you know that?"

"Heidi told me about it a few days ago. She was killed last night, at her apartment in Scottsdale. I arrived there as they were bringing her body out."

O'Halleran raised her eyebrows just a bit. But she continued to type. Then she picked up the disks, took one and inserted it into her computer, and stacked the others neatly nearby. "Well," she said, "I guess it's time to see what's on these."

I couldn't see the images on the screen. O'Halleran went through each of the disks. She made notes on a pad of Post It notes, sticking one on each of the disks as she took them out of her computer.

She looked up and said, "You were right, Travis. The images on the disks do constitute child pornography. And the fact that they happen to appear on disks that also have the financial files of Desert Diamond is circumstantial evidence that could tie someone at Desert Diamond to one or more crimes. Our problem with this, my problem really, is that they are not in the possession of anyone at Desert Diamond. And while I might be able to find a judge, even on a Sunday afternoon, who would give me search warrant, I am reluctant to go into a business establishment like Desert Diamond and seize their computers. That would create some big time media attention. I don't mind that and neither does the County Attorney. But before we do it, we want to be sure we're right. So I need more. What else do you have?"

"Two things, Gail." I took my tape recorder out of its case and placed it on O'Halleran's desk. "This conversation took place about an hour ago. George Welty is the head of security for Desert Diamond." I pushed the PLAY button.

I watched O'Halleran as I replayed my conversation with Welty. Toward the end, a half smile crept over her face and she looked up at me.

"Travis, I believe you just tried to blackmail that man," she said.

"I just hope you'll wait until I trade him disks for cash before you arrest him, Gail."

"Wait a minute, Travis," Allison interjected, speaking up for the first time, "is that all you want out of this? You get a thousand bucks and some second tier guy at Desert Diamond gets popped?"

"I'll be honest with you, Allison. It won't bother me a bit to take a grand off of these guys. They literally destroyed my house last night, so I think it's only fair that they help a little with the redecorating." O'Halleran's eyes went up with that one. It was a part of the story she hadn't heard and I could tell she didn't like surprises. "But more importantly," I continued, "I need Welty to think that I'm only in this for the money. If he starts to think that there's any other reason to be meeting me at two in the morning in a parking lot, then he's not going to show."

"And besides the money, why are you meeting him in a parking lot at two in the morning?" O'Halleran asked me.

"I'm hoping that once I hand him the disks, copies of the ones you've got, you're going to arrest him, sort of like a drug buy in reverse."

"That way I've got the disks connected directly to Desert Diamond. Okay. Now what's this about your house?"

"Last night at Heidi's apartment I ran into Ragsdale. He knows I'm working on a story that involves the murders, or at least Charlie Gonnerman's murder. But when I showed up at the scene last night, well, he wasn't happy. I'm a little closer to his investigation than he would like. So he wanted to talk. Apparently while Ragsdale and I were having a little chat at the Scottsdale PD, somebody was going through my house, tearing the place apart looking for something."

"You know what they were looking for?" O'Halleran asked.

"I figure it was those disks. But they were at my office, not my home, so that's where I went next. I think I was followed when I left my house, but I'm pretty sure I lost whoever it was. Then I spent the night at my office, just in case anybody showed up there."

"Okay, Travis. You said you had two things that might improve our chances of getting a search warrant. One is that tape. What's the other?"

"Yesterday I talked with Ted Humphries. He's the systems administrator at Desert Diamond. He told me that Delbert Geetus had him install a modem on his office computer a few months ago so he could access some bulletin board services. I assume you know about BBSs."

O'Halleran nodded so I continued. "The Desert Diamond office only has two modems that connect to outside telephone lines. One's on a dedicated computer that swaps financial information with their S&L operations in Texas each night. The other is on Delbert's. Humphries is smart enough to know that Eldon and Delbert would have no qualms about letting him take the fall if something illegal is found on their computers. And since I told him about Heidi being killed, I think he's probably pretty scared. So he's hiding out in a hotel somewhere. But I've got his pager number, and I think he'll talk with you, but you might have to promise him you're not going to indict him or anything. I had to get him scared enough that he would tell me everything about Desert Diamond. At this point he thinks whatever you find on the Desert Diamond computer system is his responsibility."

"Okay, Travis. I'll be gentle with him. Now tell me about the murders."

"I can tell you what I know, and what I think, but in fairness, you probably ought to be talking to J.R. Ragsdale, too. He's the detective who's got the cases."

"Oh," she grinned, "I'm going to talk with Detective Ragsdale. As you probably know, I primarily work computer crime. But if there's a connection between these disks and other felonies, then I want to know the whole story when I'm putting my case together, and I'll tell you right now that the County Attorney will let me follow this wherever it leads. So, first tell me the facts. Then tell me what you think, especially about how the four cases – the three homicides and the child pornography – all fit together."

CHAPTER 48

I laid it all out for O'Halleran, from the moment Heidi first walked up to my table at Lucinda's to my plan to meet with Welty late that night. It was after five when we finally wrapped up our meeting. I gave O'Halleran my card so she'd know how to reach me. I was hungry and O'Halleran said she was going to talk with J.R. Ragsdale to coordinate their investigations before she started calling judges on a Sunday night to get a search warrant. So she walked Allison and me to the door.

I asked Allison if she wanted to get a bite to eat. She thought it over for a couple of seconds and then said she'd better get home and make sure her notes were in order. She wanted to be ready when the big Geetus story finally broke.

I was ready for dinner and something cold to drink, but I had to stop at the office to drop off my tape recorder. I checked for phone messages. There was one from Humphries. "Travis, I've got something you need to see, man. I'm putting it on a floppy. I'll leave it with Buddha. Pick it up there. Somebody from the County Attorney's office paged me. I'm not ready to talk with anyone, yet. Take the disk to them after you look at it." No "Call me back later," or anything like that.

When I got to the Indian Bend Tavern I asked Buddha if Ted had been in that day. "He was here. Left about an hour ago."

"Any chance he gave you something to give to me?" Buddha reached into his shirt pocket, pulled out the disk and handed it to me across the bar. As he did he raised his eyebrows as though he were asking me a question about the disk. "Ted's sort of a computer whiz," I replied, trying to sound convincing. "He's helping me with a project, but he doesn't want his boss to know he's moonlighting."

"Got it," Buddha confirmed with a knowing smile.

"We appreciate your assistance with this," I said as I slipped the disk into my own shirt pocket, "and your discretion." I took a twenty out of my wallet and dropped it in Buddha's tip jar. I was so hungry that I almost ordered one of those greasy quesadillas, but I was even hungrier to find out what was on the disk that had produced this cloak and dagger exchange.

"A pleasure to be of service," Buddha said as I headed for the door.

On my way back to my office and against my better judgment, I stopped at El Gallo for a California Burro.

Back in my office I flipped on the computer and started in on the burro. I put in the disk. There were two files on it. One was named read1st, so I opened it up. It was a note from Ted.

Travis, the other file is a series of email messages. I pulled them off the computer at work when I accessed it remotely today. Within the office we send inner-office mail electronically over the computer system. I copied these from Heidi's e-mail account. I thought you and the police would find them interesting.

I spent the next two hours staring at my computer screen and periodically munching the California Burro, while I voyeuristically read through three months of e-mail messages between Heidi Charlayne and Delbert Geetus. When I had talked to O'Halleran, laying out the case for her, I thought that I had it all pretty well figured out. But after looking at Heidi's emails, I wasn't very sure at all. So I did the only thing I really knew how to do. I opened up the Charlie Gonnerman file on my computer, added the new information, and looked at the links and the sequence of events, trying to solve the puzzle with new pieces thrown onto the table. Then I called J.R. Ragsdale.

O'Halleran had said she'd be talking to Ragsdale. That was all well and good. But I had new information that pertained to one of his cases. I felt obliged to keep him informed personally. Somebody else answered and said Ragsdale was out of the office. I was offered the option of leaving a voice mail message. So I left a message, letting

216

Ragsdale know about the meeting with Welty I had set up for later that night, and also about the email messages that Humphries had put on the disk.

I suddenly felt very tired. Maybe it was the previous day and night catching up with me. The huge burro I had just put away probably didn't help much. And once again, I had no home to go home to in order to get some rest. So I made sure the door to my office was locked. I set the alarm on my digital watch for 1 a.m., shut off the lights and once again propped myself on the floor of the corner of my office with my .45 on the floor next to me.

I slept without interruption until the beep beep beep of my watch said it was time to get moving again, to go out and face the night. I pulled the canvas bag out of the desk drawer, and threw my tape recorder, a box of computer disks and my .45 inside. I was badly in need of a shower, but that would have to wait. I had business to attend to, and I couldn't go home anymore.

CHAPTER 49

I walked out the service door of Suite 16 just a little before 2 a.m. I'd arrived about a half hour before. Rafer let me hang out while the band packed up their instruments. There were only a few vehicles in the parking lot, most of them vans. With all the gear they need for a gig, musicians tend to own vans.

I was reminded of the vans driven by several sergeants I knew in the Army: darkened windows, plush interiors, great sound systems, no back seats, cargo area padded and covered in colorful linens – perfect for entertaining ladies one might meet at the club. We called them boogie vans.

It was still hot outside, though the temperature might have slipped below the century mark sometime after midnight. I stood in the shadow of the overhead awning, against the back wall of the building. A dark blue late model Lincoln crept into the parking lot. It moved toward the far corner of the lot, then turned slowly and came to a stop pointed toward the exit. Tinted windows prevented me from seeing who was inside.

I stepped out of the shadows and walked casually across the parking lot toward the Lincoln. When I got to the middle of the lot I stopped and waited. It was their turn.

The passenger door opened and a large figure stepped out. As he walked toward me I had only a few seconds to do my assessment, to identify any weaknesses or vulnerabilities. He wasn't showing me any. In his left hand he carried a bank deposit pouch. In his right hand he swung a large tire iron. I wasn't looking to get my tires changed.

Behind him I could see the electric window of the Lincoln roll down, revealing the hardened features of the man behind the wheel. He kept the engine running.

I knew I wouldn't have much time. When the big guy was close enough to hear me I said, "How's it going, Larry? Leave your truck somewhere? Canal, maybe?"

Big Larry raised the tire iron, but I wasn't in range unless he was thinking of throwing it at me. "You fucking punk," he moved closer. I began to circle to my right, moving away from the tire iron, while I watched him move, watching for some vulnerability, something that would allow me to survive if he somehow got in close enough to do damage. It was time to go to work.

"Let's talk business, Larry. You're in deep shit and getting deeper. Right now you've got one chance to get out. After tonight your ass goes down and I won't be able to help you."

"What the fuck are you talking about?" He turned, following my movement. There was just enough confusion showing on his face to tell me I had a chance.

"Think about it, Larry. The cops have witnesses that can put you and Charlie Gonnerman together on Saturday night. That makes you their chief suspect on a charge of murder one. But it's not too late. You could still cut a deal."

His expression changed, if ever so slightly. I was trying to find some little window into Larry's head, hoping to slip in just a hint of doubt – just enough to create the possibility that I could turn him. Now I had to either shit or get off the pot.

"Tell me how it went down, Larry. Tell me about Charlie. Maybe it wasn't even you who killed him. But you're the one they're looking for, Larry. You're the one they're going to fry. So tell me what happened and I'll help you."

He continued to turn as I slowly circled. Then from the Lincoln a gruff voice with a Gulf Coast accent called out, "Goddammit Larry. Stop fucking around and get those disks." Larry glanced toward the Lincoln, looking confused.

I held out the box of disks in my left hand. "They're right here, Larry. Just tell me why Charlie was killed. What was so damned important that you had to kill him for it?"

From the Lincoln, the voice called out louder this time, "Damn it, Larry, come on. Do it!"

"What was it for, Larry? Why did you have to hit him so hard that it killed him, Larry? Tell me why you did it."

I could see the sweat on his forehead slipping down toward his eyes. From the corner of my eye, I saw the Lincoln start to roll very slowly, moving closer. And the voice again, losing patience, "Larry, goddammit!"

"Why'd you kill him, Larry?"

"Larry, get the fucking disks now!"

"Why'd you kill him, Larry?"

"Larry, goddammit!"

"I didn't kill him!"

"You were there, Larry. Tell me what happened."

"Larry, don't you say a fucking thing!"

"Tell me what happened."

"He wouldn't tell us."

I heard the Lincoln come to a stop somewhere behind me. The voice from the Lincoln called out, "Goddammit Larry, don't you say another word." I kept turning, wanting the Lincoln back in my field of vision, but keeping eye contact with Larry.

"So you kept hitting him?"

"Not me."

"You were there, Larry."

"I just held him while Mr. Welty tied him to the chair. He said he was just going to interrogate him."

"Where, Larry? Where were you?"

"In a house in Diamond Rio, still under construction. Welty kept hitting him, asking him where the disks were and how he got them. But he wouldn't say. Finally, Mr. Welty hit him so hard, it lifted the chair right off the floor. His head hit the concrete slab. With his hands and legs tied to the chair, there was nothing..."

My peripheral vision caught the back door of one of the vans fly open. Everything shifted to slow motion — someone screaming "Gun!" and the gravelly voice yelling "Larry, shut the fuck up!"

Larry's huge frame jerked as one, two, three, four rounds from Welty's gun slammed into him. Instinct had me flat on the parking lot. It was only the gritty heat of the asphalt that told me I was down. Low-crawling toward Larry as fast as I could, I caught just a glimpse of Wayne Henderson, the cowboy cop, sprinting across the parking lot, yelling at Welty to drop his weapon, while at the same time drawing his own and then firing at the open driver's side window of the Lincoln.

A heavy hand pushed down on my back, and I looked up to see Joe Diaz, holding me flat on the asphalt with his left hand while he covered his partner with the gun in his right. "Looks like you got yourself into some real shit this time, Travis. You're damned lucky that motherfucker in the Lincoln didn't try to blow *you* away." Then, feeling the hard object at the small of my back, Joe pulled the tape recorder out of its pouch and said, "And what do we have here?"

"Just a little audio to complement the videos you were taking, Joe. Now, if you wouldn't mind, I'd like to get my face off of this fucking parking lot."

CHAPTER 50

J. R. Ragsdale and I sat facing each other in a booth in an all-night diner just a few blocks from Suite 16. Each of us needed the opportunity to fill in the missing pieces and round out the jagged edges of the story that brought us together one last time.

"Okay Travis," Ragsdale said, "since you're the hot-shit journalist who's got his prints all over this case, tell me why. I know who's dead. I'm pretty sure I know who did the killing. But I don't know why. I offer you the opportunity to enlighten me."

"According to Larry's last words, Charlie was killed by Welty. I don't think he meant to kill him. It just went down that way." I took out my tape player and handed it to Ragsdale. "There's the recording of my little chat with Larry. It should complement the tape that Joe and Wayne shot from the surveillance van."

"And the reason Mr. Welty was beating up on Mr. Gonnerman?"

"He wanted to know where Charlie got the disks with the Desert Diamond files on them."

"I take it that Mr. Gonnerman wasn't telling them because he was protecting his sister, Ms. Charlayne. And according to Deputy County Attorney O'Halleran, those disks contained images of a pornographic nature involving children."

"That's what I've been told, Detective. I haven't seen them."

"And Mr. Gonnerman was planning on making the existence of those files public information?"

"No. I don't think so, Detective. He didn't know what they were. So he made copies of the disks and took them to A-1 Computers to see if they could figure out what those files were."

"Thus our connection to Mr. Pelosi."

"Exactly."

"And why did Mr. Pelosi end up lying in the middle of Pima Road with a bullet in his head?"

"Pelosi saw that he had two sets of files. One set was the Desert Diamond financials. The other set was the kiddie-porn. He thought that he could demonstrate to Desert Diamond that they had a security problem, and he figured that the pornography would be sufficiently embarrassing that he had a little leverage. So he tried to sell his services to them. Based on my short discussion with him, I'd say that his personality clashed with the genteel Southern culture of the Geetus organization, though I don't really know. But he's the one who told Welty that Charlie had been in possession of the files, and I'm guessing that Charlie told Pelosi that the disks he was giving him were copies of the originals."

"So," I asked, "you figure it was Welty who shot Pelosi?"

"Completely off the record," Ragsdale replied, taking another sip of coffee, "the coroner found a .380 slug in Pelosi's skull. I think you'll find that it was also a Walther .380 that Mr. Welty was using as he was attempting to kill your friend Larry this evening."

"You think Larry's going to make it?"

Ragsdale shrugged his broad shoulders. "He might. He's a pretty big boy. The .380 is not an especially powerful round. I'm truly hoping that he does pull through and that, once the facts are presented to him in a calm and rational manner, he'll decide that it's in his best interest to cooperate in the on-going investigation of criminal activity within the Geetus organization. I'll bet Ms. O'Halleran, being the extremely competent prosecutor that she is, has already contacted the U.S. Attorney to look into the financial dealings of the Geetus family's little savings and loan operation, too."

"Then there's Heidi's murder," I said.

"I wouldn't be at all surprised if the slug the forensics team took out of the wall of her apartment also turned out to be a .380," Ragsdale replied. "You want to tell me why she had to die?"

"Welty figured out that she was Charlie's source for the files. Something the Desert Diamond's system administrator, a guy named Humphries, said may have tipped him off. Welty's an ex-cop. Maybe he just put two and two together."

"And just what was it in those financial reports that made Welty want to kill everybody who might have had a look at them? Political contributions? I don't get it, Travis. Everybody makes political contributions. Why do a bunch of people have to die?"

"It wasn't the numbers. At least I don't think so. Geetus didn't care who knew about the contributions. Charlie was trying to show that there was a connection between the contributions and the water study. He thought that the voters would be outraged if he could show that Geetus bankrolled Sandy Dominguez who, in turn, found a way to delay release of the water study so Geetus could sell more subdivisions. But Geetus didn't care. Not about that."

The waitress came by and warmed up our cups. Out the window there was just a hint of the coming light on the northeastern horizon. Another blistering hot day was on its way, and the memorial service for Charlie that evening.

"So if it wasn't the numbers, what was it?"

"Prestige, Detective Ragsdale, prestige."

"Now you have me truly mystified, Travis. How does a series of murders translate into prestige?"

"It's ironic, in a way, Detective. Old man Geetus has enough money to buy a whole stable of politicians. So it eats at him that he hasn't been invited to join the Phoenix 40. And I think he is acutely aware that Delbert is only one generation removed from his father's white trash roots and Florida real estate scams. He wanted the prestige he thought would come by having a son in Congress. That was the plan – Delbert would run in two years with help from Congressman Sandy Dominguez, and all the other political favors his daddy would call in. And being part of Delbert's immediate family, the old man could dump all the money he wanted into getting his boy elected to Congress."

"Well Travis, pretty much everybody I know comes from, how should I say this, somewhat humble origins. And Lord knows we could all use a little more prestige. Doesn't mean we go around shooting people. What am I missing?"

"Humphries made a copy of some communications between Heidi and Delbert. These were in the form of electronic mail—he called them e-mail. And he copied them from the Desert Diamond computer files so I'm guessing they're still there on the computer."

"I got your voice mail message about that. But not being much of computer geek myself, I thought it best to get some help from Gail O'Halleran. I assume she's going to have a search warrant for the computer files sometime later today, by the way. So what were these messages?"

"Apparently Heidi and Delbert were having a little relationship outside their normal business responsibilities."

"You don't say," Ragsdale said with a straight face.

"Afraid so, and not very original either. He kept implying that his marriage was on the rocks, that he was going to get a divorce, that it was just a matter of proper timing and working out the details in terms of the business and the kids. He dragged it out for months."

"It saddens me to hear that such a thing could happen in a good Christian family," Ragsdale said.

"At some point not too long ago, Heidi got impatient and gave Delbert an ultimatum. Either he files for divorce or Heidi was breaking it off. The civility of their discourse headed down hill from there. Heidi suggested that Delbert couldn't get elected Dog Catcher if word of those pictures on his computer were to get out."

"So she knew about them, too."

"I guess so. But I don't think that Delbert took her seriously until she submitted her resignation a couple of days ago. Maybe he got scared. I'm guessing he went to Welty instead of his old man. He explained the problem to Welty, and Welty said he'd take care of it."

"You think Welty told the old man?" Ragsdale asked.

"Hard to say. Welty was extremely loyal to Eldon. After all, Eldon hired Welty after he was canned by the Bay County Sheriff's Office. But I'm guessing Welty would also try to protect the old man by not telling him."

"Well, Mr. Welty won't be telling Mr. Geetus anything anymore. Officer Henderson managed to hit him three times while on the run. That is fairly impressive shooting."

"I should probably thank Officer Henderson. Welty might very well have decided that once Larry went down he should empty his magazine in me."

"Travis, you went down so fast I thought that Welty got you with the first round."

"Well, you know how it is, Marine. Habits you learn in combat don't break easily."

"Nothing wrong with that. You're still here to talk about it," he said, looking me right in the eye.

I lifted up my coffee cup and offered a toast. "Absent companions."

Ragsdale touched his cup to mine. "Semper Fi," he replied.

He reached for his wallet and began to take out a bill, but I stopped him. "Let me get this, Detective," I said, unzipping the bank bag I had picked up from the parking lot next to where Larry lay bleeding. "I've recently come into some money."

Ragsdale glanced at the money bag for a moment. Then he stood up and said, "Let's get out of here, Travis. Thanks to you I have a shit load of paperwork to do."

I thought about going back by the wreckage that was once my home. The memorial service for Charlie was coming up that evening. I figured that Elena Sanchez would be there. I owed her a wash cloth, but I didn't feel like combing through the debris in my house to find it. Since I had a bag full of cash, maybe I should get her something nice. After all, she'd been very nice to me.

So I went to the office. I had two stories to write, and two publishers who were waiting for them.

EPILOGUE

(From the August 1992 issue of *Outdoor West*)

Ascending Higher
By Travis Jefferson

The climbing world lost one of its brightest young stars with the death earlier this summer of Juliette Skye Valdez.

I was with Juliette the day she died. We had just finished a climb in the mountains of Colorado. A light rain was falling as we topped out, gathered up our gear and started back down.

Juliette slipped during the unprotected down climb, falling over 100 feet to the ground below.

These photos of Juliette were taken at the Denver Climbing Gym the day before she died. They are a testament to the grace and beauty she brought to the sport of climbing...

###

You can connect with Avtar online at:

www.facebook.com/avtar.khalsa.writer

He is currently working on a dystopian novel about the disintegration of the United States of America, as well as the next Travis Jefferson mystery, *The Kenai Connection*.